MARDI GRAS MYSTERIES

EDITED BY SARAH E GLENN
MYSTERY AND HORROR, LLC

DEDICATION

This book is dedicated to Deanna Familton. Her love of Mardi Gras is an inspiration to us.

TABLE OF CONTENTS

CAFÉ DU MOAN

Robert Allen Lupton

Rachel woke up in her car with a pounding headache. She gagged at the sweet stench of vomit and something else that her foggy brain couldn't identify. Two half full (or half empty) plastic tumblers were in the console. She picked one up and sniffed it. The pinkish slop in the tall thin fluted glass was a hurricane.

She gagged again at the cloying smell. Visions of closing down Pat O'Brien's piano bar last night danced in her head. She held her head to keep it still. The nausea was too much. What time did she leave the damn bar? It's hard to close down a tavern that never closes, but hey, yesterday was Mardi Gras, and she and her friends gave it hell.

She sniffed the warm slurry. The scent of rum and passion fruit was almost sickening, but it wasn't the sweet undercurrent playing backup to stale vomit.

Rachel checked her clothing. Vomit free. "Beers Beads Boobs" was emblazoned on the T-shirt. She vaguely remembered buying it at a shop on Decatur Street and proudly changing into it while she danced with a ragtag group of street performers in Jackson Square. She'd twirled her University of Oklahoma shirt on one finger like a stripper, and tossed it into the crowd.

Sunlight reflected off the river and glinted on her streaked windshield. She shaded her eyes and looked outside.

Her Honda was parked in the parking lot between the Café Du Monde and the Mississippi River. The vomit smell came from outside her car.

The night was coming back to her. Rachel had split up with Anna and Kaylee sometime after the dueling pianists played "Saints" for the fiftieth or sixtieth time. Anna had headed off with a lawyer from Chicago, and Kaylee found a group of Tulane University Tri-Delts to be her new best friends. She left, saying they were going to catch a streetcar to an after party somewhere near Audubon Park.

Rachel stepped out of the car and stretched. She was supposed to meet her friends for *café au lait* and beignets before they drove back to Oklahoma. She winced at the rising sun and checked the time on her cellphone. 6:30 AM. If she remembered right, she had thirty minutes. She could walk to the café, wash up, use the restroom, and drink a couple cups of coffee before the girls were supposed to meet her.

She looked in the side mirror. Her hair looked like the Bride of Frankenstein on drugs, and her makeup was even worse. Her breath bounced from the mirror. *My God*, she thought, *it smells like a river rat crawled in my mouth and died.*

The girls had locked their purses and travel bags in the trunk. Rachel thought, *Bottled water. Wash my face, brush my teeth, and take a jar of aspirin. I've got time to do that.*

She staggered around the car and stepped on a sharp rock. Shoes, where the hell were her shoes? The trunk was locked. Hopefully, their stuff was still inside. She didn't see the luggage they'd hidden under blankets before sunrise yesterday, before they'd hurried to Canal Street to watch the Krewe of Zulu Parade. A day of beads, booze, and doubloons. They'd come back to the car and stashed their booty and changed shirts a half dozen times.

There was more in the trunk than Rachel expected. Anna was in the trunk, and so was their lawyer friend from last night. Both were naked from the waist down and festooned with beads and doubloons. Their throats were cut.

2

Anna's face and back were covered with blood. Stunned into silence, Rachel stepped away from the car. Her feet stuck to the cold asphalt. Her footprints glistened in the tacky blood on the pavement.

She took out her phone. Rachel was pretty sure that 911 was the same in New Orleans as it was in Oklahoma. Before she dialed, a voice called out. "Hey girl, where you been? We were supposed to meet for coffee and beignets at 6:30. You had too much fun to remember. *Boomer Sooner* and *When The Saints Go Marching In.*"

Kaylee carried three cardboard cups of coffee and a white grease-stained sack with so much powdered sugar inside that a small cloud puffed out when it brushed against her thigh. She wore a couple hundred Mardi Gras beads and a disgustingly cheerful expression.

Kaylee held out a cup of coffee, but Rachel didn't move. Kaylee took Rachel's hand and put the coffee in it. "Lord, girl, you were drunker than Cooter Brown last night. Sober up. Where's Anna? We got to get on the road. I've got an Econ class at nine tomorrow."

Rachel dropped the coffee, and the brown liquid mixed with the congealing blood under the car. Rachel said, "Anna," and pointed into the trunk.

Kaylee said, "Damn, Rachel. What have you done?"

"I woke up about fifteen minutes ago. The last thing I remember was Anna leaving with this guy. I think he's a lawyer. You left with a bunch of Tri-Delts from Tulane to catch the Saint Charles streetcar to some party near Audubon Park."

"Rachel, that was about one this morning. What did you do?"

"I kept ordering hurricanes. I don't remember anything else until I woke up in my car."

'Why did you kill Anna? I thought you liked Anna."

3

"Stop it. I'm calling the police. Then I'm gonna brush my teeth and wash the blood off my feet. I don't think you'll make your Econ class tomorrow."

The uniformed NOPD officer who answered the 911 call looked in the trunk. "You two sit right down in the back of my patrol car. I gotta call a detective."

Detective Fiona Guidry parked next to the Honda with Oklahoma plates, took a sip of coffee, and climbed out of the car. She yawned. Most folks didn't realize that Mardi Gras in New Orleans wasn't a day; it was a season. She leaned back in the car and logged into her computer. Twenty-three days without a day off, and seventy-six hours overtime last week. She put her sunglasses in her pocket and walked to the patrolman. "Morning. Where's the body?"

"Two bodies, Detective Guidry. They're in the trunk. No disrespect, but you look exhausted."

"I am. I worked the streetcar wreck last night. Some moron from Kentucky plowed into a streetcar in the Garden District. Killed six people. I came straight from there. You have a couple suspects?"

"I don't know about suspects, but the dead woman's friends are in my patrol car."

Fiona looked in the trunk as best she could without stepping in the blood. She turned to the uniformed officer. "Who found the bodies?"

"The brunette. Her name is Rachel, Rachel Ferguson."

"Bring her to my car. She probably killed them. Half the time, the person who found the bodies is guilty. I hope so. I'd like to get home and see my kids before they leave for school."

Rachel slid into the unmarked car. Fiona introduced herself. "I know this is hard, but I need to ask some questions. You'll have to help me find out who did this. Anything you can remember will be useful."

4

"Yes, officer. I don't remember much. We started Monday night with the Proteus and Orpheus parades, and then drank until yesterday morning. We made it to Canal Street on Mardi Gras morning in time for Zulu and partied though the Rex, Elks, and Crescent City parades. Pat O'Brien's after that. We'd been awake since we left Oklahoma Sunday night. Can I get my bag out of the trunk? I've got to brush my teeth and clean up. My head is killing me."

"Sorry. SCIS, that's Scientific Criminal Investigations Section, is backed up this morning. Everything in the trunk is evidence, and it won't be released for God knows how long."

Rachel searched her pockets and found her driver's license, two credit cards and eighty-seven dollars in cash. "Can you take me to a drug store?"

"I know it sucks, but I can't. You can't clean up until SCIS checks you out. Walk me through the whole day. Take your time."

Rachel went through it twice. Fiona asked, "The dead man. You said he's a lawyer. How do you know him?"

"I don't really. We met him at Pat O'Brien's last night. He bought us drinks for a couple of hours. He paid for song requests. One of the piano players knew all the women's power anthems. We sang 'I Am Woman,' 'I Will Survive,' 'Roar,' 'Invincible,' and 'Fight Song' for a couple hours. We were having a great time, but sometime after midnight he and Anna decided to leave for a little one-on-one time."

"What about your other friend?"

"Kaylee. She left right after that. Said she was going to an after party with a bunch of Tri-Delts from Tulane."

"Tridents."

"No, Tri-Delts. Delta Delta Delta, it's a sorority."

"So you stayed at O'Brien's, and Kaylee left with a bunch of girls right after Anna left with the dead man. That sound right?"

Rachel wiped tears from her face. She blubbered, and then rubbed her nose on her shirt sleeve. "Yes, lady. That's all

I remember. My head is fricking killing me, and the inside of my mouth tastes like roadkill. You gotta let me get to a toilet before my bladder bursts."

"There's a public toilet about two hundred yards toward the ferry landing. I'll have the uniform walk you there. A small grocery is across Decatur Street. He'll let you buy a toothbrush and brush your teeth. You can buy coffee. Don't wash your hands. If you wash your hands before SCIS checks you out, I'll lock your Okie ass up for a month."

Fiona sent the uniformed officer, Marcus Duronsolet, with Rachel. Fiona opened the rear door of Duronsolet's patrol car. "It's Kaylee, right? Step outside. We can talk while we wait for SCIS to arrive. Tell me about last night. Rachel says the three of you were drinking at Pat O'Brien's after the Crescent City Krewe parade. Start when you got there."

"Yes, Officer. The place was packed. Yesterday was Mardi Gras, you know."

"I live here. I know."

"Well, we waited outside until about ten. We met this nice attorney from Chicago, Lawrence Thibodaux. He slipped the manager a hundred dollars and got the four of us a table in the piano bar. He told the waiter to bring hurricanes for the ladies and Jack Daniels straight up for himself."

"Did he now?"

"The waiter's name was Clarence. He said, 'Clarence, I'm a fearful man. I get frightened when I don't have alcohol. You won't like me when I'm frightened.'"

Kaylee continued. "One of the piano players was a lady who knew all the women's power songs. Larry kept tipping her and she kept playing them. Larry danced with all three of us. A bunch of sorority girls from Tulane starting drinking and singing with us."

Fiona turned the page in her notebook. "What sorority? Do you remember any names?"

"They were Tri-Delts. I think one of them was named Peggy."

6

"Okay. What time did you leave the bar?"

Kaylee moved behind Fiona's car and faced west. "Do you mind? The sun is in my eyes. Anna and Larry left just after midnight. Rachel wanted to stay in the piano bar, but I left with the Tri-Delts. We took a streetcar to the University. They had an after party planned at their sorority house."

Fiona leaned against her car. The breeze shifted, came in off the river, and blew the slightly rotten stench of last night's party in the French Quarter across Decatur Street, and past Bourbon and Rampart Streets. Compared to the smell of stale beer, unwashed bodies, and old vomit, the river air was fresh and clean. Fiona inhaled deeply. "What time did you catch the streetcar to Tulane?"

"We left the bar after midnight and walked for twenty minutes or so. I'd say just before one this morning. The streetcar was packed. Yesterday was Mardi Gras, you know."

"Yes, I know. How was the after party?"

"It wasn't much. I'd wound down by the time we got to the sorority house. I went to sleep or passed out on a couch. I woke up about five and caught the streetcar back this way. I waited for Rachel and Anna at the Café Du Monde until about 6:45, bought coffee and beignets for everyone, and walked here."

The SCIS van pulled into the parking lot. Fiona met the techs. "Process this girl first. Her name is Kaylee. There's another girl on a potty break. She'll be right back. Two bodies in the trunk of that piece of crap Honda with Oklahoma plates. I'll be in my car. I gotta call my kids and then review my notes."

Fiona lit a Picayune cigarette: strong, and hard to buy outside of New Orleans. Folks in the squad room considered smoking the brand a prerequisite for being a detective, the same way that World War Two pilots only chewed Beechnut Gum. She opened the search engine on her phone and entered Delta Delta Delta Tulane University. The search showed no results. She tried three more variations and gave up. There wasn't a Tri-Delt chapter at Tulane.

Kaylee was lying about the sorority. That made two lies. The St. Charles Streetcar line was closed after midnight last night. Fiona had worked the wreck that shut it down. Nobody lies to a detective in a murder investigation without a reason. *Don't jump to conclusions*, thought Fiona. *Could be the girl just snuck off with someone for a little slap and tickle and is ashamed of it. She wouldn't be the first girl to wake up in a strange bed the morning after Mardi Gras. Relax. Let SCIS do its job.*

The tech said, "We're finished with Kaylee. Interesting. Probably cleaned up in the last couple of hours. I put her in the van and hit her with the ultraviolet light. Biological traces on her shirt, necklace and rings. I took swabs. Could be blood or it could be that our girl got laid last night. Could be both. Won't know until we get the lab results."

"I appreciate it. What about the bodies?"

"The guys with me got the bodies. I'm gonna check out Rachel now. What should I do with Kaylee?"

"Put her in my car."

Fiona ground out her cigarette out on the crumbling pavement and walked to the rear of the Honda. "Hey guys, what do you know?"

"Morning, Detective. I'm Carl. Two dead, both with their throats cut. Weapon looks like a broken hurricane glass. Pat O'Brien's gives you the glass as a souvenir when you buy the drink."

"Thanks, Carl. I live here. Tell me something I don't know."

"They were standing up when they were killed. The guy was right behind the girl. His blood splattered all over her hair and back. He collapsed on the girl and they fell forward into the open trunk. The killer just reached in, slit her throat, levered their feet into the trunk, and closed it. The woman bled out on the carpet."

"So, they were standing directly behind the car. He was right behind her and someone just walked up and slit his throat without him noticing."

"Detective, they aren't wearing any pants. We won't know until we finish the lab tests, but I expect these two were going at it like minks in a mud pile when the killer caught them. We found most of the broken hurricane glass. Looks like the glass shards are covered with fingerprints."

"You got ID on these two?"

"Just the guy so far. His wallet was in his pants. They were next to the bodies. His name's Joseph Aboud. He runs an insurance agency on Tchoupitoulas Street."

"Interesting. The girls said he was a Chicago lawyer. Either they're lying or he was. I'm gonna talk to Kaylee again."

Fiona decided to go bad cop on Kaylee this time around. Call her out for her lies, get her panicked, and see where it went from there. A guilty suspect's first story was usually a rehearsed piece of art, but once it went down in flames, the second story was more like some crap a six-year-old made up to stay out of trouble.

Fiona turned on her recorder, sat it on the dashboard, and read Kaylee her rights. "Girl, you been lying to me. I can't help you if you keep lying. This is a murder and when you lie, it makes you look guilty. First, I know you didn't go to any damn Tri-Delt house at Tulane University, because there isn't one. Second, you didn't take the streetcar down past Audubon Park after midnight last night because there was a wreck and the streetcar wasn't running. What you got to say for yourself?"

Kaylee didn't say anything, she just cried into her hands. Fiona pushed. "Them tears don't mean crap to me. I want the truth. Your jewelry and shirt lit up like a Christmas tree under the ultraviolet. You washed up real good, but not good enough. There's blood or semen traces. For your sake, I hope you got laid last night and that's what you're covering up. You need to tell me the truth."

Kaylee blubbered. Fiona waited. "Yes, I had sex last night. Larry, that's the lawyer's name. We snuck into a closet at Pat O'Brien's. Anna and Rachel thought we'd gone to the restrooms."

"I thought so. That's not a crime. Larry left with your friend, Anna, after you and he did the deed in the closet. I bet that pissed you off. I know you followed them. I know you were drunk. I know you didn't plan to hurt anyone. You followed them to Rachel's car and killed them."

"No. I was hurt, but I just wandered up and down Bourbon Street until the sun came up."

"Give it up, girl. We've got the pieces of the hurricane glass you used to cut their throats. The SCIS techs say it's got fingerprints all over it. We both know those are your prints. Remember the blood you tried to wash out of your shirt? It's gonna be a perfect match for the bodies in the trunk. I know you did it and you know I can prove it. Just own what you did. You came up behind them and killed them both. It's okay. You can say it."

Kaylee almost screamed. "Yes, damn it! I followed them to Rachel's car. Anna popped open the trunk. It wasn't locked. She tossed her beads and the hurricane glasses inside. I figured she was getting her luggage. While she was bent over, Larry pulled down her shorts and dropped his own pants. The bastard. It was less than an hour since we'd been together, and he was gonna screw my friend."

"That's when you killed him."

"Damn right. He fell on top of Anna. There was so much blood. She saw me. I had to kill her, too. I lifted their feet into the trunk, tossed their clothes onto of them, walked to the river, and cleaned up."

"Where did you go?"

"I started back to Pat O'Brien's, but Rachel was passed out on St. Peter's Street. I got her up and walked her back to the car and put her in the driver's seat. I hoped she'd think maybe she did it. She never really woke up. It was about five by then. I went to the Café Du Monde, cleaned up again, and stayed there until a little after six thirty. I probably drank six cups of coffee."

"Kaylee, I'm gonna have to take you to the station and charge you. You know that. For now, I'm gonna lock you in the back seat. I need to visit with the technicians, and I've got some more questions for Rachel."

Fiona lit another Picayune and winced at the metallic tang of the harsh tobacco. "Carl, you got ID on the girl?"

"Yes, we do. She's Margaret Carson from Tulsa, Oklahoma. Twenty-two years old."

Rachel stepped away from Officer Duronsolet and looked in the trunk with much clearer eyes than she'd had earlier that morning. "Who the hell is Margaret Carson?"

Her face went white, but she forced herself to look closer. "Our bags. Our bags aren't in the trunk." She stepped back and looked at the license plate. "This isn't my car. This is a standard Oklahoma plate. I have a vanity plate that says, 'UGOGRL.' Where's my car?"

Fiona said, "You said this was your car, earlier."

"Well, I woke up in it, didn't I? I was still drunk, and it was mostly dark. You wouldn't let me go to the bathroom or even wash my face. God, my head is still killing me."

Another woman entered the parking lot from the Café Du Monde seating area. Patrolman Duronsolet stopped her. "You can't be here. This is a criminal investigation."

The woman said, "That's Rachel. She's my friend. We got separated last night."

Fiona turned toward the woman. "Who are you?"

"Anna Barnes. Did Rachel rob a bank or something?"

"Something."

Rachel moved toward Anna. "We thought you were dead. There're dead people in this trunk."

11

Fiona stopped Rachel. "Don't say another word. Let me talk to Anna. I've almost got this figured out."

Fiona took Anna to Duronsolet's patrol car. "Rachel and Kaylee say you left Pat O'Brien's with a lawyer named Larry sometime after midnight. That sound about right?"

"Well, I tried to, but Larry wanted to get another drink in the patio bar. They had this band playing college fight songs. All the chairs were full, but we sat on the ground next to a bunch of ferns and some trees. Larry said they were banana trees. Anyway, we sort of slipped back into the foliage and started to fool around a little bit, but then Larry passed out. Boy, was I pissed."

"What happened then?"

"The banana trees started playing roulette."

"I don't understand."

"They spun round and round. I followed them with my eyes and thought, *place your bets, ladies and gentlemen, place your bets.* I closed my eyes, but everything kept spinning. I woke when a man watering the plants this morning sprayed me with a garden hose. That bastard, Larry, was gone. I couldn't believe that Rachel and Anna went off and left me. I tried to walk here earlier, but I got lost and ended up on Rampart Street. One of those policemen on a horse told me how to get back to the Café. He said, "Follow all those other people doing the walk of shame this morning. Most of them are going to the Café. It's a tradition.""

"So you never left the bar with Larry."

"I never left the bar at all."

"Christ on a Honda. I'll have to take you to the station and get a formal statement. Stay in the car for now."

Fiona told the techs. "Impound the Honda. It's the murder scene."

Fiona reviewed her notes one more time. "Kaylee, I'm arresting you for the murder of Margaret Carson and Joseph Aboud. I've already read you your rights, but I want to remind you that anything you say …"

"I don't need to hear that again. Who are Margaret and Joseph? What happened to Anna and Larry?"

"Anna's fine. She spent the night passed out in a fern garden on Pat O'Brien's patio. Larry, if that's his real name, is gone with the wind."

"I didn't kill them?"

"No, you didn't kill Anna and Larry. You followed the wrong people to the parking lot. Joseph and Margaret, not Anna and Larry, were having sex when you killed them."

"So, it was a mistake. That's not a crime, is it? It's not murder when a person kills the wrong people. I can plead 'mistake' in court, right?"

"Oh, honey. Murder is murder. What you plead is up to your lawyer, but I assure you that young, drunk, and stupid isn't a legal defense, at least not in Louisiana. Judges hate it when a defendant says, "Sorry, but I killed the wrong people.""

"You're mean. I want a lawyer."

"If you say so, but wanting a lawyer is what got you into this mess."

Robert Allen Lupton is retired and lives in New Mexico, where he is a commercial hot air balloon pilot. Robert runs and writes every day, but not necessarily in that order. More than seventy of his short stories have been published in several anthologies including *Chicken Soup for the Soul — Running*, and online at:

www.horrortree.com
www.crimsonstreets.com
www.aurorawolf.com
www.stupefyingstories.blogspot.com
www.fairytalemagazine.com
www.allegoryezine.com

About 1000 drabbles based on the worlds of Edgar Rice Burroughs and several articles are available online at www.erbzine.com. His novel, *Foxborn*, was published in April 2017 and the sequel, *Dragonborn*, in June 2018. His collection of running themed horror, science fiction, and adventure stories, *Running into Trouble*, was published in October 2017. His annotated edition of John Monro's 1897 novel, *A Trip to Venus*, was released in September 2018. His newest novel, *Dejanna of the Double Star*, was published on December 1, 2020.

Visit https://www.amazon.com/author/luptonra his Amazon author's page for current information about his stories and books.

A PRAYER TO MOMUS

DJ Tyrer

I met Étienne in a bar in the French Quarter as crowds of revelers surged past outside, celebrating Mardi Gras, or gathered to watch the women flashing from the balconies above the street, and, having threaded my way through the crowd of patrons to his table, placed a bottle of Ojen and two glasses on the table before him.

"Here," I said, pouring some into each glass. "Enjoy."

He didn't touch his glass, just looked at me through the eye slits of his mask.

Étienne had the same lion mask on that he had worn the year before. It was a deep golden color and flashed when it caught the light. It might even have been gold, I don't know, it could've been; his family was old and rich and he had just the right amount of ego for it to be.

He looked down at the liqueur and, though I couldn't see his expression, from his posture I guessed he was dubious about it.

I drank mine in a single gulp.

Reassured, he pushed his mask up atop his head and sipped at his.

"Nice."

"I think we can both do with a drink," I said. "It's been a lousy year."

"Yeah." He glanced away.

My sister, Jessica, had been hit by a bus just a week ago, her death casting a shadow over the celebrations for us. She'd been dating Étienne, but they'd broken up just after the festival last year, and the anniversary of their breakup could hardly have been worse for him. Not that he seemed too cut up about it.

The police said her death was an accident, that she'd tried to cross the street without looking. I had my own suspicions. Just as I had my suspicions about why she and Étienne had broken up.

He took another sip. "I'm sorry about your sister."

"Yeah. But, it wasn't much of a surprise. The needle ..." I looked away.

"Yeah." Étienne's voice was flat.

Jessica had always had problems with drink and drugs since she was in high school. She'd been through rehab twice, had finally been clean for a couple of years until she hooked up with Étienne; she'd gone completely off the rails after their breakup. What had happened had been almost inevitable, the shock parceled out over the preceding year.

"Yeah," I said, pouring us some more liqueur.

I smiled. "I guess we both need something to lift our spirits."

I topped up his glass.

"Thanks."

"So, Mardi Gras ..."

"Yeah."

"I half-expected you not to come. Or, that you'd be too busy to see me, tossing beads to the girls."

He shrugged. "I never miss Mardi Gras."

"You're quite the connoisseur, eh? An expert?"

"I guess so." Étienne loved the celebration and had a head full of facts about the krewes and their parades, which ones had had which theme in which year, which celebrities led them, and so on.

"So, you've probably heard the story of Annette Barbarin."

"Annette Barbarin?" He shook his head. "Something to do with the jazz musicians?"

I shrugged. "I don't know. She was before their time."

"Oh. So, her story has something to do with Mardi Gras?"

Étienne leaned closer to me, across the table.

"It's a spooky tale," I said, taking another sip of the Ojen. "I think you'll like it ..."

Annette Barbarin was born into a creole family descended from a wealthy *gens de couleur* line that had inhabited Louisiana long before the Civil War. Things had begun to change as Americans moved into the state and, after the War, the pushback of the Southern Democrats had stripped away many of their rights.

Born into luxury, Annette had been little affected by the changes. For her, life went on much as normal, no matter how her father and uncles complained, even as their fortune slowly declined and their rights were stripped away.

That all changed one Mardi Gras ...

It was around the time that the white middle classes of New Orleans began to celebrate the festival, supplanting the native sons of the city. Now, the streets were filled with as many Americans as Creoles of various hues.

Annette was a beautiful young woman and had attracted the eye of a youth named Charles Brantworth. Of course, in those days of strict segregation, there was no way in which the two of them might marry, although, if they were honest, those who knew him would've said he wasn't the sort of man who cared for marriage or consent.

Having set his eye on Annette, he and some friend donned masks and cornered her during the Mardi Gras celebrations and took what they wanted and left her for dead.

17

Her father found her, and she managed to whisper the name of her attacker before she succumbed to her wounds and died.

Étienne shifted awkwardly as I told him the story, then leaned back and said, "A dark tale, but hardly spooky."

"That isn't the end of the tale. It's merely the opening ..."

I poured us each more Ojen and continued the tale.

Although the Barbarins were a reputable family and good Christians, Édouard Barbarin was as aware of the claims concerning conjuremen and voodoo priests as anyone in New Orleans, and had heard tell of the infamous sorceress Marie Laveau.

Knowing he would never get justice for his daughter through the courts, he went to the sorceress and begged for her assistance, to help him take revenge.

"Because your daughter died in misery," Marie Leveau said, "your daughter belongs to the goddess Oizys. Oizys is the sister of Momus."

Édouard Barbarin gasped at that, for the men who had formed the parade were called The Knights of Momus.

"Yes, Momus, the patron god of Mardi Gras."

Sobbing, he asked her what he should do.

"You have buried your daughter, yes?"

He nodded. That day had been the worst of his life.

Marie Leveau handed him a small cloth bag, a conjure bag or *grigri*.

"Do you know what this is?" she asked.

Édouard shook his head. "No."

"This bag contains items of power. Never open it — you have no need to know what it contains, do not want to know, and doing so will render it useless. Suffice to believe it holds the answer to your desire for revenge."

"What does it do? Is it poison?"

"It is no poison, nor a curse," she said.

"Then, what good is it? How will it help me take revenge upon that fiend Charles Brantworth?"

Marie Leveau smiled a particularly feral smile. "Oh, it will give your daughter her revenge. This is what you will do ..."

He listened and, though he recoiled at her words and shook with fear and nausea, he took the conjure bag from her and kept it safe until the following Mardi Gras and his opportunity for revenge.

Édouard Barbarin went to his daughter's tomb and pulled back the slab to uncover her coffin and lifted off its lid to reveal her embalmed remains.

Some say that she was as pretty as she had been in life, others that she had become desiccated and vile.

Either way, her father suppressed his revulsion and laid the bag upon her chest and began to chant a prayer that Marie Leveau had taught him, calling upon the god Momus to take revenge upon those who had profaned his celebration.

Then, he stood over his daughter's tomb and watched as, first, a single finger twitched, then her hand. Slowly, the corpse of Annette sat up, grave mold dripping from her shoulders, then pulled itself out of her resting place to stand before her horrified father.

In his numb fingers, Édouard held a mask, the one she had worn on the day she died, which he handed now to her and which she donned, without a sound, before turning away and vanishing into the night, heading in the direction of the celebrations.

If Charles Brantworth felt any guilt for what he had done, he had pushed it down deep inside and was out with his band of friends, enjoying the night, perhaps tormenting some other young woman who had caught his eye.

But, his laughter was silenced and, then, replaced by a croak of terror when a figure stepped out of the crowd towards him—a figure who wore a tattered and moldy dress and a mask that he found horribly familiar.

He gasped her name. "It can't be!"

She stepped towards him and reached out to seize his throat and choke him.

As the crowds cheered and partied about him, he slowly died, voiceless and alone, just as Annette had been when he attacked her.

That night, each one of his friends, those who had been with him a year before, died in the same way and Annette and her father had their revenge, and Momus received satisfaction for the way his night had been profaned.

Étienne looked up. With his mask atop his head, I could clearly see his expression. He was looking past me. There was fear in his eyes.

I didn't need to turn. I knew who was standing behind me, who had stepped out of the crowd to approach our table.

"It's a spooky story, isn't it, Étienne? Vengeance from beyond the grave. A prayer to Momus bringing justice."

He didn't reply, just continued to stare past me.

"Something wrong?" I asked.

Still, he couldn't reply.

"I went to the graveyard, today, Étienne. Visited Jessica's grave …"

"No …" He began to push back his seat.

"Yes."

"I didn't want for her to die. I promise you, I didn't want her to die."

"No? I don't think you cared whether she lived or died, did you, Étienne?"

Étienne stood and stumbled backwards into someone, spilling their drink and earning a cussing.

"Jessica, I didn't mean to …" He began to sob.

"Oh, that's not Jessica," I told him. "It's her mask, of course, but she's still in the funeral home. We haven't even buried her yet. Not that you cared.

"There never was an Annette Barbarin. I made her and her story up, although I'm sure there's some truth in it. I just needed to prime you, to see how you reacted when you thought Jessica had returned from the dead, to confirm that you were the guilty one."

I stood and shook my head.

"Jessica told me about the video you made, what you did to her. I couldn't be certain, of course, and she was never able to prove it—the police weren't interested in the claims of a drug addict—but, now, I know it was true.

"Why? It can't have been because you needed to make money, can it? I guess it was just for your own twisted enjoyment. You didn't care what it would do to her, how she would be affected, how she might react, did you? You might not have pushed her in front of that bus, but you killed her."

Étienne laughed. It was the sort of slightly manic laugh that escapes as a release for panic or fear.

"You can't prove a thing," he said, his voice loud and high-pitched. "And, even if you could, it's not my fault your crazy druggie sister killed herself."

He laughed again, less manic now.

"Your silly trick was a waste of time. What did you think I would do, run to the police and spill my guts? That I'd die of fright? You're an idiot."

"No, Étienne," I said, taking a vial from my pocket and uncorking it. "You're the fool."

I swallowed the liquid. It didn't taste pleasant, but medicine seldom does.

"I needed to be certain you were to blame, and your reaction proved it. Otherwise, I would've had to give you the antidote to the poison I put in the Ojen.

"But, I don't."

21

It was my turn to laugh, although it was more from bitterness than mirth.

"I might have made up the story about Annette, but I did say a prayer to Momus — over a 'potion' I got from an old-style conjureman. If he's right, it's undetectable. If not, there's no reason anyone would connect it to me."

Étienne began to gasp and clutched at his throat. The golden mask fell from atop his head, was trodden on by one of the revelers.

I picked up the bottle of liqueur and the glasses. "Tasted good didn't it?"

Then, I turned and slipped away into the crowd, leaving him to enjoy his last Mardi Gras, a sacrifice for the appeasement of Momus and the vengeance of my sister.

DJ Tyrer is the person behind Atlantean Publishing, was placed second in the Writing Magazine "Local Reporter" competition and has been widely published in anthologies and magazines around the world, such as *Disturbance* (Laurel Highlands), *Mysteries of Suspense* (Zimbell House), *History and Mystery, Oh My!* (Mystery & Horror LLC), and *Love 'Em, Shoot 'Em* (Wolfsinger), and issues of *Awesome Tales*, and, in addition, has a novella available in paperback and on Kindle, *The Yellow House* (Dunhams Manor).

DJ Tyrer's website is at
https://djtyrer.blogspot.co.uk/
The Atlantean Publishing website is at:
https://atlanteanpublishing.wordpress.com/

SOUTHERN DISCOMFORT

Grant Butler

Crowds didn't bother me, but this wasn't just a crowd. This was a sea of people. A horde of drunken bodies and hazy thoughts. It would normally be fun to watch, but I wasn't here for fun. I was here to work.

The great thing about working during Mardi Gras in New Orleans was that I didn't even need to make an effort to be incognito. Once I put on the mask, I had ceased to be Will Parker, private investigator, and became just another person in a Mardi Gras mask surrounded by other people in masks. It was ironic, because trying to figure out who was behind the mask is an apt way to describe my job. Mardi Gras is unique because it's one day where everyone acknowledges they wear elaborate masks in public. The reason I was down here was because a client of mine thought their spouse was wearing the mask of the loyal spouse, a common mask these days. Marriage is like college; not everyone is cut out for it.

Spouses worried about infidelity are a private eye's bread and butter. One could base an entire career off it if you so chose, especially if the nervous party has a lot of money. The best analogy is to imagine you had a luxury car and were worried about it being stolen. Now imagine how worried you'd be if you had $20,000 in cash stashed in the backseat. That's the mindset of a client who's rich and worried their partner is unfaithful.

For some strange reason, people have gotten it into their heads that a person's physical attractiveness is some sort of talisman that protects them from their partner cheating on them. I cannot tell you how many attractive women come to me, all nervous because they think their husband has their eye on someone else. Most people would take one look at these women and be like "Seriously? Your husband would have to be blind to cheat on you."

Well then that means a hell of a lot of people are blind, because attractive people get cheated on just as much as everyone else, perhaps even more so. The dirty little secret that attractive people know is that wandering eyes will not be deterred by anything, including looks. Show me a beautiful woman, and I'll show you a man who tossed her aside to screw her best friend or cousin right under her nose. And for every man who seems like a terrific catch, there's some woman out there who called him a loser and snubbed him just to get knocked up by some ex-felon.

At times I feel like a venereal disease doctor, since people pay me to discreetly investigate their dirty little secrets, but usually won't want to acknowledge me in public. But I get it. If you hire me to see if your wife is screwing your coworker, you can't exactly introduce me to your friends from work if you see me at the bar on Friday night. I've bumped into clients in their everyday life once or twice and it can definitely make for an awkward encounter. You know that sensation when you're younger and stumble upon one of your teachers outside of school? It's like that times 1000. But it's all part of the job and I don't exactly mind. Just more good stories for me when I want to entertain my friends during a night on the town. And sometimes if I get lucky, I get to travel to some choice locations while being paid for it. The only thing better than visiting New Orleans was getting paid to visit New Orleans.

The reason I was being paid to visit New Orleans, during Mardi Gras of all times, was Mr. Francis Sinclair. A wealthy hospital administrator, he made an appointment to see me on a dreary December afternoon. I can still see his face, the heavy-lidded eyes and pale skin. Not a bad looking guy *per se*, but he reeked of unhappiness.

"I have good reason to believe my wife Alexa is cheating on me and I'd like to confirm it," was Frank's response when I asked him why he made the appointment.

"Very well. What reason do you have to believe this?"

"She's been acting all secretive. And on top of that, she's been working out more and whenever she says she's doing stuff with her female friends, she's putting on new perfume and getting her hair done differently. Believe me, I love it when Alexa puts in effort to look good, but I'm not stupid. There's one reason, and only one reason a woman puts that much effort into their appearance."

"That's fair. Anything else?"

"Yes. She's been spending a lot more time visiting her family down in Louisiana. She's originally from there and we moved here to Chicago shortly after our wedding. Her family owns one of those big plantations that's only a short drive from New Orleans."

"I see. How old is she?"

"39."

"Okay."

"Is that significant?"

"Absolutely," I said. "That's right in the hot zone for when many spouses are unfaithful. I'm sure I don't need to tell you the psychological impact hitting 40 has for people."

"Got that right."

Frank agreed to my standard retainer and I made his wife Alexa my new assignment. An athletic brunette, she was an attractive woman by any standards. When Frank tipped me off that she planned to see her family for Mardi Gras, which was normal for her, I followed her here from Chicago. From the looks of it she was having a great time amongst the alcohol consuming, bead flinging, dancing partygoers. The entire city had become a makeshift dance floor. It was a wonder to behold.

No matter how many times you visit New Orleans, you never get used to the feeling. I suspect that even people who were born here, raised here, and never lived anywhere else feel that way too. It's so exotic and unique. If cities were relatives gathered together for a family event, New Orleans would be the aunt that says and does whatever she feels like and has some of the best stories you've ever heard, whether they're true or not.

The classic architecture and old-style streetlights served as the backdrop for occult shops and stores selling authentic Mardi Gras masks and beads, which were nothing like the knockoffs at Party City. And every year, all these stores got a front row seat for when people put on masks, get appallingly drunk, and occasionally expose themselves to strangers. But that's par for the course in a city called The Big Easy. The place is certainly big, but it's anything but easy. I've visited almost every major American city, and there is nowhere even remotely close to it. New York may be the city that never sleeps, but New Orleans is the city that never stops partying. Even the most famous serial killer to ever walk these streets wanted to hear some jazz while out on the prowl.

But long before a guy with an axe simultaneously taunted the city's residents and celebrated jazz, this town was the refuge of pirates, prostitutes, smugglers, and virtually every kind of misfit that was found back in the day. Not that it's changed much since then, as the city is full of interesting characters. Gourmet restaurants and jazz clubs sit right beside Voodoo shops while tourists gawk at the statue of Andrew

Jackson before signing up for one of the many haunted New Orleans tours. There's something around here for everyone. Most modern cities bend over backwards to hide their less savory aspects and occasionally sketchy histories, while New Orleans openly revels in their more "colorful" aspects. How the hell can you not love a town like that? Since the town predates Vegas by about 200 years, it's America's original Sin City.

The swamp around New Orleans is what the desert is to Las Vegas; the burying ground for things people want to disappear. But unlike the desert, you can't exactly dig a hole around here and bury something, or someone, because once it rains, it'll come right back up. That's the reason for all the above-ground cemeteries and another reason why the city is so unique. Since you can't just dig a hole and bury someone, the other option is to grab a boat and hope that the alligators are hungry. While Vegas and the Wild West had cowboy gangs, pirates were the first type of organized crime to make their presence known here in New Orleans.

The saga of cops and robbers, heroes and villains, is as old as civilization itself, but it comes in many different forms. First came pirates, probably the oldest type of gang in history, and it's still very much in existence today. Sure, the Spanish Galleon ships and Jolly Roger flags are gone, but the manner of existence is virtually unchanged. The biggest difference is that instead of flintlock muskets they have fully operational assault weapons.

Other cities claim to be founded by humble people seeking a better life. New Orleans happens to be one of my absolute favorite cities because it not only openly proclaims its history, it challenges you. The Big Easy makes no bones about the fact that many people here have suffered in both the past and present. It's no coincidence that a city with a homicide rate that has exceeded anything in Chicago or Detroit is also home to Mardi Gras, aka Fat Tuesday. That's a city that says, "Yeah we've suffered, but we're still standing and damn it, we're gonna have one hell of a party to celebrate that." Now that's a city with soul. A soul that was currently in full swing around me while I kept a low profile to watch Mrs. Sinclair while she hugged some people goodbye before leaving the bar she was at.

As I walked carefully behind Alexa, it reinforced my belief that New Orleans isn't just a city, it's a way of life. Every step you took there was something exotic to look at, some bit of history or culture just waiting to be soaked up. While that was perfectly true of other cities, here it felt different. More alive. Like the past wasn't really in the past and history was much closer at hand. Instead of lurking in art galleries or museums, it was staring you in the face, whether you liked it or not. It hung just as heavy in the air as the humidity did on this balmy night. In this town, most people seem to relish reliving their unusual history. Good for them.

Nothing embodied this more than the city's above ground cemeteries, one of which was in sight as Alexa walked past some people spilling out of a jazz club. In other places you could forget a cemetery was where someone was buried, the neatly manicured lawns and other signs of careful grooming reminding you more of a country club than a graveyard. Not here. The massive ornate mausoleums crowding each other was a constant reminder that the city's past was not content to stay on a page in some dusty book. Almost as if the land itself sought to remind people that the past quite literally would not stay buried here.

Alexa weaved her way through the streets with ease, but not once did she glance behind her to see who else was around. No surprise there. Watching someone in an unruly crowd of people is a piece of cake. No one notices someone may be looking at them when there are so many people around who've had plenty of strong drinks.

So that's why when Alexa caught the eye of a man in a red feathered mask and made a beeline for him, she was clueless that I was not only watching her the entire time, but taking pictures of it on my phone. There was no hesitation, no pause to evaluate the situation, just an instant flash of recognition before initiating contact. That meant she not only knew him but was expecting him. That was no surprise. No woman ever goes alone to a Mardi Gras event without a reason.

The mask hid his face, but I could tell he was well built and muscled. He had a shaved head and his arms bulged out of a tight black T-shirt and a few strings of gold beads sat on top of what I could tell was a toned chest. The left arm was completely covered in a tattoo sleeve, while he clutched a drink in his right hand.

They were talking close, but that was all for now. There were no affectionate gestures. None of the enthusiastic making out that countless others around here were doing. In fact, they didn't seem affectionate at all. But it was possible this was the first time they were meeting to hook up. There was no doubt she planned to meet this guy and they knew each other; the only question was: what exactly was their relationship? That was the question I was being paid to get the answer to. Suddenly, they both started walking in the opposite direction. I made sure to follow carefully, but at a safe distance.

As I followed the pair, I made sure to keep busy on my phone. Back in the old days, private investigators would kick back and chain-smoke while on a job. Aside from it being a habit, it was something they did to pass the time. But more importantly, smoking a cigarette made them look busy and concealed the fact they were loitering somewhere because they were on a job. But since I don't smoke and we're in the 21st century, whenever I'm on a job I take out my phone and scroll through it instead of lighting up a cigarette and taking a drag. While phones, social media, and the internet are addicting in their own way, a smart phone is far more useful for PI work than a cig could ever be.

While the two were deep in conversation, I managed to get a picture of Alexa's male associate when he briefly took off his mask to scratch his face. He was in his late thirties to early forties and had a tanned face with only a hint of dark stubble. I texted a picture of him to Frank in the hopes that he'd recognize him. My timing was good, as the pair stopped talking and went their separate ways shortly after that.

Frank responded about 10 minutes later.
"No idea who he is."
Regardless, I kept watching Alexa as she walked back the way she came. If the two were an item, they were doing a great job hiding it. I could tell they were acquainted, but I know the look of two people having a steamy tryst and these two simply didn't have it. But then how did they know each other, and more importantly, why were they meeting?

After some time, Alexa found her way back to the hotel she was staying at while down here. The next day, she went about her normal business by spending time with family and some female friends. But what really caught my attention was how she wasn't hiding herself down here. If anything, she was more than happy to be amongst friends and seemed to revel in the attention. Watching them all taking pictures with each other, it was bizarre. If Alexa was trying to keep a low profile down here, she was doing a horrible job of it.

Then it hit me. What if she wasn't trying to hide herself? What if she wanted to be seen out with people because she was building an alibi? But then the question became an alibi for what?

With that question in mind, I took my phone out of my pocket and dialed Frank. I was operating on pure instinct now.

"Will?" he asked when he picked up on the third ring. "What's wrong?"

"Nothing, but I have a question to ask you. Is there anything preventing you from checking into a hotel and staying for a few days?"

"Um, no, I can do that. But I don't know why I would. What aren't you telling me?"

"I have an idea. It's nothing concrete, but I think it's best you stayed at a hotel."

"Ok. But there better be a reason for it."

"There is. Whatever you do tonight, don't go anywhere that's deserted. Stay in public places, the better populated the better."

"I won't do anything tonight."

"Very good. One last thing, and it's very important. Can you change the code to your alarm system?"

"Yes,"

"Do that before you leave, which you should do right now if you can. And whatever you do tonight, do not, I repeat, *do not*, go back to your house tonight."

"Can I ask you one thing before I do all this?"

"Sure,"

"Should I be afraid?"

"Not if you do what I ask."

"All right, Will, you're the one everyone recommended to me. I'll take your advice."

"Good deal. Let me know if you need anything."

With that, I hung up and went back to silently watching Alexa go through her ordinary day. After a while she returned to her hotel while I parked down the street and kept watch. By this time, it was late. It was well after 11 pm when I received an incoming call from Frank.

"Yeah?" I answered immediately.

"The police just left my house," he began. "They were called there by the alarm company, who also notified me that my system had been activated. And when they got there, they found a man there who had a key and claimed to be a house guest. That story lasted for all of two seconds when I told them I had none and was at a hotel for the evening. But I did recognize him."

"From where?"

"From the picture you sent me of him talking to my wife last night. There's one more thing, Will. When they searched his car, they found a bunch of stuff that's typically used to blow up houses and make it look like an accident."

Grant Butler is an author from the Midwest who writes in a variety of fiction genres as well as in true crime and general film criticism. Some of his literary influences include Stephen King, Ira Levin, Agatha Christie, and Thomas Harris. Cinema is also a big influence on his storytelling and some favorite films of his are *Jaws*, *The Godfather*, *Goodfellas*, and *Psycho*.

THE STEEL PELICAN

Nathan Pettigrew

It was the first murder of 2020 in Terrebonne Parish, and the first since the Krewe of Hercules had kicked off this year's Mardi Gras season. Anna Theriot's pale blue face and forehead were still warm when a drunk couple drove upon her body at the end of Sandy Beach Road on February 16th. The clock in their Dodge Ram read ten past 3 AM, the headlights intensifying the blood from her mouth and nose, and the bruises on her neck.

A senior at Terrebonne High, her best friend was Sarah Jean Prejean who ran the bike trails near Sandy Beach Road on Mondays, Tuesdays, and Thursdays, while Sheriff Anselmo studied her every move. Emancipated from an abusive foster home at the age of sixteen, she didn't have family to celebrate her upcoming graduation with or any pets waiting in her garage apartment on Wilson Ave.

She was perfect. Anselmo sat in his cruiser on Tuesday the 18th until a quarter past four p.m. when Sarah pulled into the Sandy Beach parking lot under the brutal sun of Terrebonne—right on time. She stepped out from her emerald green Civic in a tight black and long-sleeved body suit, never failing to surprise Anselmo. In Terrebonne's humidity? Girl liked to sweat.

"Ms. Prejean," he said when stepping out. "I have some news on Anna's case."

She held her hand above her eyes as he approached her.

"I have some news on Anna's case," he said. "Some good news. Mind if I walk with you?"

"No, of course, not," she said, her amber eyes turning green when she brought her hand down.

"How have you been holding up?" he asked.

She made the sign of the cross. "Taking it one day at a time."

"Of course," he said. "Have to say, though. I'm surprised to see you still jogging around these parts given the circumstances."

"Guess I'm used to confronting my fears," she said.

"Is that it?" Anselmo asked.

The parking lot behind them was now blocked from their view by endless moss that dangled from the oak trees on both sides of the trail.

Anselmo placed his arm in front of Sarah.

"What is it?" she asked. "What's wrong?"

"Shh. That's a snake," he said.

"Where?"

He slipped on a pair of patrol gloves. Stepping forward, seeing nothing, he turned and threw a right hook into Sarah's jaw.

She couldn't move after falling to the dirt, but nevertheless, Anselmo told her to stay put. He found a decent-sized rock in the woods and brought it down against her temple. He was different from the killers he'd arrested in his time as a lawman; their eyes were always devoid of emotion, whereas Anselmo's would tear up in a fleeting moment of sadness before his new appreciation for how precious life was. His passion for ending precious life was the biggest mystery of his own life, but his indifference toward the families of his victims was no more twisted than that of the universe's.

He left Sarah's body for someone to find and questioned the young male jogger who'd dialed 911 when arriving at the scene. First showing his badge with the pelican engraved in steel, Sheriff Anselmo had the trails of Sandy Beach taped off and sent Deputy Naquin for coffee before taking the jogger's official statement.

"You okay, Sheriff?" the deputy asked when returning. "You seem confused about something."

"Fine. Just—the jogger said the parking lot was empty when he arrived."

"So?"

"The victim's car, you dimwit. She lives in downtown Houma and walked here? So, where is it?"

"How do you know for sure she drove?" the deputy asked. "Girl liked to jog the trails, after all. Maybe she liked to walk long distances, too."

"Or maybe it was stolen," Anselmo said.

One could only hope. Racking his brain, Anselmo was positive that he remembered the Civic having no passengers, only doubting himself because he'd left the vehicle in the parking lot before leaving the scene. All he could confirm at this point was that he'd left the Civic behind, and that it was gone by the time the jogger arrived to find Sarah's body.

Come morning, Anselmo spread *The Courier* across his kitchen table and flinched when his toast popped up.

Sarah Jean Prejean was all over the front page—as expected—her brutal murder now the second in Terrebonne since Mardi Gras had started and the second to occur near Sandy Beach Road. Anselmo had given a statement the night before, promising that an intense investigation was under way and asking for patience, but much to his surprise, *The Courier* revealed that Sarah Jean Prejean was the estranged daughter of Mary Herbert—Anselmo's second cousin.

"You can't be serious," he said.

What were the freaking odds?

As a young woman about to graduate from Terrebonne High, Sarah Jean Prejean looked nothing like the 3-year-old that Anselmo had last seen at a family reunion. How could he have known? She'd taken a different last name, after all. Anselmo crumbled and tossed *The Courier* before pacing his kitchen floor, his toast getting cold.

The wake and funeral were a must, not just for a lawman investigating the murder, but for a family member, and Aunt Mary broke down on the altar of Trinity Baptist while giving her only daughter's eulogy. Sarah Jean had ended up in foster care at a young age because of Mary's crack habit in those days, but still managed to make a life for herself as a young adult while working after school and weekends at Mr. Ronnie's Famous Hot Donuts on Tunnel Boulevard. She was about to graduate from Terrebonne High as a straight-A student and had reached out to Mary at Christmas to offer forgiveness, going as far as to visit the home where she was born down Bayou Black.

Her last text message was to her best friend Anna Theriot describing the effects of a something new in town called DMT—a fact that Mary Herbert wasn't privy to. Ol' Aunt Mary was the main distributor of DMT in Terrebonne Parish, having reached two subdivisions in the city of Houma and all three of the main bayous at the bottom of Terrebonne. Could that have been Sarah Jean's true motive for reaching out to her estranged mother?

Aunt Mary had a buffet prepared for guests at the reception, the fried catfish served with crawfish étouffée, white beans and rice and French bread. Anselmo wasn't the only one not eating, taking notice of the unconscious individual in the living room on Aunt Mary's sofa. Cousin Arty. A functioning alcoholic who'd worked offshore for different oil companies before getting laid off to the point of no return.

Anselmo slapped his face.

"'The fuck?" Arty sat up. "Are they all gone?"

"You remember me?" Anselmo asked.

"What? Of course," Arty said, shaking his hand. "Thanks for coming."

He invited Anselmo to sit in the armchair across.

"Still carrying the flask?" Anselmo asked.

"Why? You want a pull?"

"Why not? I'm off duty for another hour," Anselmo said.

Arty slid the silver flask from his back pocket and waited for Anselmo to take his pull before reaching out for his turn.

"How's the crime fighting?" he asked, and then he emptied the flask.

"Never a dull moment," Anselmo said, "and I'll promise you, Arty. I will find who did this to Sarah Jean."

"If you haven't, already," Arty said.

"Meaning what?"

"Meaning y'all might know more than you're willing to tell the public, but I guess it's personal for you, now."

"It's always personal in Terrebonne," Anselmo said.

"Then why no arrests? We're talking two bodies, now."

"I heard that about you, Arty. A bitter drunk not worth employing."

"Don't need employment, right now," he said.

"Is that right?"

"That's right, you asshole. You're the one who needs it. So, do your job. That is, if you can."

Aunt Mary entered the living room and put her hand on Anselmo's shoulder.

"Well, it's sure nice to see y'all together again. You're not eating, Victor?"

"No, ma'am." Anselmo stood to hold her hands. "Can't stay long."

"I understand," she said. "You have a job to do."

"Yes, ma'am."

"Better get to it, then," she said.

Anselmo had promised to follow up, but the community was growing impatient. Citizens of Terrebonne had taken to social media to point out the incompetence of Anselmo and suggested that the Sheriff's Office should seek outside help from the state—or hell, anyone who cared and was capable enough. Two murders, no arrests, and residents no longer dared to go near Sandy Beach. Some even questioned if going to the parades was still safe.

The career saver for Anselmo, as always, was Aileen Verdan—the true power in Terrebonne. As sole owner of Earhart's Bermuda East, she ran a multi-generational den of three floors for locals from all bayous and backgrounds seeking sex and drugs. She had the support of the people after saving some local businesses from the chains trying to turn Terrebonne into another corporate stop on the southern map, and she had local politicians and police in her pocket, but she no longer dealt with Anselmo directly.

The weight of this reality was almost heavy on his heart. He was loyal—through and through. He'd taken out her adversaries and even killed her father on a Christmas morning after Aileen decided the time had come to wear the crown, but now she had cut him out of her inner circle.

He couldn't get close enough to ask her why. There was always a middleman involved when it came to taking orders these days, and she'd arranged for one of her politicians in Baton Rouge to meet with Anselmo about a game plan for current events in Terrebonne Parish. A hungry bastard if Anselmo had ever met one. Agreeing to see the sheriff on the morning of Friday the 21st before Mardi Gras, the politician had a Saints platter of crabs on his desk that one of the prison trustees had boiled for him.

"So how can we shut this social media thing up?" he asked before sucking the meat from a claw.

"We can get Mary Herbert on drug charges," Anselmo said. "She's one of these local shamans pushing this new DMT

38

shit—the same shit we found in her dead daughter's apartment after Sandy Beach, and—"

"That's all you have?" the politician asked. He stuffed some crab meat into his mouth before wiping his face with his sleeve. "'Cause we're talking about a serial killer. During Mardi Gras when the state brings in the most money? And you're focused on one family and their drug problems?"

"I thought Sarah might've been connected to her best friend's murder," Anselmo said. "That's why I was following her, but what if the person who killed her is connected to this new drug in some way? We should at least put it out there that this could be drug-related and not random. Social media will pick it up."

"Fuck it. Do it," the politician said, still eating without making eye contact. "And do it fast, Anselmo. This social media thing could determine your future. If it were up to me, I'd ask for a word with the governor and we would be having a different conversation, but Aileen Verdan says you stay for now."

There it was—the name of the shot caller who no longer associated with Anselmo in private.

He'd last seen her face when watching dear life depart the eyes of Sarah Jean Prejean.

"Are you listening?" the politician asked.

"Yes, sir," Anselmo said.

"You better be," the politician said, making eye contact for the first time. "'Cause we have assholes from all over the world coming down here for Mardi Gras and the last thing we need is a serial killer on the loose. It's bad for business and bad enough that everyone's getting more anxious about this COVID thing going on in Wuhan."

"No one in Terrebonne is sick," Anselmo said. "Just scared. And both murders took place on Sandy Beach Road. Parades and businesses shouldn't be affected after this play, but I'm on it."

"Yeah, and what about what this other noise *The Courier* made regarding the mistreatment of homeless people by authorities during Mardi Gras?"

"I wouldn't worry about that one, sir. Folks in Terrebonne, like most folks in America, have more sympathy for stray dogs than they do for homeless people."

The politician ignored him while bending down to suck the meat from another crab leg.

Anselmo closed the door on his way out. "Fat fuck."

Aunt Mary rented a second home in the neighboring parish of Lafourche and had gone there to escape media attention, and probably to expand her DMT empire. Her home was a cushy apartment in downtown Thibodeaux, and Aunt Mary met Anselmo's familial eyes when walking in from a long day at the Lafourche Parish Public Library.

He knocked her out in the vestibule with one punch. He kicked her stomach and pulled a blade out before kneeling on her shoulders.

"Drug-dealing bitch. Say hi to your daughter for me."

He cut her throat, the serial killer having relocated to Lafourche Parish. That's what *The Courier* and *The Daily Comet* would report come morning — the latest murder confirming a connection in the eyes of readers, of gossipers. First the best friend, then the daughter, and now the estranged mother — all drug-related.

Folks in Terrebonne were about to find themselves in confused state of empathy and horror, but relief in knowing the green light had been given for attending the Mardi Gras parades without fear. The killings were no longer random, and no longer taking place near Sandy Beach, much less Terrebonne.

Anselmo had done his job, but hesitated to leave the apartment while remaining curious about the DMT on Aunt Mary's coffee table.

What was so special about it? Anselmo had dabbled in every narcotic that he'd arrested others for possessing, but not this stuff—not yet. The first drug to become a viral sensation in Terrebonne, local YouTubers had claimed DMT to be the answer to depression, anxiety, even alcoholism and drug addiction. The buzz was all bullshit in Anselmo's mind, but he remained too curious, wanting to know the truth behind the new show in town.

He picked up the pipe and packed it.

"Well, here goes nothing."

He took a hit, feeling no different at first, and then he inhaled another, deeper hit, hearing a high-pitched ringing that reached to a deafening level, having silenced the very concept of other sounds.

Objects and surfaces appeared more crystalized, becoming as bright as the sun—until it all became one light, and one object that broke apart into geometric shapes and designs. And he wasn't alone. Multiple entities had entered this space, appearing as jesters all laughing and dancing around him—Mardi Gras jesters—their capuchons and three-tail harlequin hats made from bright gold, purple and green light. While laughing and dancing, they communicated with Anselmo using telepathy. *We're so happy you found us. We're so happy you're here. We love you. We love you. We love you.*

And he could feel the immense warmth of their joy to see him, their genuine regard for his well-being, their compassion—emotions he knew existed but had never felt before—and certainly not from another human being. He reached out to hold their hands, but was catapulted away from them like being shot from a circus cannon. Entering a place that he could describe only as alien, he searched for words to explain his surroundings in English, French, and Italian—the three languages he spoke—coming up empty. Either way, this place felt more real than reality.

He received the gift of familiarity when exposed to a spinning circle of bright and shining souls connected by love

41

that stretched beyond the light years of any galaxy — a destination that he'd been to so many times — after life and before birth. Only he wasn't supposed to be here in this moment — another telepathic message from an unseen entity. It wasn't his time yet, and while he was welcome to stay here for as long as he wanted when his time did come, he would be encouraged to go back and try his hand at life again, for there was nothing else to do with eternity.

The life he lived now had resulted in the murders of family members, and for the first time, guilt plagued his cold heart. Another emotion that he was aware of but hadn't experienced in his life, the guilt was crushing — so sad and so much heavier than any weight he'd known up to this point. And almost as if he were the dead one, his life flashed before the eye of his mind.

Despised by his teachers at Saint Timothy's grade school, Anselmo could see through the control of religion. He could solve the math problems his classmates couldn't — a straight A student that nuns prevented from taking part in honors classes — the covered-up women too disturbed by the drawings in his textbooks. With incredible detail, a young Anselmo brought glory to Michael Myers, Jason Vorhees, and Freddy Kruger. For Anselmo, these killers had taken the place of the Father, the Son, and the Holy Spirit.

The satisfaction he'd found from killing caterpillars in the Saint Timothy's schoolyard during recess was nothing compared to the adrenaline rush of his accomplishments as an adult killer. He'd ended the precious life of three women, now, of flesh and real blood and not the green muck of insects.

Socially awkward, girls and women never took to him and neither did the single mother who'd raised him on a social worker's salary before succumbing to mental illness. She didn't have much to offer beyond verbal abuse, and she'd left him without a reason to trust a living soul. He never knew his father and never felt the desire to find him. He'd felt disrespected and abandoned by existence itself — that is until he flashed a badge with the state bird engraved in steel.

If not for Aileen Verdan, Anselmo would've been another psycho locked up. Her father had financed his campaign — a favor as Anselmo had watched out for Aileen as a deputy while she struggled to overcome her rebellious teenage years.

With newfound power and impunity, Anselmo was free to kill again but had gone too far, his family in pieces that he didn't have the power to put back together.

Back in the living room of Aunt Mary's apartment in Thibodeaux, Anselmo sat up, wiping his eyes. Groggy, but his thoughts were his own again, and his first one surprised Anselmo. He thought of Cousin Arty — the functioning alcoholic.

He checked his watch, seeing that only fifteen minutes had passed since he'd blasted off.

Fifteen minutes, but it had felt like a lifetime. Getting to his feet, Anselmo stopped in the vestibule when faced with Aunt Mary's body. Crying to the point of sobbing, he felt something that had been missing from his life until this downer of a moment. A conscience. He was finally afraid of himself, and if only he'd tried the DMT on Aunt Mary's coffee table before she had come home ... Fifteen minutes out of his day would've made the difference of a lifetime for her.

The sheriff jumped when his cell rang, and he answered. "Anselmo."

"Sheriff. It's Naquin, and we haven't located that green Civic yet. No one's seen it."

"Keep looking," Anselmo said, and then he disconnected.

Still groggy, Anselmo drove back to Terrebonne and down to her house in Bayou Black where she had allowed Cousin Arty a place to pass out.

Anselmo found him on the sofa in the living room.

"Arty," he said, nudging him. "Arty, wake up."

"Victor?" he asked, his eyes still closed.

"It's me. Come on. Take a ride with me."

"You find Sarah's killer?"

"Well, I found something, but you need to see for yourself. Come on. Get up."

"Fill my flask, would you?"

Anselmo found the flask in Arty's back pocket.

"Where do you keep the bourbon?"

"Kitchen. Under the sink."

"How original."

Arty hadn't changed his clothes or brushed his teeth while Anselmo filled the flask, still on the sofa and not moving.

"Damn it, Arty."

"I'm up, Victor. Jesus."

His body slung from the sofa like a Slinky, his feet hitting the floor and the rest of him rolling over into the coffee table.

"Jesus." Anselmo ran over and helped him up. "You okay?"

"Fine," Arty said, pushing him off. "The flask?"

"Here, damn it. I don't think you need more, right now."

"No, you're right," Arty said. "It's for later, but I plan on sleeping in your backseat if it's all the same to you."

"That works," Anselmo said. "Come on. Put your arm around my shoulder. Think you can make it to the car?"

"Wouldn't be the first time," Arty said.

Anselmo drove to his house in Broadmoor—a middle-class subdivision that pretended to be lower class. Houses were made from bricks, and while the one and two-story homes weren't as nice as the brick homes in Summerfield or Southdown West, the way folks in those subdivisions lived meant funding the appearance of money, of doing better than others and having nicer things while folks in Broadmoor had more in their bank accounts.

44

But the inside of Anselmo's house was a wreck. Microwave food cartons were piled up on his kitchen counter while his floors and windowsills had collected balls of dust. Books were stacked on both his couch and recliner.

"Here," Anselmo said, clearing a spot on the couch for Arty.

"I don't think I've — ever been here," Arty said.

"You haven't," Anselmo said. "Please. Have a seat."

He sat and was able to stay sitting up. Anselmo tossed a packet on the coffee table.

"What's this?"

"DMT."

"Damn," Arty said, sliding it away. "I already told Ma — I want nothing do with that shit."

"Afraid I'm insisting," Anselmo said.

"Insisting?" Arty asked, amused. "Meaning what? You're holding a gun to my head?"

Anselmo pulled his piece, aiming between his cousin's brown eyes.

"Call it an intervention," Anselmo said.

"Well, okay, then," Arty said. He took the packet in his hands. "How do I go about doing this shit?"

Anselmo set a glass pipe on the coffee table.

"Looks like a crack pipe, Cousin Victor."

"It is," Anselmo said. "Pick it up. Take three long hits, and no worries — I got you."

"Well, that's comforting, Cousin Victor — especially with a gun to my head."

Anselmo holstered his piece.

"Trust me," he said. "The whole thing lasts about fifteen minutes and you won't regret it."

Arty did as told, unable to move or remember where he was for a little longer than Anselmo expected — almost twenty minutes.

"Looks like you're back," Anselmo said.

"How — how long was I — ?"

45

"Almost twenty minutes."

"Twenty minutes? Are you serious?"

Arty sat up, wiping his eyes.

"Felt like a lifetime, yeah?"

Removing his hands from his face, Arty stared at Anselmo wide-eyed, and changed.

"Why did you want me to do that?" he asked.

"Felt I owed you one, seeing how you just lost your sister and mother. I mean—let's face it. I'm the only family you have left."

"Okay, but—"

"The flask," Anselmo said. "You want it?"

Arty shrugged. "Where is it?"

"Do you want it or not?"

Arty had no words.

"You're not sure, are you?" Anselmo asked. "For the first time in your life, you're not sure."

"Is that's what this is?" Arty asked. "A cure?"

"Would be irresponsible for me to say, cousin. Doesn't work the same on everyone from what I understand, but I know it's helped others."

Arty sat back, his attention on the dusty window blinds.

"You need a housekeeper," he said.

"I'll take care when there's time," Anselmo said.

"So, what—what now?" Arty asked.

"Mardi Gras," Anselmo said. "Fat Tuesday's right around the corner. Biggest parade of the year."

"That's a rough scene," Arty said, his attention returning to the dusty blinds.

"But a good test for you, cousin. Look, I'm on duty but can get you a good spot near the courthouse. You interested?"

"With a gun to my head?" Arty asked, his attention on Anselmo, now.

"Do you see my gun?"

"Okay, so let's do it," Arty said. "'Cause the way I see it? I owe you one in return if all works out."

"Well, I don't know if that's true. Arty. Just hoping to make a difference in your life is all."

"Let's just see if I can handle the Krewe of Houmas, first," Arty said.

The final parade of the year on Fat Tuesday, the Krewe of Houmas was the one that the entire city of Houma and all surrounding bayous showed up for. Arty took his place on the courthouse balcony where Anselmo had introduced him to some colleagues, some lawyers and judges and their families before leaving him behind.

Anselmo's Carnivals were a much different experience from the ones of citizens since he was elected sheriff as he was needed on the streets and required to call the shots for deputies responding to fights, public intoxication, and lewdness.

Arty would get to enjoy the better side of Mardi Gras, catching beads and laughing with children while flipping off the masked riders on the floats if they threw too little, but chances of that happening with the Krewe of Houmas were fat with most of the floats. The wealthiest of the Houma-Terrebonne Carnival Clubs, their riders threw packs of beads instead of singles and real doubloons versus the cheap coins of Krewes past.

The people of Terrebonne waited in parking lots, fields, in front of stores and fast food businesses — mostly on sidewalks and streets — while others had elevated themselves on work planks, giant scaffoldings, and some on balconies like Arty.

The wait before any parade kicked off was never a problem, and the best part in some eyes. There was more food than anyone would see for forty days. Some crawfish boils. Though mostly barbeques since the crawfish were still small and not in season. And plenty of booze.

Where Anselmo would get to enjoy a hamburger from the grill of a local if he were lucky to have five minutes to spare, Arty would see every opportunity to indulge in hard liquor.

He was standing straight when Anselmo pulled up to the courthouse to retrieve him.

"So, how was it?" he asked. "'Cause you're looking sober, cousin."

"Definitely sober," Arty said, shutting the passenger door, "and ready to repay the favor. That was the most fun I've had in a long time, man. Thank you."

"We're family," Anselmo said, pulling away.

"Hey, you remember how Uncle Boo used to own that barn down Bayou Blue?" Arty asked.

"Vaguely," Anselmo said. "I'm aware of the property because of my job, but I don't remember ever going there while Boo owned it. Who owns it now?"

"Mary," Arty said. "Or, well. She did."

The crushing weight of guilt split Anselmo's heart in two. If only he'd tried the DMT before their encounter, and if only he'd found DMT before this year's Mardi Gras season had started.

"Are you paying attention?" Arty asked.

Anselmo snapped out of it. "To the road? Yeah. You want me to head over to the barn?"

"Affirmative," Arty said. He found Stevie Wonder's "Superstition" on the radio before buckling his seatbelt and playing air drums.

The barn was well kept, the surrounding grass and shrubs all cut and trimmed.

Arty was the first to get out while Anselmo killed the engine, but he did something curious in signaling for Anselmo to get out before unlocking the barn doors.

He tossed the keys to Anselmo. "Go ahead. You'll like what's in there."

Anselmo stuck the key into the padlock and pulled the left barndoor open, able to see a covered car. He turned to Arty.

"Go ahead," Arty said. "See what's under there."

"What is this?" Anselmo asked, knowing full well what this was and what he had seen.

He came close to pulling his piece when Arty got the drop on him, pulling a Glock 17.

"Was passed out in the backseat while you killed her, and imagine my surprise when I saw the sheriff — my cousin — leaving the scene of the crime when I got out for some air."

Anselmo had no words.

"Seriously?" Arty asked. "You've got nothing to say? Would you even like to know what her last words to me were?"

"I have — no idea, Arty."

"Of course, you don't," Arty said. "Sarah left cracks in the windows and asked if I was sure if I wouldn't be dead from the humidity when she returned. Know what I said?"

"You know I don't, Arty."

"She said damn, brother. You sure like to sweat."

Arty fired two shots into Anselmo's chest, and his body exploded into fire with Mardi Gras jesters dancing and laughing around him.

Welcome back. We knew when you were coming, and we're so glad to see you again. We're so glad. So glad. So glad.

Nathan Pettigrew was born and raised an hour south of New Orleans and lives in the Tampa area with his loving wife after sharing a close friendship as residents of Massachusetts. Recent stories have appeared in "The Year" Anthology from *Crack the Spine, Switchblade* Issue 12 and at *Bristol Noir*. Other stories have appeared in *Stoneboat*, and the *Nasty: Fetish Fights Back* anthology from Anna Yeatts of *Flash Fiction Online*, which was spotlighted in a 2017 *Rolling Stone* article. His story "The

Queen of the South Side" was recently named Honorable Mention in the Genre Short Story category for the 88th Annual *Writer's Digest* Writing Competition. Other genre stories have appeared in the award-winning pages of *Thuglit*, the *Mardi Gras Murder* anthology from Mystery and Horror, LLC, and at DarkMedia.com. Visit Nathan @NathanBorn2010.

Carnival Carnage

John Kiste

Everyone in the 8th Police District, if not the entire Parish, knew that while I wasn't a practitioner of New Orleans Voodoo, I put much stock in the religion and its teachings. Even the more outré doctrines of its teachings. I always carried a leather gris-gris bag on a cord beneath my shirt, and a tiny part of me trusted the odd-numbered diverse contents to somehow keep me safe while on duty. Especially the charm that had been my wife's. In my mind, it would have been a doubly powerful charm if she had died, but she hadn't. She went back to Ohio with half our bank account after we spent Katrina huddled in the Superdome. Now I only missed her on odd-numbered days.

My surname was Glapion, the same as the famous Voodoo Queen Marie Laveau's husband, and some of my colleagues thought I was a distant relative. Though I never told them so, I am not. Like many who accept a fraction of the tenets of Mississippi Valley Voodoo, I was a practicing Roman Catholic, and even occasionally stopped by St. Louis Cathedral for special services. Nonetheless, I gave far more credence to the bizarre features of this fusion belief system of the African diaspora than was acceptable in my line of work as a police detective. It was probably why I was still a lieutenant. But that was about to change.

The whole mess began with a parade float maker who had a growing reputation: Tom Fitzhugh of Metairie. Of course, everyone knew no one could make a Rex float like the world-famous Blaine Kern. But Fitzhugh's *Jester* was a masterpiece, part D.C.'s Joker and part Poe's Fortunato. And it breathed fire. It was now legendary. A number of krewes awaited this year's parades mainly to see what he would serve up next. Buoyed by his extensive press, Fitzhugh refused to pay protection to a local crime boss, Pierre Taum-Lauren. Fitzhugh had his own security at his warehouse, and he believed his new fame would go a long way to dissuading trouble. The float maker didn't know that Taum-Lauren's syndicate was being beset by upstart mobsters, and it was imperative he make an example of someone. He ordered Fitzhugh beaten to death in his own design workshop, and a middle-aged laborer and porter named Paul Tergon saw the murder from a gantry above. He effected an escape out the window when Taum-Lauren's thugs spotted and recognized him.

Now we were holding Tergon in a safe house, and Taum-Lauren was under indictment, jailed, and strangely reluctant to post bail. It was going to be an eventful Mardi Gras. My partner, Sergeant Lucian Ellsworth, and I had been assigned to Tergon's security detail. Ellsworth was a literal delight, a great brawny black man of gigantic stature who had grown up in the Garden District, and who only ever called the holiday Pancake Tuesday — and backed up the epithet with his monstrous appetite. He was a loud down-to-earth clown, but you never doubted that in a scrape, and we had seen a few, he would be thinking of your life before his own. He had been the first cop to greet me when I had transferred from Cleveland twenty years before. I had stood up with him at his wedding. He had helped me drink my way through my divorce. Sadly, he was the one who had ended up in a month of rehab over that.

At shift's end, I grabbed takeout and headed home, choosing a roundabout route to avoid the crush of a parade. I locked my case notes and my badge and gun in my wall safe and took out some cash. Then I showered, changed, and headed for Bourbon Street. Tomorrow was the Sunday before Fat Tuesday. I knew the smell of the French Quarter was now well on its way to transforming from the beer stench it always maintained to the miasma of alcohol blended with piss and vomit. It was time to forget things for a bit. I had nothing in my professional or personal life worth holding in memory, and strong drink was a kind soul on evenings like this. The crowds were insane, and that was how I liked it. I passed street artists in chalk and street musicians in zydeco and street souses in puke. I had no thought of speaking to any of the gorgeous staggering single ladies I bumped into, and that was okay. I certainly could not foresee a relationship beginning before sunrise.

I had been wandering voodoo shops and drinking hurricanes half the night and considered myself a hard-boiled drinker if not exactly a hard-boiled cop, but when I first met Heather around midnight at the Tropical Isle, the barmaid told me she had been guzzling hand grenades for hours. There was nothing for it but to be impressed. As small as she was, this lass vacationing from Iowa, that other four-letter Midwestern state, was far less inebriated than yours truly. I slurred at her until I was able to sober up a bit, and then we went for late night po' boys and Bananas Foster at some unlicensed back room to which her friends had referred her. I was more entranced by the minute. There was an easy and kind manner hidden under her initial shyness. She did not come home with me that night, but I unsteadily walked her to her hotel and learned her last name was Corvin.

She promised to see me again. I got her cell number, and *mirabile dictu*, it turned out to be legitimate. Thus it was we each had a full dozen oysters in the French Quarter the next evening, and I had the unbelievable pleasure of carrying her breakfast into my bed the following morning. My very being felt uplifted, though admittedly the throbbing in my head was far worse than the pangs after my previous evening of ice-cold hurricanes. I think I should have eschewed the magnum of champagne I had chilled on my night table, but I had so wanted to enthrall her as she had me. Perhaps it worked, because she did agree to stay at my place for the remainder of her vacation. I kept smiling at her as I dressed and retrieved my gun and badge and notes from the safe. Though she hailed from a place of corn-fed folks, she was thin and lithe in her daytime movements, and had been beyond lithe in her nighttime ones. Moreover, she smiled back.

I arrived late at headquarters that morning, and Sergeant Ellsworth and I headed out of our jurisdiction to the lower 9th ward to look in on our witness. We had secreted him in one of the more squalid neighborhoods that had never fully recovered from August 29th of '05. The Spanish Creole architecture here had been subsumed into the French. During our drive I showed Ellsworth a picture of Heather and myself that I had asked a tourist to take with my phone. His eyes lit up with his usual goofiness, and he let fly a series of crude remarks, as I expected. He then fell to complaining that he and his underwear companion should have met her first, but I knew it was all locker room bluster. Though he often referred to himself as the Big, Big Easy, that burly idiot was actually very happily married with a young daughter and another baby on the way. I guess his underwear companion had done its conjugal duty.

Tergon was pacing the front room of the little shotgun cottage in some agitation, and the officer assigned to him said he had been nervous all night. His pale features were pinched and sweaty, his gray hair tangled, and his dark eyes darted to the covered windows with some frequency. I pushed him to a chair and sat across from him while Ellsworth carried in food and supplies with the uniform's help.

"What gives, Paul? Can I get you something? You need to take a breath." I said.

He snorted. "Any breath could be my last, Glapion. I won't be around to testify. I got word before you picked me up that Taum-Lauren knows I saw everything. He'll have some professional in town by now."

"That's why you're here. Nice and quiet and out of the way. Even my boss doesn't know where we're keeping you. Another week, and Pierre will stay behind bars, and you can start fresh far from here. That's what you said you wanted."

"What choice do I have? They're coming for me whether I testify or not. Even as I watched them kill Fitzhugh, I knew when they spotted me on that catwalk that my life was over too. I ran. I should have kept running."

"Maybe. I'm not gonna lie, Paul. Why didn't you?"

He shrugged. "I suppose I owed Fitz something. He was my best friend. He gave me my job. Fool should have just paid his protection. None of this would've happened."

Paul Tergon's life in Louisiana was certainly over, but I doubted Pierre Taum-Lauren had enough contacts elsewhere to ever track him down in witness protection. Still, this poor little porter had never been anywhere else. All he understood was now in his past. He was not a young man. I knew the remainder of his life would be no picnic. I never dreamed how little there would be of it.

I had two other active cases on my plate, so I called Heather from the office and asked her to meet me at nine at The Gumbo Shop two blocks off Bourbon Street. The long day had irritated and frustrated me, but all was forgotten when I saw her luxuriant black tresses in the rear of the restaurant. Her uncomplicated smile cheered me, and her almond-shaped blue eyes gleamed at me happily from the dim corner. Once we ordered, I vowed to learn more about her while sober.

"I'll start," I said. "I'm divorced, no kids, I drink far too much, and I've been a cop since I left college — without graduating. I am done. Now you ..."

She blushed. "For a start, I've never ever slept with anyone on the second date. Before this trip, the craziest thing I ever did was ... this." She turned over her slim wrist on the table. A small raven tattoo flapped its tiny wings there as she flexed and spun her thumb. "I wore long sleeves for a year afterwards because I was too embarrassed to show anybody, especially my dad." She paused. "My parents are farmers. I had three years of accounting in college, quit last spring, and will — probably — go back in the fall. I teach a business course at an unsuccessful community college, and a couple girlfriends wrote out a full itinerary for my first ever vacation alone. Everyone should see the Carnival once, don't you think?"

I laughed. "We folks in New Orleans mostly call it Mardi Gras." I paused. "But I agree. That's why we originally came. And while we were partying, a good position opened on the force. My wife ended up hating everything about the South. Me — I became a voodoo enthusiast. You smile, but I've seen things. One of my best friends is Madam Morel."

She gasped slightly. Sure, it sounds corny, but that gasp was adorable. "I've heard of her!"

"If she is not an actual Voodoo Queen, she's at least a grand duchess. She's adjusted my mojo on a number of occasions. But enough. Are you involved with someone?"

She stared right into my eyes and took a bite from her plate.

My heart tried to move around the andiron that had fallen on it. "Oh," I said. It was not a question.

Then she grinned. God, she was beautiful. "He's a cop in The Crescent City," she said, laughing. "Seems like a nice guy." I laughed too. Then my phone rang and our night crashed around us.

Thirty minutes later, I was standing over Paul Tergon's bloody body in the little 9th ward safe house. There had been nothing safe about it. Paul had been impaled through the throat by a long iron needle and bled out, choking on his own arterial spray. The officer who had been guarding him had never heard the back window removed, and was himself stabbed in the lung. He was expected to survive, but even in his pain was most apologetic about losing his charge and about lying unconscious for hours until his relief arrived. This young policeman was better known to me than most. His name was Flynn, and he also was an adherent of voodoo. I was able to talk to him by midnight, though he was drugged and barely lucid. I began to think he followed the religion's darker factions, for he insisted from his hospital bed that the assassin had been a wild, black-cloaked demon. Before passing out again, he also swore that the killer had worn a gris-gris bag that shimmered from within and emanated bad mojo. Of course, he was in shock. Still, I never mentioned that we had found a cloth doll next to Tergon with a long, beaded pin in its neck.

I had told Heather I would probably not be home tonight. That alone had broken my heart, for she was leaving the day after Fat Tuesday, which at one in the morning was now today. Another Mardi Gras. A new type of loneliness descended upon me. I knew I would never have the courage to ask her to stay. I had nothing to offer her. I spent far too many nights like this one, and I wanted a whisky more often than not when finished. And of course she was much too young for me. Better she return to school and make a life near her family. But God, I would miss her. More than I had ever missed my wife, though I had been in this girl's company only a few hours. I touched my breast and felt the leather pouch beneath. Though reluctant to admit or accept it, I understood that good things were for others.

I needed to focus on the murder. The lateness of the hour be damned. I phoned Madam Morel. She grumbled at being awakened, but agreed to meet me at New Orleans Cemetery No. 1. She was a funny old bird; most ladies of the spirit would demand a tryst at the Glapion crypt, where Marie Laveau is reputed to be buried, and where tourists scrape triple Xes into the stone. Others doubt that her body is here, but none of this mattered to Madam Morel. She always met me at the strange pyramid Nic Cage built in the graveyard, just because she adored it.

I watched her round shiny brown face studying mine as I approached, and her manicured fingers dropped from her colorful sleeves and shook something toward me that looked suspiciously like a chicken bone. "You are trailed by some bad juju," she said.

"No shit," I grunted, slapping the plate affixed to the pyramid which translated 'Everything From One.' "Officer Flynn was stabbed earlier by a cloaked man he thinks is a bokor. Damn, but I'm inclined to believe him. Would Pierre Taum-Lauren hire a male voodoo witch?"

She rubbed her chin. She never accented the Haitian undertones of her voice, but I always caught them. "He is a believer. I can imagine him wanting to harm the souls as well as the bodies of his enemies."

My voice involuntarily dropped to a whisper. "Madam, you know strange things happen around the bayou all year, but things seem to get extra nuts for me during the Meeting of the Courts. I wanted to bring something wholesome to my life, but it's all gone wrong. I can scream 'to hell with mystic societies and to hell with hoodoo voodoo!' but something is just not normal tonight."

She put a finger to the side of my nose. Her whisper was lower than mine. "You might even call it *paranormal*, eh?"

I was reluctant to answer. Certain aspects of the killing smacked of weird, though. Any hired hitman might hide beneath a flowing cloak to avoid identification, but few hitmen stabbed their targets and collateral victims with long iron needles, and fewer wore juju and dropped off voodoo dolls at the scene. They came to town, shot someone, and took off back to Vegas or Chicago or New York.

I discussed what details I could with my sage friend for an hour but felt no less anxious when I headed home. There I found a note that deepened my depression. "I left some things at the hotel, since the room was prepaid. I hope to see you before my flight tomorrow. Please call." The horror of it was, I probably could not see her a final time. I needed to report in. My text messages insisted.

I finally met with the police chief late Tuesday afternoon, expecting at least a severe reprimand, but all he said, I swear, was, "We are now in the special section of Hell where the toilets get dirtier as you clean them." That little *tete-a-tete* has me flummoxed to this day. I could only shrug when I exited to inquiring looks from Ellsworth, nor was I allowed much time to contemplate the odd philosophical tidbit. We had a call, and the address was one of the properties of Pierre Taum-Lauren, who was still in a cell on the first floor.

We arrived at his industrial warehouse just before twilight to find two of the crime boss's thugs swimming in puddles of their own blood. One was already deceased, but the other one had been stabbed by several needles in such a manner that he was bleeding out slower. His description of their assailant matched Officer Flynn's on every salient point, making me believe that this assassin wanted us to hear these eerie descriptions. Something was shining in the gris-gris bag when the light caught it, and the cloaked killer was upon them with no notice. Before the hoodlum was carted out to die in the ambulance, he mentioned one other, commonplace bit of information. Knowing he would not survive, he freely noted that Taum-Lauren had gotten a phone call before we arrested him during which he had argued that a particular fee was far too high and would require renegotiation.

No wonder the gangster had not posted bail. At least we had an obvious motive to hold on to, regardless of some of the trappings of the case. I had almost grasped a sense of normalcy again when I saw a large metal coin in the blood on the warehouse floor. Wiping it clean, I found inscribed upon it crossed scimitar-like machetes below a flaming urn within a triangle. My mind twisted a bit once more. This was a charm for Loa Ogoun, warrior and god of iron, to ensure the winning of a battle. And these needle weapons were all made of iron.

"Kind of a vengeance token," said Ellsworth, examining it closely. "Our hitman didn't get what he was promised. I don't get it either. Who shafts a crazy hired gun?"

"Yeah," I agreed. "Especially this one. Double insane — or something more. But clever. Why kill the muscle? Unless …"

"It's to learn where Pierre is," finished Ellsworth.

We made record time getting back to the 8th District, but as we were pulling around the alleyway, we got a radio call that Taum-Lauren's jail cell was afire and that he had a big hole through the middle of his chest. And that was when my mojo flipped.

Ellsworth and I both looked into the alley that abutted the cells, drawn by the flames belching between the bars of a broken cell window. If we had not been in this exact spot at this exact moment, we never would have seen the flowing black cloak dashing away into the dark. The mouth of the alley was blocked by two askew dumpsters, so we leapt out and sprinted after the figure. The stones were slick between the overarching buildings and we were forced to dodge trashcans and pallets and chunks of old carpeting. Ellsworth's bulk played against him after a block, and I outpaced him and began to gain on the billowing form ahead. Suddenly the silhouette pivoted and spewed flames at me from his arm. Amazed, I threw myself to one wall, and the fire exploded against some cardboard boxes, igniting them.

Confused as to what had happened, I had the presence of mind to aim and fire into the middle of the form. My gun went off, but the shell had no effect on *its* movements. *It* moved toward me. My throat tightened. I was the best shot in my company. I emptied the gun into its head and body. It simply stopped and raised its hand once more. Fire spouted forth again. I would have been hit by the speeding flame, but Ellsworth yanked me to the left at the last second and the projectile again burst beyond me. The momentum caused Ellsworth to stumble against an iron railing, and as I watched the killer raised its arm beside the wall and my friend began to spasm horribly and fell to the pavement.

I clutched at my shirt beneath which my gris-gris pouch lay and was overwhelmed by the realization of how ridiculously impotent my own juju was. It was as though reality had kinked, and this creature had keyed into impossible forces. My head began to swim. Would I be willed into unconsciousness as well? My faith and beliefs split and shattered. Then Sergeant Ellsworth, tough guy to the end, was moving beside me. I realized he had only received a heavy shock from an electrified section of the railing that our prey had earlier wired into an old wall fuse box and just switched on.

Ellsworth was sighting in on the cloak while a jumble of thoughts frothed in my confused mind. Would his shot be any more effective than mine? Still, he had not been dropped by conjured lightning. I could now see the large alligator clips attached to the bottom of the metal rail frame, and the cables trailing away. The other "magic" may have had its origin in similar light shows. Still, I had shot the being point-blank in the torso and in the head. And I *could* see something glittering in the dark through a hole in its gris-gris bag.

Ellsworth pushed me again as another flaming projectile exploded from beneath the cloak. It missed us. "No dying on Pancake Tuesday!" he yelled. Then he fired back. And, unlike my bullets, his had the desired effect, catching the villain in the shoulder and spinning the cloaked figure to the alley bricks.

A uniformed officer burst into the opening behind us, gun drawn, and as a group, we approached the squirming body. Ellsworth picked up an oversized flare pistol that had clattered to the stones, and checked to be sure it was now empty. I didn't notice. I was transfixed by the tattoo of a raven that stood out on an uncovered wrist. I bent and pulled aside the dark hood. Heather's blue eyes gazed back at me fiercely.

I suddenly knew why this was the City that Care Forgot. Fate didn't give a fig for the gash that opened deep inside me. My lover, the out-of-town assassin. She had followed me down Bourbon Street that first night, probably bribing our barmaid to say she had been drinking for hours. The second night she had drugged my champagne, broken into my cheap safe, and replaced the bullets in my gun with blanks. She had read my case notes and certainly followed us to the safe house the next day. She would have been already gone if Taum-Lauren hadn't welshed on her contract when he feared arrest. Letting him live would have been bad for her reputation among her peers.

More than half of New Orleans is below mean sea level. I felt as if I were personally underwater as they wrapped her wounded shoulder and handcuffed her. She never blinked, and she never looked away. I saw Ellsworth pull the wires free of the old building fuse box. "She certainly planned ahead," he said, also without looking at me. "Dolls and needles and amulets — fire and lightning — and what's shining in this bag?" He pulled at the leather pouch around her neck and the cord snapped, spilling the contents onto the oily ground. Thirteen strings of bright gold, green, and purple beads of metal glittered in the shadow.

As they led her past me, she watched my face closely. I saw a coldness in her eyes now, but no magic. I felt I had to say something. "So, the contents of your gris-gris weren't the products of hell-spawned evil?"

"Oh, I dunno," she smiled wickedly as they led her away. "I had to show my tits to get them."

John Kiste is a horror writer who was previously the president of the Stark County Convention & Visitors' Bureau and a Massillon Museum board member. He is a double-lung transplantee and organ donation ambassador, a McKinley Museum planetarian, and an Edgar Allan Poe impersonator who has been published in *Third Flatiron*, *With Painted Words*, *A Shadow of Autumn*, *Modern Grimoire*, *Dark Fire Fiction*, *Six Guns Straight from Hell 3*, *Theme of Absence*, *The Dark Sire*, NonBinary Review's *H. G. Wells* and *The Odyssey* anthologies, Jolly Horror Press's *Coffin Blossoms* anthology, and whose work was included in Unnerving Press's *Haunted Are These Houses,* and Camden Press's winner of the 2019 Preditors and Editors readers' poll for best anthology, *Quoth the Raven.*

CRESCENT CITY SYMPHONY

Jetse de Vries

—sonata: look the storm in the eye—

Special Councilor Trevor B. Lemurel lets out a sigh of relief as the plane's landing gear hits the runway. It's been a rough ride, and things have only just begun.

"Welcome to Louis Armstrong International," the captain says over the intercom. "I've just been told we're the last flight allowed to land."

It's not Lemurel's intention to travel towards an approaching hurricane, but an unexpected turn of events necessitated his urgent trip to the Big Easy. Normally stationed in Washington DC, Lemurel's talents are needed for a certain undertaking, an operation so delicate he will get the details on a 'need-to-know' basis. Right now, he only has his airline ticket and a hotel reservation. Presumably he'll get some updates after he's checked in at the Mazarin.

Torrential rains combined with severe gusts of wind pound the French Quarter in April already, thanks to climate change. Yet the citizens of New Orleans seem oddly defiant as Mardi Gras is still taking place—bars bursting at the seams with people, floats in the overcrowded streets, and more beads than brains—many more. Even the Mazarin seems fully booked, which is just as well, according to Lemurel. No better place to get lost in than a crowd.

Lemurel also can't help but notice that despite the relentless downpour, the streets are not flooded. The new storm drains seem to work fine, and judging by their revelry, the burghers of the Big Easy seem to have faith that the rest of their coastal defenses will withstand the worst of Hurricane Ivana, as well. Ivana is strengthening into a Category Five hurricane over the unseasonably warm waters of the Gulf of Mexico, its bullseye aimed as unwaveringly on the Crescent City as its notorious predecessor Katrina.

The political pressure to justify the huge cost of the 'once-in-a-10,000-years' coastal storm defenses is so immense that no evacuation was ordered. Come hell, high water, and the storm of the decade, New Orleans would sit through this one and show the world where their taxpayers' money was spent. Since one of his ancestors was a survivor of the 1953 North Sea Flood, Lemurel can sympathize. *Like the Delta Works*, he thought, *once but never again*.

Other matters require his attention, though, as he enters K-Paul's Louisiana Kitchen to meet his contact. He spots LeJeune at a lone table in the far corner of the legendary establishment, wearing his era-perfect costume of the Jazz Age — to the intense envy of many a hipster.

"Jean-François," Lemurel says, "*Comment ça va?*"

"*Pas mal*, Trevor," LeJeune answers in kind, "*tout bien considéré.*"

Initially, their conversation is all polite and generic, their impeccable French not quite out of place in this particular locale. They order an exquisite meal and take their time to enjoy it with a bottle of fine wine. It is only after they've moved to the backyard — that now features a hurricane-proof, retractable roof — to enjoy the cognac and cigars that they get to the point.

"Your target stays at the Ritz-Carlton Suite," LeJeune says, "deeply incognito."

"Who is he?"

"A retired CEO-cum-politician whom we shall name ... T —" LeJeune says after exhaling a whiff of Cuban smoke.

"Interesting," Lemurel says after a sip of excellent XO. "I thought he was touring a few European countries."

"That was what everybody — including certain agencies — were supposed to believe," LeJeune says, "and act upon. And we will, if your mission succeeds."

"Which is?"

"There's more than one who can play the doppelgänger game." LeJeune casts a casual look at the cognac swirling in his glass. "Your mission is twofold. You need to swap Mr. T-0 with Mr. T-1, then deliver Mr. T-0 to a specific spot."

"Which spot?" Lemurel says through a series of carefully crafted smoke rings, "and where's Mr. T-1?"

"Mr. T-1 will be in the Fantastic Suite of the W tomorrow," Lejeune's look couldn't be more disinterested, "and here's the spot." He quickly shows Lemurel a card with something written on it, then sets fire to that card with his cigar.

"Is his wife with him?" Lemurel asks as he puts down his empty glass. "Or other family members?"

"He's alone," LeJeune says, his index fingers mimicking quotation marks, "a 'business' meeting plus a night out with the boys. Excepting his security detail."

"Obviously." Lemurel nods slightly. "It will be done."

As Lemurel walks back to his hotel, he wonders how Lejeune keeps his costume in such perfect shape through this flying storm. But it's just a temporary distraction while his subconscious works at the mechanics of the upcoming job. Getting Mr. T-0 out of his suite is one thing. Going back to the scene of the crime to replace him with Mr. T-1 is an altogether different kettle of fish. Yet, as his surface thoughts drift off into wondering how bad the storm will be tomorrow, a plan slowly emerges.

He needs to do a little reconnoitering and squeezes himself through the throng of the French Quarter. He has a cocktail at the Alibi, checks what's playing at the House of Blues, has an Abita Amber at Cajun Mike's. As the howling winds shake cocktail glasses, rattle window sills, and roll hats over the crowd like tumbleweeds on cobbles, the mood is positively rambunctious while fear is swept away like spindrift on a stormy sea: Mardi Gras *über alles*.

On the one hand, the incoming hurricane complicates matters quite a bit. Mr. T — and his doppelgänger — are tall, heavyset men, so carrying them in and out will be no mean feat. On the other hand, Ivana's onslaught together with Mardi Gras will provide plenty of cover and distraction. The carnivalesque atmosphere gives Lemurel an inkling of what to do.

He heads back to the Mazarin, trying to get there before he is totally soaked, hoping certain places will be open tomorrow. He has some shopping to do.

— adagio: calm during the storm —

Early the next afternoon, through the torrential downpour and intense gusts, Lemurel checks a few costume and mask shops that, to his surprise, are still open. At Fifi Mahony's, he buys one Harlequin costume for himself and two Court Jester outfits for 'friends', making sure to pay for them with cash. Then he visits a Mardi Gras social club — the Krewe of Endymion — and convinces them to run a special errand for him, paying a preposterous amount of cash for the privilege.

After that, he checks a number of local machine shops outside town until he finds one that has the equipment he's looking for, even if it needs a few tweaks to fit his particular application. Thankfully, they can get that done just before dinner.

Unlike last night, he has a light dinner and heads back to his hotel room in the Mazarin to prepare for his midnight heist-and-swap. Then he heads for the W where there is an urgent, top secret delivery. There will be little sleep tonight — if any — but the anticipation fuels the fire in his underbelly. *This* is what he's here for.

— andante: in the eye of the storm —

As the eye of Ivana crosses the French Quarter, Lemurel makes his move. It's impossible to remain unsighted in a city that never sleeps — let alone at Mardi Gras — so he decides it's better to hide in plain sight. A minor turbulent event might go unnoticed in the eye of the hurricane, especially if one tries to blend in.

Time to begin — what Lemurel sardonically referred to as — the dance of the four hotels: a *commedia dell'arte* for a Harlequin and a pair of Court Jesters. Or a Four-Square in Four Acts. First act at the Hyatt. In the Petite Queen Suite, inconspicuously guarded by a few fellow compatriots, Lemurel hypnotizes the person who is referred to as Mr. T-1, then dresses him in a Court Jester's outfit, which nicely complements his Harlequin costume.

After cities like San Francisco, Oakland, New York, and Miami started to sue — with increasing degrees of success — the big five oil companies for willfully ignoring the effects of climate change that they were aware of at a very early stage, the principle of 'the polluter pays' started to include climate change, and — as it transcended national borders — eventually became a criminal offense under the rules of the International Criminal Court in The Hague.

Under that new jurisdiction, the ICC issued a warrant against Mr. T —, who was a fervent climate change denier both as CEO of a major petroleum company and as an appointed cabinet member. As the USA — who had originally signed but then withdrawn from the ICC—would not extradite him, it seemed Mr. T— could enjoy the rest of his life in splendor in his mansion in Texas. The world was taken by surprise, however, when it was announced that Mr. T— accepted an invitation for a series of lectures in Europe. Almost as if the wanted Mr. T— dared a confused world to arrest him.

Under hypnosis, Mr. T-1 follows Lemurel out of a side entrance of the Hyatt onto a crowded street. Then they walk half a block to the Courtyard by Marriott for the second act. As inconspicuously as possible, Lemurel takes Mr. T-1 to the top floor. There, through the fire escape stairs, he takes him up to the roof and quickly into the service closet of the hotel's elevator, where Lemurel has already stashed two more costumes and a battery-powered electrowinch.

Lemurel puts the doppelgänger to sleep and changes into his second outfit—that of the Hunchback of Notre Dame. He ties the battery-powered electrowinch to his back, effectively hiding it in the costume's hunch, and stuffs the second costume in a fake paunch.

Surreptitiously he makes his exit from the service closet, then moves to the edge of the roof to show his disguise to the partying crowd in the streets, needing a launch of a few firecrackers to draw their attention. He takes a few bows, performs a number of clownish moves, and then climbs up the wall of the Ritz-Carlton, in full sight of the cheering crowd. The eye of Ivana is passing over the French Quarter, and for about twenty minutes it will be eerily quiet.

However, the moment he reaches the top floor of the Ritz-Carlton, he disappears out of sight, in preparation for the third act. He doesn't have to wait long, as he's already seen the Krewe of Endymion—all dressed up as Harlequins just like him—make their way into the Ritz-Carlton, throwing out jelly beans to the reveling crowd like their lives depended on it.

While his prepayment was already very generous, Lemurel's upped the ante by promising a considerable bonus to Krewe members who make it all the way to the Ritz-Carlton's top floor (and prove it through a few selfies with room numbers and/or guests). Most of them do, as the hotel's staff is outnumbered and outclassed by the professional merry-makers, and most of the guests seem to enjoy the Mardi Gras invasion, especially when they find out that the jelly beans have a secret filling—the brown ones filled with bourbon, the yellow ones with margarita, the blue ones with blue curaçao and the green ones with true-to-life absinthe.

On the top floor, they become the problem of Mr. T—'s security detail. The hefty bonus incentivized all of them, and Mr. T—'s protection personnel have their hands more than full trying to handle them. In that mad crowd, one extra Carnival character does not stand out, *if* he is found.

Outside of the Ritz-Carlton suite, unseen by the distracted security detail, Lemurel breaks in, the muffled creak of the ancient window lock lost in the wild revelry noises from the crowded corridors. He's in the deserted dining room and makes his way towards the bedroom. Mr. T— is there, dressed, awake, alone and not at all surprised to find the Hunchback of the Notre Dame has entered his room.

"Twenty years ago," Mr. T— says, apparently in a good mood, "I'd join you guys and party all night." He waves his hand towards the exit door. "But now, I need my beauty sleep. If you could join the rest of your party and leave this old man alone ..."

"No problem," Lemurel says, "but first I need to show you this."

He quickly takes out his tablet, preset to show the most mesmerizing and fast-hypnotizing pattern known to humanity. The pattern looks very pretty and enticing, yet becomes irresistible with the right combination of words.

"Say it is too late," Lemurel says, barely distinguishable from the noise in the corridors, "Prepare to see the way it falls apart. Give up, let it come down, and see the decisions we make."

Mr. T—'s eyes become glassy as the hypnotic spell takes hold. Lemurel orders him to partly undress and put on the Cardinal suit—complete with carbon fiber body harness and hook—that Lemurel brought with him, which goes with the Hunchback character. Lemurel helps him.

"We'll go outside," Lemurel the Hunchback says, "where we'll bow to the crowd and then swing down like Spiderman." The hypnotized Mr. T-0 nods as if in agreement, and out they go, Lemurel making sure to close but not lock the door to the balcony.

— scherzo: Sturm und Drang —

They walk to the edge of the roof, where Lemurel and Mr. T-0 the Cardinal—impelled by Lemurel and the hypnotic trance—take a quick bow to the audience below. Lemurel anchors the electrowinch's rope to a nearby chimney, tests its strength to his satisfaction, and then wastes no time hooking himself and Mr. T-0 to it. He grips the unresisting Cardinal, tightens the rope, and then jumps off the roof while slowly unreeling the rope through the electrowinch.

Under the encouraging cheers of the street crowd, they swing down like superheroes and land safely on the roof of the Courtyard by Marriott. It takes all Lemurel's strength, and then some. But somehow he pulls it off, and after landing safely they take their parting bow to the audience below. Quickly, Lemurel leads the heavily hypnotized and slightly euphoric Mr. T-0 to the elevator's service closet, well out of sight of any onlookers above and below.

Inside, his doppelgänger—Mr. T-1 the Court Jester—is awaiting in a similar hypnotic trance that is beginning to fade. Before the original Mr. T-0 can be surprised, Lemurel sedates him with an anesthetic syringe.

The whole operation took ten minutes flat. Now onwards to get Mr. T-1 back into the Ritz-Carlton Suite. It already took all Lemurel's strength to get the original down, so it will take the small yet powerful electrowinch's battery pack to get them back up. With both hypnotized, Lemurel orders them to swap costumes, and helps them to speed up the process. Once that's finished, Lemurel wakes the doppelgänger from his hypnotic slumber with a carefully preconditioned double snap, and leads him out onto the roof of the Courtyard by Marriott.

At its edge facing the crowd below, they wave and take a few enticing bows. Then Lemurel the Hunchback quickly connects the electrowinch to the still-hanging rope, tests its security, and up they go, under loud cheers. In the far distance, Lemurel sees the hurricane's eye wall approaching; there are only a few moments of relative quiet left. Using the electrowinch's momentum, Lemurel swings the two of them over the Ritz-Carlton's ledge, both his muscles and the foundation of the anchoring chimney creaking under the combined weight of the two jokesters.

A final bow to the maddening crowds, then Lemurel and Mr. T-1 sprint to the Ritz-Carlton Suite, which they enter seconds before Ivana's eye wall passes over the luxury hotel. Nobody's in there yet, as Mr. T—'s security detail is — hopefully — still busy clearing away the last of the Krewe of Endymion.

He tells Mr. T—'s doppelgänger to undress, helping him in the process. Then he tells Mr. T-1 to go to bed and to sleep. To be certain, Lemurel sedates him with an anesthetic syringe as well. He pulls the covers up to the slightly snoring Mr. T-1's chin, swiftly picks up the Cardinal's costume and gets out, closing the door and then — with a trick of the trade — locks it from outside.

In this way the security detail may only find out about the swap the next morning. By then, the real Mr. T— should be long gone.

— presto: a teacup through the tempest —

Outside, Ivana is battering the French Quarter once more. In a matter of seconds, Lemurel gets soaked to the bone but doesn't care much. The crowd in the street has dispersed — probably moved on to safer indoor spaces where plenty of drinks are served — and the drenched Hunchback does not bother to introduce himself to them a third time. Instead, he gets down as fast and as unnoticed as possible through the flying storm.

With a quick snap command, the rope unlocks at the chimney, and Lemurel reels it in with the remaining battery power. Down below, he sees an empty pickup truck approaching. He takes careful aim — the small and heavy electrowinch will not be moved much by the wind, even at hurricane force — and throws it in the pickup's trunk.

Onwards into the elevator's service closet to change back into the Harlequin outfit. As Mr. T-0 already wears the Court Jester costume; Lemurel wakes him up and hypnotizes him again. He leads his quarry down the fire escape stairs, the rattling of their steps drowned in the fury of Ivana's gusts and relentless deluge.

At the bottom of the stairs, he leads Mr. T-0 into the nearby parked rental car. Once his quarry is snug in the passenger seat's safety belt, Lemurel sedates Mr. T-0 one more time and starts driving. He carefully moves through the thick crowd, which gradually thins as he moves away from the French Quarter. He takes his time, drives around the Big Easy at random to make sure he isn't followed. Once he's satisfied that nobody's tailing him, he heads for his delivery point.

It's an amphibious house at the shore of the Mississippi, on the edge of the city. Amphibious houses became part of New Orleans and the Louisiana coastline at large once people realized these — when carefully anchored by

74

self-tensioning winches—could not be flooded, and were tested as hurricane-proof.

This particular amphibious house—the *Robespierre*—was owned by an eccentric Creole family who used it for art exhibitions and soirées for the artistic demi-monde. Unbeknownst to them, the amphibious house has a double bottom. On the river side of this double bottom there is a watertight hatch with a quick-connecting, high tensile rubber seal that can connect to a similar watertight hatch on a mini-submarine.

In deepest secrecy, this connection was only used to get certain people in and out of the United States. The butler—signaled by Lemurel—is already at the rental car's passenger door before Lemurel has switched off the engine.

"Ah, Monsieur L—," the butler says, all apologetic as if the cyclone was his fault, "You and Monsieur T—, who has passed out, I see—are still drenched. Let me get you something dry right away."

He carries the sleeping Mr. T— out of the car and they enter the boathouse via the second—barely visible—ramp and a side door out of sight from the partying crowd. Through a small corridor they enter the secret double bottom of the amphibious residence. The ceiling is low, so they have to crouch, yet somehow the butler manages to drag the unconscious Mr. T— in with him.

"You've done this before," Lemurel says in admiration.

"*Pas de problème,*" the butler says.

On his haunches, LeJeune is inside next to the watertight door, eyeing a sparsely lit panel. "Excellent timing, Lemurel," he says, "the *petite DeGrasse* is approaching."

"Fine," Lemurel says, "my job's done. I'm leaving."

"You don't want to see your, well, package delivered?" LeJeune says.

"No, I leave that to you people," he says with a nod towards the butler. "I'd rather park the rental car far away from here, to remove any possible trail."

"Always the professional," LeJeune says, "Many thanks, and until we meet again."

"Until we meet again," Lemurel says and takes his leave.

After he leaves, Mr. T—the original—is delivered to the crew of a mini-submarine that has entered the Mississippi in all stealth. Staying mere centimeters above the bottom, they barely noticed the hurricane raging above the surface. The securely anchored Robespierre made connecting the airlock routine, and they're away in scant moments.

As carefully as it made its run upriver, the *petite DeGrasse* moves downstream, taking extra caution not to be detected. After a few hours, it leaves the Mississippi and enters the Gulf of Mexico. A few hours later, well outside the USA's territorial waters, the *petite DeGrasse* meets its mothership, a latest-generation submarine of the highest stealth class, docking in its underwater bay. While it does not carry nuclear weapons at this time, the payload that is delivered to it will be quite explosive in a completely different manner. A *force de fracas* rather than a *force de frappe*.

The *DeGrasse* then heads for a select island in the Caribbean, where the original Mr. T— is set on a plane to Europe. In the meantime, Mr. T-2—the doppelgänger to replace the doppelgänger—is officially arrested—much to the relief of the double doppelgänger—on behalf of the ICC. A trial date is announced well after the arrival of the real Mr. T— in Europe.

— coda uno: after-party —

The beers and cocktails flow freely in the Krewe of Endymion's clubhouse, and the atmosphere is very merry, indeed.

"Everything was going swimmingly as we made our way up to the top floor," one Krewe member says, "and initially, things were fine up there, as well."

"Especially as we explained to the guests how spiked our jellybeans were," another says.

"But then this bunch of bouncers came out of the Ritz-Carlton Suite," the first one says, "Ordering us to leave immediately."

"And we would've gone, if they'd asked gently," the other says, "but they bossed us around as if they owned the place."

"Still, things might've remained calm if one of them didn't push Little Jake up the wall," the first one says, tapping said Jake on the shoulder, "well in sight of Jonah and Boyd."

"No shit," one the Krewe's members who increasingly regrets that he didn't join that particular outing, eyeing the afore-mentioned, freshly retired American football player and ex-welterweight champion.

"Then it was clobberin' time," the huge ex-Saints player says, "as nobody pushes Lil' Jake like that."

"We're sorry about the damage," another Krewe member says, "but they left us no choice. And we'll settle it with our bonuses, right?"

"Yes," the rest of the Krewe says, "one for all and all for one!"

"That won't be necessary," the club secretary says, "as I just received a huge donation from the same source that provided our bonuses. 'For unforeseen expenses,' it reads, 'and a job well done'."

— coda duo: after-effect —

As Mr. T— is led before the court in The Hague, enabled through the assistance of a service that shall not be named, a few diplomats go through a carefully whispered exchange.

"This should not have been necessary," one says, his affable expression remaining as if painted on his face, "You could have taken his double, which would have been a win-win."

"How so?" the other says, his amiable bearing slightly broken by a somewhat superior smile.

"You still would have gotten your trial," the first one says, "and our protest would have been much more muted. Everybody happy."

"The majority amongst us decided not to settle for an empty *j'accuse*," the second one says, "and wanted the actual culprit to face justice."

"Too bad," the first one says, "now our diplomatic relationship suffers a huge strain."

"It's gone through much worse, in particular during the President that shall not be named," the second one says, "and otherwise a precedent would have been set; meaning the truly rich can avoid standing trial through surreptitious means. Making this trial a façade, not an actual deterrent. The super-rich would not change their ways."

"They never will," the first one says. "Everything I've said is purely off the record, of course, but you can quote me on this: you cannot cure the intense greed of the super-rich. It's a disease stronger than cancer, it's anchored in them like a genetic trait."

"Then the only way to stop them is the actual threat of standing trial," the second one says. "QED."

— coda tres: aftermath —

'NEW ORLEANS WITHSTANDS IVANA'

The Times-Picayune headline reads. "Three dead," the article continues, "which can be read as *only* three in comparison with Katrina's body count of eighteen-hundred-and-thirty-three. On the other hand, it could have been two less if those Mardi Gras revelers had just stayed inside. Without the Carnival celebrations, we might have lived through Ivana without having to bury anyone. Which is what we hope when the next hurricane — inevitably — arrives. This seems to be a price our revelers are willing to pay."

[...]

"Apart from the dead and wounded, the city and its wide environs withstood Ivana admirably. So far, the estimated 125 million dollars damage dwarfs in comparison with Katrina's estimated 250 billion dollars. 'This alone has made the 80-billion-dollar investment in hurricane-proofing absolutely worthwhile," Mayor LeCorbusier says, 'and we can only urge other cities on the Gulf Coast to follow our example.'"

— *coda quattro: afterglow* —

Lemurel sits down at the table in *Dieu du Ciel*, facing LeJeune who is — as usual — indistinguishable from a Prohibition-era gangster. At this meeting in Montreal, he's looking forward to a great meal with — if possible — even greater drinks. His eyes, though, almost roll out of their sockets when the waiter sets their beer flight on the table.

"...fifteen, sixteen, *seventeen*," Lemurel says, counting, "that's insane."

"There are so many fantastic beers here," LeJeune says, "and I couldn't choose. Now I don't have to."

"At this rate we'll be drunk before dinner." Lemurel says, flashing a sardonic smile.

"They're only small glasses," LeJeune says, "and we have not had time to celebrate your — let's call it — Crescent City Symphony."

"That's true," Lemurel says, "but I suppose we're not here just for that."

"Correct," LeJeune says, "there's this gentleman staying at Hotel Le Crystal ..."

Jetse de Vries — @shineanthology — is a technical specialist for a propulsion company by day, and a speculative fiction reader, editor and writer by night. He's also an avid bicyclist, total solar eclipse chaser, single malt aficionado, metalhead and intelligent optimist.

His new website: https://www.the-future-upbeat.com

MY VOLKSWAGEN FOR A STRING OF BEADS

Lorraine Sharma Nelson

Sonali Sen pushed forward through the throng of revelers watching the parade floats, the music a heady mix of rhythm and blues and zydeco. Add in the roar of the crowd and that New Orleans was currently experiencing a heatwave, unusual for this time of year, and it was all she could do not to scream. Her dress clung to her, damp with sweat, the humidity pressing in on her as she maneuvered the crowd.

She finally reached the modest doors of *L'Auberge*, the tiny boutique hotel where she and her best friend, Josette Everard, were staying. Clutching the bag of feathered party hats, beads, and noisemakers against her chest, Sonali ran up the wrought-iron steps to their second-floor bedroom. Jo was going to die when she got a look at all the cool party stuff she had bought.

She rooted around in her purse for the room key, but couldn't find it. Sighing, she knocked on the door. "Jo, let me in. I need to pee." No response. "Jo? Come on. Open up. I'm not kidding." She banged on the door with the flat of her hand, then pressed her ear against it. Even through the thick wood, she could hear the party on the street below. *Godammit. No wonder she can't hear me.* She dropped the bag by the door and went back down to the front desk.

The desk clerk pushed the door open and Sonali preceded him in. "I'll check your minibar," he said, grinning. "You ladies might need the alcohol re-stocked."

Sonali stepped past him into the room. "What's Mardi Gras without a *Sazarec* or three, right?" she said, referring to one of the city's most popular drinks. She glanced around the small, cramped room and saw the top of Jo's flaming red hair peeking over the chaise lounge on the small wrought-iron balcony.

"Hey? Wanna see what I got?" she said, stepping outside and wincing at the noise below. She tapped Jo on the shoulder.

No response.

She shook her friend's shoulder slightly, and watched in horror as Jo slowly listed to the side. "Jo?" she whispered.

With legs suddenly shaky, Sonali squatted beside her. She took one look at Jo's glassy-eyed stare and scrambled back. "Jo? Ohmigod, Jo?"

Sonali barely registered the activity around her as she sat hunched over in the room's only armchair, her arms wrapped around her knees.

"Ms. Sen?"

She raised her head. A man knelt beside her. "Are you all right? Would you like something stronger than water? A *café au lait*, perhaps?"

She stared at him, uncomprehending.

The man turned to someone standing beside him and said something in a low voice. She heard the person mutter something back and footsteps rapidly retreated. "We'll get some *café* into you. It'll help," the man said.

Sonali's gaze swiveled to him. Who was he? And who were all these people in her room?

"Ms. Sen, I'm Detective Aubin Benoit, of the New Orleans Police Department."

Police department?

Suddenly, everything clicked into place. *Oh no. Jo. Please, no. No. No. No.*

"Do you understand what's happened?"

She nodded, her breath hitching.

Concern flickered in his clear, green eyes.

The *café* appeared at his side. He took it and, gently lifting her hand from her lap, wrapped it around the cup. "Take a sip. You'll feel better." He smiled gently. "Nothing beats our *café* with chicory."

Sonali sipped, grimacing as the hot liquid burned her tongue.

"Better?"

She nodded, only because he seemed to need a response.

"Good. Now ..." His eyes searched hers. "Can you tell me what happened here?"

Her hand trembled, sloshing hot, milky coffee on her sundress.

"Here. Let me." The man took the cup from her stiff, uncooperative fingers, and set it down on the side table. "Ms. Sen, I know this is very difficult for you, but I need you to tell me what happened."

"Jo's dead. That's what happened."

"Yes, I'm very sorry. She was your partner? Friend?"

"Friend," Sonali answered, wincing at the word *was*. "My best friend."

Detective Benoit nodded. "Again, I'm very sorry."

He waited. Sonali got the impression that he was a man of infinite patience. Up to a point.

"I ... I went out to buy some fun party stuff. Beads and such."

He nodded, his gaze urging her on.

"When I got back, she wouldn't answer the door. So I got the guy at the front desk to let me in and ... and there she was." Sonali shuddered, the taste of the chicory-blended coffee filling her mouth. "Ex—cuse me." She scrambled to her feet and hurried to the bathroom.

When she got back, the only person in the room was the detective. He stood facing the balcony, hands in his trouser pockets. He turned at her approach.

"I—I'm sorry," she said, wrapping her arms around her waist.

"No apology necessary."

"What now?" she asked.

"Do you want me to call her parents?"

"No. I'll do it. I don't ... I don't want them to hear it from a stranger, you know?"

"Of course." He looked at her, his gaze searching. "Will you be all right? Do you need help taking your luggage to your new room?"

"No. Beau said he'd do it."

"Beau?"

"The front desk clerk."

"You understand why you have to move, right? Until we know exactly how she ..."

"Yes, of course. No problem."

He hesitated a moment longer, then strode toward the door. Held it open for her. She took a deep breath and preceded him out.

"I'll walk you to your new room."

"That's not necessary."

"I insist."

At her door, his gaze met hers. "I'll be in touch as soon as I know more. In the meantime, please—"

"I'll call if I remember anything else," she finished for him. "Thank you."

"Goodnight, Ms. Sen. Please try to get some sleep."

She listened to his steps as he walked away.

And felt very much alone.

Sonali hung up the phone, tears streaming down her cheeks. Telling Jo's parents that their baby girl was dead was the hardest thing she'd ever done. Mrs. Everard's scream was something she would hear for the rest of her life. They would fly down to New Orleans the next day, and Mr. Everard would make arrangements for Jo's body to be flown back to New York for the funeral. On the verge of even more tears, Jo was profoundly grateful when they were interrupted by a call from Detective Benoit. She hung up, grateful that he'd be able to give them the details she couldn't.

Sonali was scrolling through the photos of past trips she and Jo had taken, when the phone rang, startling her.

"Ms. Sen?"

"Hello, Detective."

"I'm sorry to disturb you, but there's been a ... development ..."

"Development? What does that mean?"

"I'd like to meet with you and the Everards. I can pick you up on my way, if you like."

"It's something bad, isn't it?"

"I'm not at liberty to discuss it now."

Sonali took a deep breath, a tight knot forming in the pit of her stomach. "Fine. I'll be there, but I'll drive myself."

"Thank you for seeing me," Detective Benoit said to the small gathering in the Everards' suite. "I know this is not the time, but it's important."

"Whatever you have to say, Detective, please just spit it out. My wife and I would like to take our daughter back to New York for the ..." His voice trailed off.

"Yes, of course." Benoit cleared his throat. "Based on your information about Ms. Everard's weak heart, the coroner originally thought that she might have had a massive stroke. But the autopsy you requested, sir—"

"I didn't want one," Mrs. Everard whispered, her voice cracking. "I didn't want my baby cut up like a Christmas goose." She glared at her husband, but he stared woodenly at Benoit. Sonali wasn't sure he even heard his wife's accusation.

"It revealed that Josette was poisoned." Benoit said softly. "I'm truly sorry."

The silence echoed off the walls, deafening.

"Poisoned?" Sonali whispered. "But … how? When?"

Benoit shook his head. "We don't know yet, but rest assured we will." His glance took in all three people staring at him. "You have my word," he added.

A low keening sound came from Jo's mom, and turning to her, Sonali saw that she'd turned ashen. Her husband, looking equally shaken, turned to Benoit.

"I'd better get her up to bed. Please have the front desk send a doctor."

"Of course. Again, please accept my —"

"We don't want your damned platitudes," Mr. Everard snapped, helping his wife to her feet. "You find the culprit, you hear me? You find whoever did that to her." He glared at Benoit, nodded once to Sonali, and helped his wife up to the second-floor bedroom.

Deep in thought, Sonali turned to Benoit when he broke the silence. "Are you all right?" he asked.

"All right? You just told us that Jo was poisoned. Murdered. What am I supposed to say? Yeah, I'm peachy?"

"I have to ask," he said, ignoring her sarcasm, "where did you stop on the drive down from New York?"

"I … I don't remember. Rest stops. Gas. Food."

"Anything else? Please think, Ms. Sen. It's important."

"The only other stop was at one of the labs she works with. She's a chemist, you know? I dropped her off and went to buy more snacks for the rest of the trip."

"Where was this?"

"Memphis. The pharmaceutical company she works for has a lab there, and she stopped in for a quick meeting."

Sonali could almost hear the wheels turning in Benoit's head. "How long was she in the meeting?"

"About an hour. Maybe an hour-and-a-half, tops."

Benoit nodded. "Thank you, Ms. Sen. You've been very helpful."

On the way back to *L'Auberge*, Sonali's head buzzed. She knew what Benoit was thinking. *Jo's meeting at the lab.* While she was there, something happened. Something that got her killed. But what? Benoit didn't say what she was poisoned with. Maybe he thought that didn't matter.

Even though Mardi Gras was officially over, people still milled around on the streets, partying and drinking. It was impossible to get to the hotel, so she parked her VW Bug two streets over, across from a very popular restaurant, The Suckling Pig, and walked the rest of the way.

Back in her room, Sonali used the in-room coffee pot to heat water for a cup of tea. Standing at the balcony, watching the throng of people below, she felt a twinge of envy. They all looked so happy and carefree.

Her gaze traveled over the crowd, stopped, then retreated back. *There.* That man with the shock of white hair talking to the pretty, half-naked girl in the cropped top and short skirt. Who was he? Why did he look familiar? She saw him remove the string of beads he wore, placing them around the girl's neck instead. Saw him stroke her cheek ...

And then it hit her.

Sonali tore down the stairs, heart thudding. She burst out the front doors, her gaze going to where she'd seen him no more than a minute ago. Gone. *No, no, no. Wait, the girl.* Sonali saw the bright red skirt sashaying away from her, down the side street where she'd parked her car. She dashed after her, dodging people this way and that.

She caught up to the girl outside The Suckling Pig. "Excuse me, please."

The girl turned, and Sonali realized she was older than what she'd thought. "What d'you want?"

"Just some information. That man you were talking to a couple of minutes ago," she gestured behind her. "The one who gave you that string of beads —"

"What about him?"

"What's his name?"

"How would I know?"

"He gave you that string of beads." Sonali gestured to the multi-colored plastic beads around the woman's neck.

"So? It's Mardi Gras. A lot of guys gave me beads this week."

"How much for them?"

That got her attention. "What?"

"The beads. How much do you want for them?"

The woman's eyes narrowed, a thin smile spreading across her face. "What you got, hon?"

"I don't have my purse with me. Hold on." She glanced at Delilah, her battered, red VW Bug, parked across the street. "Maybe I have something in my car. Wait here." She trotted over to the Bug, jiggled the handle, kicked the lower right corner of the door twice, and yanked with all her might. The door squeaked open, as if protesting this treatment. Sonali slid into the driver's side and reached into the glove compartment. She sometimes kept a twenty-dollar bill in there for emergencies. And this sure qualified as one.

Nothing. All she came up with were two protein bar wrappers that Jo had stuffed in there. Sonali groaned. Now she remembered. She'd used the cash for sundaes and a bottle of wine, which still sat in her room. Unopened.

"So? What's it to be?"

Sonali looked up to see the woman leaning on the door, peering inside. "I thought I had some cash in here, but I don't. If you'll come back to the hotel with me, I can pay you."

"How much?"

"Ummm … I don't have much cash on me. I can give you ten."

The woman straightened and took a step back. Thinking she was about to bolt, Sonali scrambled out of the car. But, the woman was still there, head cocked, hands on hips as she scrutinized the Bug.

Uh oh. I don't like the way she's eyeing Delilah.

"I'll take it."

"What?"

"Your car?"

"My *car?*"

"You want the beads?" She held up the string with a pinky.

"Yes, but —"

"Then I'll trade you the beads for the car."

"Are you insane? I'm not giving you my car for a string of beads."

"Fine." She shrugged, turning away.

"No, wait." Sonali sprang after her.

"Well?" The woman raised her eyebrows. "Make up your mind. I haven't got all day."

"Look. I may be able to scrounge up twenty. How's that? Twenty bucks for a cheap, plastic string of beads."

"See, the way I figure it, you really want these beads. The only way I'm parting with them is for that hot little number."

"But … she barely runs. We made it down here by the skin of our teeth."

"We?"

"My friend and I."

The woman smiled. "But you did make it." She fingered the beads, her gaze on the car.

Godammit! Sonali took one last beseeching look at Delilah, committing all her dents and scratches to memory. "Okay, fine. She's yours. But, don't say I didn't warn you."

"No take backs." The woman held out a hand for the key.

"The key's in my purse back in my room. Come on."

The woman's eyes narrowed again. "No tricks."

"No tricks." Sonali led the way back, justifying the bizarre exchange. She needed those beads. For Jo's sake. And if it cost her the divine but damaged Delilah, then so be it. It was just a car. It could be replaced. In about three to four years, when she'd saved up enough money to buy a new one.

Back at her room, the exchange was made: the key for the beads. Sonali watched as the woman flounced toward the elevator, humming under her breath. *Of course she's happy,* she thought peevishly. *She just made the most amazing trade of all time.*

"You want me to do what?" Benoit looked at Sonali as if she'd lost her mind.

"Examine these beads for fingerprints."

"I can tell you right now yours are on there."

"I know that."

Benoit's dark brows pulled together. "I gather this has something to do with Jo's death?"

Sonali nodded.

"Are we looking for anyone's in particular?"

"A colleague of Jo's who works at the Memphis lab. I saw him on the street giving the beads to a woman."

"There's a chance his prints aren't on file, and even if they are, they may not be detectable among the countless others who've touched those beads."

"I know that, but ..."

"Fine. I'll see what I can do."

"Thank you, Detective."

Sonali's eyelids drooped, but she forced them open. She needed to stay awake. Benoit promised to call her as soon as he got the results.

When her cell did ring, she jumped, then pounced on it like a cat on tuna fish. "Hello? Detective?"

"Yeah. I have the results. There are more than three sets of prints on the beads. It's been around."

Sonali's heart lurched. "So it wasn't much help?"

"On the contrary, we checked out all the prints that are in the data base, which turned out to be four of the six sets."

"What did you find?" Sonali's heart started to thump.

"Three of them belonged to men, one to a woman. All of them spent time in jail ..." Benoit paused, and Sonali wanted to shake him.

"And?"

"Not *and*, but. Only one of them works in a pharmaceutical lab in Memphis. He'd been picked up for starting a brawl in a bar up north near the Mississippi border, and had to spend two weeks doing community service."

"What's his name?"

"Do you know a Daniel Van Buren?"

Bingo.

"Detective, I believe he killed Jo."

"Based on what, the beads? Or the fact that he works in the lab she visited on your trip?"

"Both. Listen, I think he followed us down here."

"Why? He could be here for Mardi Gras."

"Just listen. Last year, Jo briefly dated some guy who worked in her lab. He made her uncomfortable with his intensity and when he started getting possessive after their third date, she broke it off. But, he wasn't having any of that. He called her cell constantly, begging her to take him back. Kept saying she was his soulmate and he couldn't live without her. Then he started turning up outside our apartment building."

"Did she call the police?"

"Yes, but they said they couldn't do anything because *he* hadn't done anything. What is it with you cops? Why do you act after it's too late?"

"Please focus, Ms. Sen. You were saying?"

"Just that life was a nightmare for both of us for about a month, then by pure luck he got transferred to the Memphis lab. Jo was so relieved that we went out to celebrate."

"Did you ever encounter him?"

"Just once. Briefly."

"Then how do you know the man you saw is Daniel Van Buren?"

"Because, Detective, he has one very distinct feature."

"Which is?"

"He looks like Steve Martin, you know, the actor. His hair's completely white. Jo remarked on the resemblance when she first started dating him. And also how long and lean he was. Gangly. The man I saw on the street flirting with the woman I got the beads from looked like a gangly Steve Martin."

"You could see him that clearly from your balcony?"

"Yes. I mean, it was his hair that caught my eye."

"Ms. Sen, you do realize none of what you've told me is grounds for arresting someone, let alone accusing them of murder?"

"Please, please bring him in for questioning. I guarantee it's the same guy."

She heard a heavy sigh. "Look, we'll interview him in due time. We plan to interview all the victim's co-workers."

"Her name is Jo."

The line fell silent for a moment. "Sorry. You're right. We'll interview all Jo's co-workers. If he's guilty, we'll nail him. Now, is there anything else?"

"So bottom line is, you're not going after him right now. I traded my car for nothing."

"I have no idea what you're talking about."

"Never mind. Good night, Detective."

"Goodnight, Ms. Sen."

Sonali hung up, head buzzing. They were going to interview all of Jo's co-workers. How long would that take?

And what about Daniel? He killed Jo. She was convinced of that. The time to nail him was now. Not days, or weeks, from now.

Her lips pressed together. If the good detective thought she was just going to sit around waiting, he was very much mistaken.

She reached for the phone, and after doing a quick Google search, dialed a number. "Hello. I'm trying to reach Daniel Van Buren."

"Daniel isn't in for the week. May I take a message? He usually checks in every day, and he's due to call in soon."

"This is Jo, from the New York lab. Can you tell him *nice try?*"

"Nice try. That's your message?"

"Yes. He'll understand."

After she hung up, Sonali reached for her purse. *The Masher*—a deterrent against attacks—sat in the bottom of her purse. She pulled it out, testing the weight of the heavy iron rod. Small in size—no more than six inches long — it packed a powerful punch.

Sonali placed the rod beside her on the couch, turned the lamp off, and settled back to wait.

One hour ticked by. Two. Her eyelids drooped.

Then she heard it.

A footstep.

Another.

Instantly alert, Sonali's heart jack-hammered against her ribs. What was she thinking, luring Jo's killer up to her room? She sat facing the front door, clutching the rod. *Why didn't I call Benoit? What the hell's wrong with me? This is by far the stupidest thing I've ever done. Well, this and trading my car for a string of beads. But still ... this ranked right up there.*

"Hello, Sonali."

She whirled, almost falling off the couch.

The setting sun outlined his profile, giving his snow-white hair a golden halo.

93

"How ... how did you get here?"

He smiled. "I have the room next door. I love this city, don't you? It's so easy to jump from balcony to balcony."

The room next door. He'd been right beside them all along. "How do you know my name?"

"Josette, of course. When she stopped in the lab she mentioned that the two of you were on your way down here for Mardi Gras. Sonali. Such a pretty name. Is it common in India?"

"I ... I don't know."

"No matter. I've been wanting to meet you. Josette showed me a picture of the two of you in Central Park. You're quite a looker, but I'm sure you already know that, don't you? Every beautiful woman knows she's beautiful."

"What do you want?"

"I want those beads you got from Claudette."

"I ... I don't have them."

Daniel took another step into the room. "You're lying. Where are they?"

"I don't know. I ... I lost them."

"Oh, honey. I wish you hadn't said that." He advanced further. She saw him stoop beside the lamp. Heard a click, and the room was flooded with soft light.

She could see him clearly now, dressed in baggy blue jeans and a white short-sleeved tropical shirt decorated with bright flowers.

"You killed her, didn't you?" she said, scrambling off the couch to face him. She gripped the rod tightly behind her, thankful for the folds in her sundress, which effectively hid it from view.

She took a small step back toward the door.

"Stop."

She froze.

"What did you want with those beads?" His voice was dangerously quiet.

She shrugged, tried to force a smile. "They were pretty. I thought they'd make a good souvenir."

He chuckled. "Nice try. Most people don't trade their car for a string of beads. Now," he took another step forward. "I'm going to ask you again, and if you're smart, you'll tell me the truth. Why did you want those beads?"

"Because they had your fingerprints on it. I'm sure you figured that out, didn't you? Or else you wouldn't have bothered coming here."

He smirked. "I wanted to meet the woman who had the audacity to claim to be my dead girlfriend."

"She wasn't your girlfriend. She couldn't stand you."

Daniel's face flushed red. "She was mine. My soulmate. We were fated to be together. She just couldn't see it."

"You poisoned her, didn't you? When she stopped in at the lab on the way down here?"

"Very good, Sonali. Although I shouldn't be surprised. Josette wouldn't be friends with an airhead."

"Why? You said you loved her."

"*Because* I loved her. It was the only way to keep her to myself, don't you see? She couldn't understand that we were meant for each other. I couldn't take the chance that she would fall for someone less worthy of her. I had to stop her before that happened."

Sonali shook her head. "How? How did you …?"

He shrugged. "It was simple, really. The receptionist went to fetch a cup of coffee for her. I followed her into the kitchen and offered to take it to Josette. I then slipped a cocktail of sodium cyanide and a couple of other special ingredients into it."

"Special ingredients?" Sonali whispered. *Just keep him talking.*

Daniel grinned. "Yep. One to mask the bitter almond taste of the cyanide, and the other to slow its absorption rate, so that it would be hours before she died. I call it the *Dan Slam.*"

95

Sonali fought a wave of nausea. *Get a grip, dammit. For Jo's sake.*

"Clever, don't you think? I knew that by the time it took effect you'd both be long gone. No one would suspect me."

"I did."

His eyes burned into her. "Too bad for you."

Adrenaline zipped through her. *He's going to kill me.* Too late, she realized the extreme danger she was in. She'd been cocky, thinking she could handle him. Control the situation. Too late she realized you can't reason with a sociopath. *What now?* She'd never make it to the door. He'd pounce on her before she could take a step. Her hand gripping the rod felt slick with sweat. The muscles in her wrist ached from the intensity of her grip.

In a dreamlike state, Sonali watched Daniel advance toward her. He moved slowly, taking his time, a smile on his face. He was enjoying this. Savoring the moment.

"I came to check on her while you were at the store. I should have waited and taken care of you too," he said, raising his hands to her. "Two for the price of one."

His hands brushed her hair as he reached for her neck.

The touch triggered Sonali into action, and she swung.

A sickening thud.

A groan.

Daniel stumbled back, then advanced again, looking dazed. The blow to his head had slowed down his reaction time, and when he reached for her a second time, she was ready.

Sonali swung again. Another thud as the rod made contact with the side of his head. Something warm and sticky hit her arms. Like a warm summer rain.

Blood.

She watched in horror as Daniel slowly sank to his knees, his eyes glazing over. Then he folded to the floor, legs tucked under him.

Sonali stared at him. Had she killed him? *Oh God!* Her intention was to bait him into admitting his guilt. If he attacked her, she'd planned to defend herself with the Masher. But her goal was to injure him. Incapacitate him.

Not kill him.

The rod, sticky with blood, slipped from her hand. Numbly, Sonali reached for her phone. Dialed Detective Benoit's number.

"Benoit."

"Daniel Van Buren is here, in my room. I think I killed him."

She heard Benoit swear. "I'm on my way."

"He'll be fine." The medical examiner motioned for the paramedics to wheel Daniel away. Sonali slid a glance to the prone form on the stretcher, his head swathed in bandages. She winced. Who knew she was capable of violence?

"Are you all right?" Benoit's gaze narrowed on her.

She shook her head, suddenly cold. Shivering, she dimly acknowledged Benoit guiding her to the couch. He plucked the crocheted throw draped over it, laying it gently over her shoulders.

"Better?"

Her eyes filled with tears and she blinked them back. "Thank you."

"Why did you do it, Sonali? Why lure him to you? You had to know he'd hurt you. Or worse."

"I had to do something. I owed it to Jo."

"We would've caught him, you know."

"I know, but not soon enough." Her gaze shifted to her phone in his hand. "Is that enough?"

"His confession? Yes. It was smart of you to record everything."

She managed a shaky smile. "It's the only smart thing I've done since I've been in your city."

"I disagree. Without you getting those beads, we would never have had his prints." He paused, cocking his head as he looked at her.

"What?"

"Did you really trade your car for them?"

She nodded.

"Jo was lucky to have you for a friend."

"Delilah was ready to fall apart anyway."

"Nevertheless. It was an act of love and loyalty on your part."

Sonali's eyes burned, but she refused to cry in front of him. "No. I was the lucky one. She was an amazing person. She brought out the best in me." A wave of loneliness and despair hit her. "And now she's gone."

"You never gave up," Benoit said softly. "I think Jo saw *you* for the amazing person *you* are. I've been in this business a long time, and I can tell you honestly, I don't know a single soul who would have traded their car for a string of beads."

She summoned a smile. "You're giving me way too much credit."

Benoit matched her smile. "You caught your best friend's killer, Sonali. I'm still furious with you for putting yourself in danger. But, I'm also impressed as hell."

Sonali's smile widened. "In that case, I'll take a *café au lait* now, please."

Lorraine Sharma Nelson grew up globally, constantly having to adapt to different cultures. She loved writing stories, and used it to escape from the reality of always being the new girl in school. She is a board member for UNICEF New England, which works to save the lives of children all over the world, and the Vice President for Sisters in Crime New England, which promotes the ongoing advancement, recognition, and professional development of women crime writers.

Lorraine's short stories have been published in sci-fi, fantasy, horror, and mystery/crime anthologies, and usually feature an Indian protagonist. Two of her sci-fi stories, "Get Carter," and a Star Trek story, "Tribbles and Woes," have won awards. Her most recent publishing credits include a horror story, "Mister Peepers," which appears in the *What Monsters Do For Love, Vol. III* anthology, and a mystery, "The Case of the Watery Wife," which appears in *Sherlock Holmes and the Great Detectives*, the first mystery she's written involving the famous sleuth. She is currently working on her first novel. You can find her on the following social platforms:

Twitter: @loneriter

Instagram: loneriter

Website: www.lorrainesharmanelson.com.

SPELL CHECK

John M Floyd

"Are you kidding me?" Trevor Sanders asked. He looked as if he'd bitten into a lemon.

Catherine Weeks ignored him. Both of them were staring up at the sign above the shopfront: MADAME ZOUFOU—QUEEN OF VOODOO. They were half a dozen blocks off Canal Street, near the west edge of the French Quarter and away from the biggest crowds, and it was about as cold as it ever got, in this part of the country.

"Don't tell me *this* is where you said you wanted to go," he said.

"It won't take long. We got two hours before the biggest parades."

Trevor let out a bored sigh and carefully smoothed his long blond hair. Neck muscles bulged above his jacket. "Voodoo?" he said, still frowning. "Who cares about voodoo?"

Louis LeBlanc, a dark-haired man in his twenties sitting behind the cash register on the other side of the shop's window, couldn't hear the girl's reply, but he could see her, and the guy too, standing there in the afternoon sun, looking up at the sign. "Mama?" he called. "Incoming."

In the small office twenty feet away, beyond the shop's cluttered shelves and islands of dolls, charms, candles, books, drawings, and masks, an older woman lifted her ballpoint pen and glanced up from the paperwork spread out on the desktop in front of her. "Good," she said, through the open doorway. "Old? Young? Wealthy?"

"Young couple. Maybe seventeen. One looks sweet, one looks like a doofus."

On the floor beside the woman's desk was sprawled a big, ugly Siamese cat. In a chair on the other side was sprawled a small, attractive young woman about Louis's age. Loudly she said, without looking up from her iPad, "Says the boy psychologist."

"For your information," Louis called back, "I'm an excellent judge of doofusism."

"I don't doubt that," the young woman said. Texting away.

"Quiet, both of you," their mother said. She had already gone back to writing the checks for the monthly bills. "Louis, if dey come in, show to dem de new Saints sweatshirts," she called.

No sooner had she spoken the words, than the little bell over the street door dinged and the teenaged couple entered the shop.

Catherine Weeks stopped in front of the counter. "Madame Zoufou?" she asked.

"I'm her son, Louis. People are always getting us mixed up."

The girl blushed and grinned. "I meant, is Madame Zoufou in?"

"Indeed she is." Louis pointed, smiling too. "Right through that door."

She turned and said, "I won't be long, Trevor. Look around a minute, why don't you?"

"Right," he mumbled. "That should be fun." He and Louis locked eyes, and after a moment of glaring, Trevor turned away, took off his coat, flexed his biceps, and stared sullenly out the window at the street.

Catherine walked into the office. The woman had put away her paperwork and was sitting there with hands folded on the desktop, a ring on every finger. The two studied each other.

"Wot con I do for you?"

Catherine cleared her throat. "I've, ah, I've heard you have something I'd like to buy. My name's Catherine Weeks."

"You may call me Madame Zoufou. Take a seat. Dis my daughter Evangeline."

The two young women nodded to each other as Catherine sat.

"How is it you hof heard of me?" Madame Zoufou asked.

"My mother's hairdresser. Roxie. She told Mom you're sort of famous. Mom said Roxie seemed a little ... scared of you."

"I see. You hof come here on the advice of a bue ... a bue ..." She looked at her daughter.

"Beautician," Evangaline said.

"A beautician. Is dot wot you are saying?"

"I suppose so, yes."

"And do *you* be scared of me, Miss Weeks?"

Catherine shifted in her seat. "Maybe just a bit."

Madame Zoufou nodded. "So. Wot is it you won from me?"

Catherine glanced at the door and back again. "Well—it's sort of ... embarrassing."

Out in the shop, her friend shouted, "Hurry up in there, Cath. I've had enough of this dump."

"That's Trevor," she said.

"Yes. Wot a charming young mon. Feel free to close door."

Catherine looked relieved. She rose and pushed the door shut.

After a pause, Madame Zoufou said, "Dis mon, dis Trevor. Wot you doing wit him?"

"What do you mean?"

"You in high school, de two of you?"

"Yes ma'am. In Metairie. We'll graduate in May."

"You do not seem much alike."

Catherine's face reddened. "We're not. I'm sort of plain, and shy, and Trevor ... well, he's popular, and he's on the football team, and—"

"Wot I mean is, why is it you here wit him now? Today?"

"Oh. Well—it's Mardi Gras. We're, ah, we're going to take in the parades and then a movie—"

"Did he osk you to go wit him, or did you osk?"

"Actually, I asked him."

"And are you be paying for his ticket for—how you say?—admission to dis movie?"

"Well, yes. How'd you know that? What happened was, he's a little short on cash and—"

Madame Zoufou nodded. "I onnerstan. So, again, wot is it you won from me? You won me to turn him into frog?"

Catherine's eyes widened. "What?"

"Or dog, mebby? Dog is reliable, helpful. Cat, not so much." As if on cue, the Siamese beside the desk looked up and hissed, wrinkling her nose and showing her teeth. "I could turn him into, say, chihuahua."

"Mama," Evangeline said, "don't joke about things like—"

"Who is joking?"

"No," Catherine blurted. "No, what I want is something to ... to make him ..."

She paused, a pained look on her face. Madame Zoufou and her daughter waited.

"... to make him love me," Catherine said, blushing furiously. "Or at least like me."

A silence passed.

"Do you have anything like that?" she asked.

"We hof many tings for sale here. Salves, oils, potions, all kine of tings."

"A potion. Yes, that sounds good. Something I could feed him, maybe, or get him to drink —"

"No," Madame Zoufou said, deep in thought. "For dis you need a spell. An incan ..." She glanced at her daughter.

"Incantation," Evangeline said.

"Yes. We bring him in here, dis Trevor, onn put upon him dis spell."

"You mean, like, speak words that'll make him —"

"Words, yes. But not speak. Words on paper."

"How would that work?"

"Evangeline, my assistant person, she will write down part of love poem once used in sacred marriage rite. Dis mon of yours, he will read doze words while you stand present here in dis room wit him."

"And ..."

"When he finish reading de words, de spell take effect."

Catherine frowned, thinking hard. "And he — Trevor — will love me, then?"

Madame Zoufou raised both eyebrows as if surprised by the question. "He will adore you. Never leave you, never look at no one sept you. For rest of his life. He will worship you every moment, overswamp you wit giffs, osk you permission fore he do anyting or go anywair, sing songs of love to you all de time."

Catherine swallowed. "Oh God, that sounds perfect."

"But ..." Madame Zoufou's dark eyes narrowed. "But dair are two tings I muss tell you, first."

"What kind of things?"

"Well, spell like dis ... it be much expensive."

"That's no problem," Catherine said, whipping a checkbook from her purse. "My daddy's Sherman D. Weeks — he owns a hundred hotels. I can afford it."

Madame Zoufou paused, as if wondering how to continue. Finally, she said, "Other ting is, I not know dis mon Trevor, but I see him outside door for a minute, hear him speak. Onn wen I see or hear someone, I know tings, dawn osk me how, but I know certain tings bout him. I believe dis mon will do someting evil next day or two. Probly tomorra. Sairdy."

"Sairdy?"

"Saturday," Evangeline said.

"Probly Sairdy aftanoon, or night, dis Trevor will go to a place, liddle building on corner, tall flashing sign, big oak tree to one side. Word on front winda say MARTIN, or mebby MARLIN. You know dis place?"

"Marty's," Catherine said, frowning. "It's sort of a café, near where we live."

"You mon will go dair onn rob dem of dair money. Wit two idiot frinns of his."

Catherine's eyes were popping. "How do you know this?"

Madame Zoufou shrugged, shook her head.

Evangeline said, "She doesn't know how she knows. It's the wildest thing I ever saw — neither Louis nor I can do it. But believe me, she's seldom wrong."

"You're wrong about this," Catherine said, her cheeks flushed. "You must be."

"Mebby so. Hope so. But I won to tell you wot I see."

"Why? Why are you telling me this? You want to me stop it, is that it? Stop him from robbing this place, committing this crime —"

Another shake of the head. "I care notting bout dis café, nor bout dis Trevor neither. He steal from dem, hokay wit me. I not be policemon. I juss say you need to tink it over, fore we do dis."

Catherine looked as if she were about to pass a kidney stone. For a long moment she stayed quiet, staring at the floor and wringing her hands. Then: "This spell, you said it would make him love me, listen to me, do my bidding." She looked up. "Maybe I could change him. I could tell him not to do whatever this bad thing is he might do."

The old woman spread her bejeweled hands. "Dot is up to you. You won to, we do it."

Catherine straightened her back. "I do," she said.

Evangeline seemed about to speak, but her mother gave her a look. After a silence, Madame Zoufou pointed to a small cabinet in the corner of the office. Evangeline stood, opened one of the drawers, and took out an old fountain pen, an inkwell, and a blank sheet of what looked like parchment, which she spread carefully on the desktop. She glanced at her mother, received a nod, hesitated, opened the container of ink, and dipped the point of the pen inside.

As Catherine watched, mesmerized, Evangeline carefully printed the first four lines of *The Love Song of Shu-Sin*, as translated from ancient Mesopotamian texts. When she reached the bottom of the sheet she paused, looked at Catherine and said, "What does he—Trevor—call you? Catherine? Cathy?"

"Everyone calls me Cath."

"With a 'C' or a 'K'? The writing of this name is extremely important."

"C-A-T-H."

Evangeline wrote the name and blew softly on the paper to dry the ink. "Done," she said. Though she didn't look particularly pleased.

Madame Zoufou fixed Catherine with a steady gaze. "Dot will be one dousand dollars."

Catherine looked back and forth between mother and daughter. "Shouldn't we wait to see if it ...?"

"If it wot?"

"Works?"

"It will work," Madame Zoufou said. "But you muss pay now. Ofterward, dis mon of yours be covering you wit kisses, be crazy in love. De two of you will won to leave fast, no time for pay."

Catherine nodded, and trembling with anticipation, scribbled the check and handed it over. "We'll call it a spell check," she said, in a giddy voice.

Madame Zoufou examined it, nodded again, and said, "Call to young mon to come."

Catherine opened the door, took a deep breath, and said, "Trevor? Step in here a minute."

Trevor appeared in the doorway, scowling. "It's about damn time. What do you want?"

"Trevor, I'd like you to meet—"

"I don't care who these stupid people are. Let's get outa here."

She took the sheet of paper from Evangeline and held it out to him. "Come in here and read this, first." To Madame Zoufou she said, "Out loud?"

"No. Juss read it. Silent."

For a moment it seemed Trevor might refuse. He stood there glowering at all three of them. "What is this?"

"It's sort of a poem," Evangeline said to him.

More hesitation, more dark looks. Finally, he stepped closer, snatched the sheet from Catherine's hand, and looked down at it.

"Read it all," Madame Zoufou said. "Every word, all de way to de end. Den both of you may go."

Everyone waited while Trevor read what Evangeline had written. When he was done, his sour, surly expression was gone. He looked up from the paper. His face was glowing, happy, excited.

"Our bizness is done," Madame Zoufou announced to Catherine, who didn't seem to hear her. She was gawking at Trevor, her eyes wide as quarters.

"Oh my God," he blurted, to the room in general. "I'm in love!"

***

Two minutes later, the three LeBlancs stood together at the shop window, looking out into the street.

"What the hell happened back there?" Louis asked.

Neither Evangeline nor her mother answered. They were still staring, their breaths fogging the glass. Madame Zoufou was fuming; Evangeline just looked thoughtful. Out in the narrow street, Catherine Weeks was walking along on the sidewalk beside Trevor Sanders, and gaping at him in open amazement. Trevor, his face a picture of pure bliss, didn't seem to know she was there. He was holding the Siamese cat in his arms and covering it with kisses from head to tail. Even from here, inside the shop, Madame Zoufou and her children could hear his voice. "I love you, I love you," he was saying, over and over. "I'll love you forever."

Catherine looked a bit distraught, and more than a little dazed—but not enough to have left her check behind. She'd said a surprisingly colorful word or two and snatched it from Madame Zoufou's hand before leaving.

"Did you hear what I asked you?" Louis said to his mother. "What happened in there?"

Madame Zoufou sighed. "Your silly sister cost us one dousand dollars."

Evangeline was still focused on the window. She didn't appear upset in the least. "I made a spelling error," she said.

Her mother snorted. "You con say dot again."

"How could a misspelling cause *that*?" Louis asked. A grinning Trevor was whirling around and around now from one side of the street to the other, his long hair flopping, one arm around the cat and the other hand holding its right paw, stretched out. The cat looked thoroughly bored. "He's a pretty good dancer," Lewis added. "I think that's a polka." He then said, to his sister, "What kind of spelling error?"

"I just left out an 'h,' at the end of a name," she said. "An honest mistake."

"A costly mistake," her mother observed.

"Not costly for Catherine," Evangeline said. "Besides, Mama, you never liked that cat, and now she'll have a home where she's ..."

"Wair she is wot?"

Evangeline grinned. "Loved," she said.

Her mother snorted. She seemed about to leave, then said, "Get on dot phone of yours onn find dis Marty's place, in Metairie. Warn dem dot dis butthole might show up dair tomorra."

"Okay. But I thought you said you didn't care."

If Madame Zoufou heard her, she made no sign of it. She had already turned and was marching to her office. On the way, she pointed and said, "Louis, put dem Saints shirts out front like I tole you."

Evangeline remained at the window, watching and smiling.

Outside, in the street, Trevor had switched to a waltz.

John M Floyd's work has appeared in more than 300 different publications, including *Alfred Hitchcock's Mystery Magazine*, *Ellery Queen's Mystery Magazine*, *The Strand Magazine*, *The Saturday Evening Post*, and three editions of *The Best American Mystery Stories*. A former Air Force captain and IBM systems engineer, John is also an Edgar Award nominee, a four-time Derringer Award winner, the 2018 recipient of the Edward D. Hoch Memorial Golden Derringer Award for lifetime achievement in short mystery fiction, and the author of nine books.

BEHIND THE MASK

Jay Seate

1955

New Orleans is an odd combination of the familiar and the strange, as intoxicating and exotic as the mix of humanity that inhabits it. On Canal Street during Mardi Gras, I crossed paths with someone unique in a strip club named the Mad Hatter. While two uniforms cuffed a dancer called Charity and placed her in the back of a patrol car, a shimmering red blouse appeared next to me. In it was a ravishing brunette who was put together like a Greek statue with arms.

"Excuse me." Her voice was low and husky. "Charity's a good kid. Give her a break."

I swiveled toward the woman. Her red blouse revealed the tops of alabaster breasts stacked as nicely as feathered pillows. The rest of her was just as delectable, built like a comic book character come to life. "And you are?"

The female observed me with green-eyed solemnity. "Stella Barton. I'm the den mother around here."

"Head stripper, huh? Well, Stella, it appears one of your cubs got careless at home and let a butcher knife slice through a guy's neck instead of the watermelon."

"The cad she's been living with? He's dead?"

"Charles LeBeaux. As dead as Gypsy Rose Lee's comeback."

Stella's bosom swelled. "She's better off, but you're wrong about Charity. She's a rabbit. She'd run first."

"This is New Orleans during Mardi Gras," I reminded this red-lipped doll. "Impulsive behavior is practically expected. We'll be taking your statement at a later time, Miss Barton."

"Would you ask Charity to call me the minute you finish working her over? She'll need a place to stay while your boys are playing around in her apartment."

"Unless the boys downtown decide to book her tonight," I said, more interested in Stella's shape than her words. "We'll let her make a phone call when we're through."

"See that you do, Detective ...?"

"Peters. Detective William Peters."

Stella shot me a look designed to drop charging elephants, all business and sass. Then she turned on a dime and walked away with a swaggering wiggle that said, "I'm your wildest dream." Feral catnip. I stuck a Camel between my lips, thumbed open my Zippo, and leaned the cigarette into its flame. Stella's sculpted torso probably drew more customers into the Mad Hatter than a hole in a window screen draws flies. I idly wondered how many poor slobs had braced her over the years only to discover a cougar rather than a kitten.

I followed the black and white in my unmarked car and thought about all the dames like Charity who'd snapped due to some abusive piece of garbage. I knew well the savagery of which humankind was capable. But my mind returned to the luscious form of Stella Barton. She was the kind of female who could make a man climb walls. Her body spoke not only to sex, but to hopes and dreams. The fresh source of sustenance tantalized me.

After spending most of the night grilling Marilyn Goosebaum, a.k.a. Charity, asking if she knew anyone who might benefit by turning the dearly departed Charley into a morgue job, we let her go. I knew she hadn't committed the crime. Most of these naive girls from small towns wouldn't see the evil in Jack the Ripper if you showed them pictures of his six dead hookers.

A Packard Coupe picked Charity up. I went home to my small riverfront apartment which was slowly sinking into the Mighty Mississippi. A breeze rippled through the trees, carrying a whisper of death along with the scent of the river. It was Friday, a busy night for brawls. I idly wondered how many drunken Cajuns would carve one another into 'gator bait by Monday morning.

A lonely foghorn somewhere upriver reminded me of twisted hopes and broken dreams, a longing for something which seemed just out of reach. I fought the familiar tug of a dangerous thirst. Instead, I indulged in two of my three vices: Booze and the Blues.

The next morning, I called Miss Barton and requested her presence at the station. She arrived in the late afternoon. She looked prim and proper compared to the night before, more like a society dame who'd just come from a Garden District soiree than the madam of a strip joint. Still I sensed something otherworldly about her — a mistress of the occult; a white voodoo queen? In The Delta, strange things were part of life and dealing with them were part of every day. Stella's raven hair was pinned up, highlighting her long neck. The fading sunlight from a window wrapped around her nicely.

She spent an hour and a half telling everything she knew about Charity's whereabouts on previous evenings and what she knew of the deceased, now residing on a slab in the morgue as cold as a dime's worth of baloney with a big smile carved into his neck and a red tag tied around his big toe. Her gaze was cool and detached. I talked calmly, making sure not to ask pointed questions. The whos, wheres, and whens fell sensually from her mouth.

"Thanks for not giving me the third degree," she said so pleasantly I almost believed her.

"You mean the spotlight and the rubber hose? We got rid of those a couple of months ago."

"I mean for taking me seriously. Most of you gumshoes take me for a high-class bimbo."

Another cigarette died and was entombed in an ashtray. A thin trail of moisture glistened in Stella's décolletage. I tried to keep my eyes trained on hers, but that little wet trickle got in the way. Even as she sat in the metal chair, Stella Barton moved with the sensual promise of what could be, every inch of her shouting, "Female."

"So, are there any more questions, Detective Peter, or can I go home and take a hot bath?"

"That's Peters, Miss Barton." I had no other reason to hold her except to wonder what kind of underwear she wore to complement the garter belt and hosiery most dames sported these days. "That's all for now, but please —"

"Don't leave town, like they say in the movies," she said petulantly.

"I was going to say, call me if you think of anything else that might help."

"Sure thing, Peters." She stubbed out her fifth butt, uncrossed her legs and stood. "I'll call the minute the real killer confesses to me."

There were enough bodies loitering around the station to cast a De Mille epic. I led Stella past the normal assemblage of cops, boozed-up rednecks, and hookers, through the heavy scents of sweat and musk to the double doors leading out of the station.

"Maybe we could have a drink some night you're off," I heard myself saying.

Stella stared at me, her eyes dancing with frantic energy, as if she could see into my soul. A wry smile softened her features. "In my business there aren't any nights off except Sunday. I don't much care to drink on my night off."

"Maybe dinner, then?"

She eyeballed me from beneath long, sooty lashes. "You know where to find me, Detective."

Stella sashayed down the steps toward her Packard Coupe, the same vehicle that collected Charity the night before. That sway could not only stop traffic but make it go backward. Her smart mouth hadn't done much for me, but the way she moved sure as hell did.

The earthy tones from a distant saxophone floated on a zephyr. *Damned fool, asking her for a date.* I listened to the staccato of Stella's high heels attacking the sidewalk, growing fainter with each deliberate step, mocking me. A burp of smoke curled from her Coupe's exhaust as the vehicle disappeared into the haze of twilight. The moon was a golden glob of honey camouflaged just slightly in a cradle of cirrus clouds. The breeze off the river caressed my face like a woman's hands. I breathed deep and tasted the fragrance of the city. It was a night made for contact of some kind.

Stella was no tramp who would do a guy for postage stamps, or support some yoyo like Charity had apparently done. She was a sliver under my skin, like something stuck to my shoe that I couldn't scrape off, but I forced my attention back to the homicide case. If you let your mind drift too far, somebody will steal your wallet.

I muddled through some bureaucratic paperwork and then slung my jacket over my arm, put on my snap-brimmed fedora, and left the station. Although my stomach was getting sore at me, there was an uncomfortable undertow to my thoughts. I drove by the Mad Hatter, wondering if I really wanted to see Stella's metamorphosis from her sweetheart streetwear into some sleazy getup which surely included pasties and a small slip of material over her garden of delight.

The backbeat of a drum and of laughter emanated from the place — two earthy, fundamental sounds of New Orleans. Across the street, a cone of sallow light from a streetlamp illuminated two figures standing in a doorway. I could almost smell the scent of warm bodies and cheap cologne. I hung a Camel from my lip and reached for my lighter. I held the shiny object, turning it over in my hand, rubbing my thumb against its smooth surfaces and thought how Stella's skin might feel.

I lit up. The tip flared red in the gloom as I inhaled deeply, letting the nicotine wander soothingly through my lungs. I exhaled slowly, wishing the escaping smoke would expunge a few of my demons along with it. My thoughts leapfrogged from Stella to Charity, to the corpse in the morgue with the new mouth carved into his neck like a homemade party mask, to the violent nature of the human species. I looked again at the couple in the doorway. I was overwhelmed with emptiness, tortured by loneliness and an urgent hunger, realizing the laws of lust are as immutable as the laws of nature. Then I flipped the cigarette out the window, dropped the clutch and drove away, letting life move on for everyone else.

On the river, a lone horn wailed a single note, deep and mournful. And the tug of my third vice was stronger than ever.

The phone rang at six Sunday morning, cutting through layers of sleep like a cat's claw. I bolted upright into wakefulness, tripping over a bad dream. My eyelids snapped open like a runaway shade.

"What?" I asked, already knowing the answer.

At 8 AM, I was at the crime scene. A street cop started a rambling dialogue of the situation.

"Do me a favor, Sarge. Pretend I'm your wife and skip the foreplay," I told him.

"Here it is. Another slug was opened up at the throat last night, cut from ear to ear, just like the last one."

I nodded and entered the room where the fresh kill rested. The body lay splayed on the kitchen floor with a gaping funhouse grin under his chin, a lifeless lump. His dead skin was the color of rain-soaked newspaper, his lifeblood spilled like oil through a blown gasket, a grisly Mardi Gras mannequin.

I decided to revisit the queen of the Mad Hatter, one Ms. Barton.

10 AM in the French Quarter. I parked my jalopy in front of a marble statue of a Confederate soldier covered with red, gold, and purple streamers to accompany the pigeon droppings. A wisp of steam rose from wet pavement, reminding me of things left unburied in a city carrying something otherworldly from its nooks, crannies, and above-ground cemeteries. This was a town shrouded with superstition and only as safe as the strength of its levies. But the soul of the city — *Vieux Carre* — had a strong, resilient heartbeat.

The elegant decadence of Mardi Gras hung in the air like overripe fruit to accompany those feelings of otherworldliness and passion — all of it a reminder of why I stayed in this mosquito-laden parish.

A group of kids with party masks resting on the tops of their heads strolled in my direction. When they saw me, they quieted and parted, going on either side of me like a stream around a boulder. I felt sure they sensed something better left undisturbed. I reflected on the thin line between life and death, between these kids and the scene I'd witnessed only hours before. It's a flimsy mask that divides beauty and ugliness, between innocence and a bloodbath. But this wasn't the time to dwell on how quickly the barrier could be penetrated. I had other fish to fry.

Beyond a wrought-iron gate stood a courtyard draped with wisteria vines and dappled with shadows from an ancient live oak. It dripped tattered banners of dusty Spanish moss. A wind chime hung on a branch. It tinkled in a faint breeze. *Ghost music. A serenade for the dead.* I climbed the balcony to Stella's bungalow and knocked on the door. The metal peephole opened. A greenish-gray eye the color of fine

Burmese jade studied my face. I listened to locks disengage and a chain slide free.

Stella looked at me with a lazy smile. My subconscious could smell the nicotine on her lips, which called to me like a naked woman riding a wild stallion.

"It *is* Sunday, Detective Peters, but couldn't you have called first?"

She wore an elegant silk robe which sculpted her body into an amazing thing. She might as well have been wrapped in a package that read, *Danger: Handle with Care*. Her business, after all, was to elicit the very response I was having.

"Are you alone?"

"Isn't everyone?"

"You look like a million bucks," I told her.

Small upturns lit the corners of her mouth. "In Confederate money maybe, this time of day."

A sense of humor. A radio sat in a corner of the bungalow's living room. Big band music for lovers was playing. It wasn't the blues, but it wasn't bad.

Stella turned the radio down. "You know, detective, you could see more of me than this for a buck a drink at the club."

She looked more beautiful than the photo of the movie star that graced the cover of *Silver Screen* laying on an end table. "Don't get me wrong, doll. I'm not looking to see you that way. I mean ..."

"Relax. I guess I'd rather have you show up than a couple of thugs with bent noses and eyes like bloodhounds. Sit down and I'll pour you a cup of coffee, unless you would prefer something stiffer to soothe whatever ails you."

"Coffee's fine." I sat on one end of the living room sofa. Stella returned from the kitchen with two steaming cups of java and sat on the opposite end, a fresh fag lodged between her first and second fingers. The sight made me hunger for a Camel, but I merely took a sip from the cup and watched the languid ribbon of smoke rise alongside her face, forming a hypnotic sway that pleaded for company.

"Can you tell me where Charity has been since you picked her up at the station?"

"Yes. She stayed with me that night, and then with a friend last night. Why?"

"There was another homicide last night, not far from where Charity and her chum, LeBeaux, were shacked up. This guy's throat was slashed from ear to ear with a straight razor, same MO as LeBeaux. If your friend can confirm Charity's whereabouts, she might be in the clear."

"I'm sure Janie will say Charity and she were together the entire time. So this clears her?"

"Let's just say whoever did the deed last night got their cutting lessons at the same school."

Stella took a deep drag on her cigarette and exhaled slowly, seductively. "That is very good news. Not about another stiff, I mean the fact that it had nothing to do with Charity."

My gaze traced its way up Stella's long neck to her eyes, deep icy pools that sparkled through the greenish-gray landscape. "There is another connection. The type of character this stiff happened to be."

"You mean another loser, working over his old lady, someone who deserved what he got?"

"That's pretty close."

"The fewer like them, the better." She placed her smoke in an ashtray, raised her arms, and ran her hands through her hair as if to comb out whatever thoughts lodged in her pretty head.

"Let me tell you a story," Stella said. "I had a cute little trick working for me a couple of years back. She was taken in by this sweet-talking customer. I told her he was bad news, but she was headstrong, hadn't been around much. Can you guess what happened?"

"I have a pretty good idea."

"He ended up torturing and killing her." Stella's inner volcano was beginning to smolder. And still, she was beautiful. "Thanks to a magnificent job by your cronies at NOPD, they never caught him."

"Take it easy, Stella. I sympathize."

She observed me closely. "Sorry, flat fo ... Bill. I guess that's a little harsh. Your job isn't easy, scraping victims off the walls and trying to find their killers, but what has your case got to do with Charity now?"

"Nothing. It has to do with you."

My sentence hung in the air between us. Stella's hands dropped from her black mane. "Look. I don't know what your angle is, but I'm just a hardworking gal looking out for my girls," she said with an edge that could have cut a diamond. "Whatever you're trying to buy, Peters, I'm not selling. I'm not looking to get cozy with a cop. Get the picture?"

"In Technicolor, but I've been looking for *you*, Stella. In fact, *you're* exactly the person *I've* been looking for."

"What makes me so special?"

I looked at the stubborn set of her jaw and dove to the heart of the matter. "Get this news flash and hang on to it. I found something at the crime scene this morning. A tube of lipstick. I believe I could make a strong case about who it belongs to."

"That's ridiculous."

"There have been several murders around town in recent months. Some cut, some shot. There's been a similarity to all of them—men who abuse those weaker than themselves. Pretty, isn't it? Just the kind of man you profess to despise, guys who you'd as soon cut up as look at, bottom-feeders who deserve what they get."

Stella jumped to her feet, nearly upending the coffee table. "Now wait a minute, buster, you can't hang this rap on me. I can find alibis a mile long and two miles wide concerning my whereabouts on almost any night you pick."

"Maybe, but I'm guessing your fingerprints are all over that little gold tube, and maybe a cigarette butt with your brand of war paint."

"You really think I would kill because I have a low opinion of men who use women? If I wanted to do some joker in, I'd poison the SOB. You can't mean you'd let me take the fall ... wait a minute." She dashed to the far side of the room and picked up her purse.

I stood and walked up behind her. I was pretty sure she didn't carry a heater inside her bag, but you can never be absolutely sure of anything when dealing with a cornered female.

"When did you take it?" she asked angrily. "When I used the powder room at the station, or when you escorted me out? I wasn't carved out of a wet mouse turd yesterday, ya know."

I took her by the shoulders and spun her toward me. "Simmer down, doll face. Don't pop your cork."

She held out her wrists. "Are you going to cuff me? I bet you like to play with handcuffs?"

"Don't worry, sister. I won't tell if you won't." I took her hands in mine. "I'm not planning to give the evidence to the lab boys."

"Did you pull that little stunt because you believe I'm a murderess?" Her tear ducts were on the verge of springing a leak.

"If I pulled a stunt, it's because I like the way you think. And even more, I like the way you look. We're not on opposite sides. I admire your swagger, your shape, the cut of your jib."

"I don't understand. What about the murders?"

"I think you will appreciate me all the more when I tell you last night's murder was necessary to give Charity an alibi."

Stella looked at me with curiosity.

"I've established an alibi for one of your little chickens. Last night's execution should keep the NOPD from dropping on the Mad Hatter like a bunch of dive-bombing pelicans. And I'm not going to implicate you."

"I still don't get your angle. Why the phony evidence?"

"I know you're the woman who can replace one of my three vices with something more wholesome. I hate those little punks that smack women around as much as you, and I have more names on a list I keep in my noggin. That's an important thing to remember. Never keep anything that will tie you to a crime. Protecting you and your girls from further accusations isn't too high a price to pay, is it? Nobody knows I'm following up with you and nobody needs to. We're on the same team, you and me."

"So you swat away the bad guys like they were mosquitoes?"

"Like the scum they are."

"A rogue cop just looking out for my best interests as long as I play ball, huh?"

"Looking out for *our* best interests. The only justice in this world is what you create yourself, *chere*."

Stella looked at me in a new light. "You're a very strange man."

"One of a kind. Aren't you the lucky one?"

"They say there's something in a man's eyes that always gives away his vices. I think I can see it now."

"My vices have rather large appetites." She now knew the power I could wield. What we knew could land both of us in water hot enough to boil crawfish. She looked trapped, but I wanted her to feel the thrill of a new relationship enriched with an enticing secret. "Relax. It'll be good, you'll see. We will be a rhapsody. Moonlight and magnolias."

Stella's face reflected resignation as if suddenly realizing she'd struck a deal with the devil. Her voice took on the quality of a caress. "I get it."

I lit two Camels with my trusty Zippo. I was glad I had her, but she had me also, not that anyone would believe her. She was quite a prize, but others would see no more than an uptown stripper who fell for a flat foot investigating a homicide.

Stella's radio was playing Bennie Goodman's rendition of *Begin the Beguine*. It seemed like the right song for the two of us to start a relationship on. While her mind would always be a work in progress, I could possess her body which might help on nights when she, a little booze, and Billie Holliday seemed too little to replace my urge to play a different kind of rhapsody, to make the city a safer place for women.

That's all I've done, really. Not such a terrible vice, but perhaps the hours of pretending to investigate acts I've committed could be better spent with Stella, willingly or unwillingly, in my arms.

The veil of cigarette smoke was thick in the air, forming an undulating cocoon around the two of us. The room suddenly seemed as small as a phone booth. She had nothing to say about my plans for her. A lot of talk always means lies. It goes along with the protective mask everyone wears, not just on Mardi Gras, but year-round.

Stella opened her eyes slowly as if they were the counterbalanced lids of a doll's eyes. It conjured up an image of something beyond the rational, spooky even to a man who had done the things I'd done. An odd stillness came over her.

"I'll cook up a couple of steaks, Bill," she finally said. "I have a special spicy Cajun sauce I think you'll like."

Jay Seate stands on the side of the literary highway and thumbs down whatever genre comes roaring by. His storytelling runs the gamut from *Horror Novel Review's Best Short Fiction* to the *Chicken Soup for the Soul* series. His memoirs and essays report fact, while his fiction incorporates fantasy, suspense, or humor featuring the quirkiest of characters.

JUSTICE FOR ALL

MR DeLuca

"I know the masquerade ball is the biggest night of the year for our town, but I still think we should've canceled it." His face clouded over.

"Something as minor as the death of the mayor wouldn't cancel the event of the year, Wes." Theodore leaned across the diner counter he was wiping down and lowered his voice. "Especially when everybody thinks it was an accident."

He stared at his burger. "Little do they know …"

"Watch your volume, I've got customers here. You never know who's listening."

"You're right."

A tourist in an oversized purple, green and gold sweater approached them. "I'm sorry, I couldn't help overhearing—"

Theodore bored his eyes into the woman as Wes gripped his burger so hard the ketchup oozed out like thick blood and splattered on the plate.

"I don't think you heard what you thought you heard, ma'am," Theodore said coolly. "Eavesdropping is a terrible habit."

"I know, and I'm so sorry about that, but I was just on my way to the parade when I overheard you two talking about a masquerade ball. Is it open to the public?"

"Yes and no."

"Yes and no?"

Theodore interjected. "We have a unique charter. Our town forefathers were so keen on Mardi Gras that instead of independent mystic societies hosting their own invitation-only balls, everyone in town automatically receives an invitation to a town-sponsored ball."

"You don't pay for tickets?"

He snorted. "Oh, we do, ma'am. In our taxes."

"Ah."

"There are an allotted number of tickets sold to out-of-towners, but those sold out early, months ago. It's gotten pretty popular, especially these past few years when the ball became more and more extravagant. Our mayor saw to that."

"So it's not public per se, but it's not like the private New Orleans krewes you've probably heard about," Wes concluded.

She nodded. "I went to New Orleans last year for Mardi Gras and did the whole French Quarter bit. This year I'm looking for a, shall we say, calmer experience."

"Then you've come to the right place," said Wes.

"Well, thanks for the information. Sorry to have interrupted you." She turned toward the cash register near the exit.

"Wait." Wes reached into his coat pocket and pulled out a folded, slightly crumpled paper with gold embossing.

"Take my invitation. It's for general admission, so it doesn't have my name on it. And remember to bring a mask. They won't let you in without it, and they won't let you remove it either, so make sure you're comfortable in it."

She looked stunned as she gingerly took the ticket. "Are you sure I can have this?"

"I think you'd enjoy it more than I would. As for the parade, the best spots left by this hour should be right in front of the hardware store, make a right out of here and walk two blocks. And welcome to our town."

As she said goodbye, they heard her murmur, "Wow, such nice people live here."

After she left, Theodore asked, "What did you do that for? You're town council; you can't *not* show up to the masquerade ball. And what about Marcia? I don't think your wife will appreciate your giving your ticket to a strange woman."

He shrugged. "She knows I'm not going anyway. I'm tired of always having to wear a mask, and yes, Marcia was not happy with me about it. If it's going to cost me my position, so be it. I think this ought to be my last term, anyway. Besides, I figure good karma can't hurt, given the situation we're in."

When Wes walked in the front door, his wife whirled past in a royal purple blur. "Good, you're home. I know you usually have a council meeting right before the ball, so you'd better hurry. Especially this year." She tsked. "It's a shame. I know we didn't really like him, but he was still a person. One of us. And to drown like that." She tsked again. "A tragedy."

Her dress swirled as she turned back again toward from whence she came. Her mask was in an elaborate Venetian style and matched her dress shade exactly. "I don't know why all of a sudden, this year, you're refusing to wear the matching mask I bought for you. They won't let anyone in without a mask, even a town council member. It's the rules."

Wes shifted uncomfortably. "I told you, I'd rather not hide and masquerade as someone I'm not."

"That's why they call it a masquerade. Ah, you must be getting old; you're getting so stubborn. Just make it to your meeting on time and don't make the others late. You know Theodore's temper —"

The phone rang upstairs. Saved by the bell. "I'll get it."

As he picked up, he eyed his wife fluttering about downstairs, and mustered the friendliest voice he could, given his frame of mind. "Hello, Wes speaking."

127

"It's Candace. There's a … grave issue right now, if you catch my drift."

He kept the same tone, albeit while wearing a pinched expression. He turned away so his wife couldn't see his face. "I understand."

"Can you talk now?"

"Yes, yes, Marcia is here."

"Okay. I'm just finishing up at the shrimp cannery. Call Theodore and tell him to meet by my boat instead of in the municipal building. Judith and Sebastian will already be there."

"All right. See you then."

"Bye."

He replaced the phone.

"Who was that?"

"Captain Candace. She says hello."

"How far out are you taking us, Candace?" Theodore mused aloud as he watched the darkness swallow the coastline. His mask was so loud that if it had made sounds, it would dull the roar of any wave. "Prying eyes and ears can't watch or hear us this far from shore."

Candace paused. She had faux peacock feathers adorning her otherwise simple gold mask. "Not far. Close enough that if the waters get rough, we can turn back, but far enough that no one can recognize this boat from shore if they happen to be out. We don't need to arouse suspicion why we're meeting so far from everyone, especially with the news about to break."

Judith leaned against the railing and pulled her wrap tighter around her shoulders. She donned a purple, green, and yellow classic comedy mask. "I doubt either will happen. It's a beautiful night, and almost everybody's at the ball."

Her husband Sebastian replied quietly, in his complementary tragedy mask, "Mardi Gras usually is. We should all be at the ball right now, instead of here making contingency plans."

"Contingency plans?" Theodore clicked his tongue. "His body surfaced on the beach, the police took him, and the ME will rubber stamp that he drowned, whether purposefully or accidentally. Case closed. So why are we meeting?"

Sebastian, Judith, and Candace looked at each other.

"It's gone," Judith finally admitted.

"What's gone?" Wes asked.

"Wallburn's corpse. It's gone. Sebastian found out from his contacts at the police department that the body's gone. His editor will be running it as front-page news tomorrow. She wrote the article herself and will be spreading the news like wildfire at the ball tonight, in part to drum up sales tomorrow. But you know Clarisse; she loves being first in the know and letting everyone else know it, too. She's already started."

He nodded his confirmation, presumably on all accounts.

Theodore leaned against the boat's railing. "What do you mean, 'it's gone'? A dead body doesn't move by itself."

"No kidding." Candace drummed her fingers against the ship's wheel. "Wallburn appears when we want him gone, and disappears when we want him to stay."

"Sounds like his tenure as mayor."

"This isn't funny, Theodore." Wes fidgeted with the hem of his jacket. "What are we going to do?"

"Quit panicking, for one. Your paranoia is making me nervous."

"If he'd stayed at the bottom of the ocean, he'd still be missing and we would have been safe. If he were with the examiner, the case would have been closed as a suicide or accidental drowning or something and we still would have been in the clear." Candace bristled. "But some sicko stole him."

"What a way to draw attention," Sebastian said. "The police will start digging and investigate as if it were a homicide. The town council members will be the first on the list. Everyone knows we hated him. And you know what? Whoever took him had to have known what we did."

Candace finally stayed the dinghy and joined the others congregated at the helm. "Well, we had a good rationale for what we did. If the mayor continued his recklessness, the whole town would've been bankrupt in two years."

Judith looked off in the distance. "Property values would have plummeted, stores would've closed, unemployment would skyrocket. The town charter's loopholes allowed him to redirect more of the budget to a bigger and better masquerade ball, one that never came close to being covered by ticket sales. He was talking about using the Volunteer Fire Department's funds for a fancier tableau for next year's ball."

"Trust me," Theodore said. "Our hands were tied, and we couldn't get public support because our masquerade ball is as old as sin. We start planning the day after Mardi Gras, for Pete's sake. People wait around all year for it. It's even more popular than Christmas. I hear people talk all day long at the diner, and the event is our town's pride and joy."

Wes murmured, "You're right about that."

"But it's not worth destroying our lives for it. We were being absolutely selfless," Theodore said proudly.

"Not quite," droned Wes.

"Killing a man is not selfless," Judith agreed. "Though it was for the right reasons."

Sebastian nodded. "It's not admirable, but it was justifiable. We had no other choice. It was either Wallburn's death, or the town's. Though I'm not proud of what we did."

"We?" Candace interjected. "You crushed the pills and sprinkled them in the shrimp and grits, Judith made sure to mark the poisoned bowl, Wes convinced Wallburn it didn't taste funny, and Theodore was the mastermind behind the whole plan. I was barely an accessory, supplying the shrimp from my cannery."

Before anybody could counter, Sebastian held up his hand and said, "Well, I don't think the police will look at it that way. We were all involved, so we'd all go down."

Theodore clenched and then unclenched his fists. "I don't know what you all are worrying about. It was common knowledge that Wallburn liked swimming past the buoys. Missed the Olympics by a hair, and always regretted blowing his best chance out of town. He used his popularity to be mayor for the past twenty years, but he was never truly happy. He was friendly in public, and mopey everywhere else. The man was depressed, and the police chief knows it."

"That's true," Candace conceded. "Even if the medical examiner discovered that he had swallowed a handful of sleeping pills just before he drowned, he would have ruled it a suicide."

"You see? There was no connection to us for anyone to find. We should've just gone to the ball and had a good time. The tradition of bread and circuses would've done its job, distracting the masses from reality. I say we turn back before our absence arouses suspicion."

Judith and Sebastian looked at each other. "I think it's too late for that," she said, rummaging through her gold and green tote. "We overheard during the parade that people are already placing bets on which council member did Wallburn in. Clarisse got the word out fast. That's why I visited the masquerade ball earlier." She placed the colorful cake on the table. It was purple, green, and gold, and reminded Wes of the woman from earlier.

Wow, such nice people live here.

Candace looked at Judith. "You stole one of the king cakes?"

"They have plenty. They always make more than enough, as insurance for accidents."

"Or theft," Candace offered wryly.

"If you're that hungry, I would've fed you for free at the diner."

"Ha, ha, Theodore. It's not to eat. It's to slice."

The boat bobbed up and down. Except for the gentle swooshing of the waves, everything, and everyone, was silent.

"You're thinking of dessert at a time like this?" Theodore asked in mock disbelief.

"More like a game," Sebastian offered. He looked nervously at his wife before addressing the group again. "We were talking. Everybody and their mama's going to know by tonight that the mayor wasn't in, you know, an accident. We thought it'd be best if one of us confessed."

"Confessed?" Theodore snapped. "Are you nuts? They have nothing on us."

"Honestly, it's a matter of time before they do," Sebastian said. "We're not criminals. We never pulled off a murder before. We left something incriminating behind, and now that they'll be looking into it, it's only a matter of time before they find it."

"So what is this 'game' you're talking about?" Candace asked darkly.

"Well," Judith said, "you all know that each king cake has a plastic baby baked into it. You cut the slices, and whoever finds the baby supposedly has luck for the rest of the year. We thought, to make it fair, we'd cut the cake among us and whoever gets the baby, has to, um, turn themselves in. That way we don't all take the fall."

"That's practically Russian Roulette!" Candace cried.

"Uh uh. No dice," Theodore said. "How do we know you two didn't rig it? You probably baked it yourself and know where the baby is. I wasn't born yesterday, you know."

"No, we didn't rig anything," Sebastian protested adamantly. "And in good faith, we'll let you cut first."

"No. I don't think anyone needs to confess. I don't care what you say, that was a perfect crime. The ocean washed away whatever evidence, and without a body there's not much they can do anyway. I'm not playing."

"Me neither," agreed Candace.

Judith motioned to Wes, who was faced away from the group, leaning partway into the lifeboat and toward the sea. "Wes, convince these two that they're no forensic scientists and are putting us all in danger with their pigheaded stubbornness."

Thereby commenced the bickering. The argument among the four was so heated, so garbled, and so verbally violent that nobody immediately noticed that Wes had turned around, pulled a revolver from his inside coat pocket, and pointed it squarely at the group. His hand did not shake. "The second time I reached into my coat pocket today to pull out something. How different each situation is," he said wryly.

Theodore held out his hands. "Wes, my friend, what are you doing? Let's be reasonable."

"Reasonable? I'll give you reason, for why I'm doing this and why it's for your own good. You're murderers!" he yelled in a strong, clear voice. "We're all murderers! I'm a murderer! And I want everyone to hear it. I want everyone to know we're acting like we did nothing wrong—like we're noble saviors or something. Meanwhile, a man is dead.

"I knew about the whole horrid scheme the entire time and said nothing! I could have prevented this. But no—I participated in it! It's been eating me alive every day. And not one of you feels remorse. It's disgusting," he practically spat.

"But we are sorry," Candace said. "We didn't want to kill him—"

"—we had to," Sebastian finished. "You need to understand that."

"I don't understand any of it." Wes' stoic demeanor disintegrated as he began sobbing. "I stole the body last night from the ME's office, and hid it in my toolshed."

"Why? And why right before the ball?"

"Because, Theodore, as Mardi Gras came closer and closer, I couldn't stop thinking of what the holiday is really about. At its core it's about misbehaving, acting greedy and gluttonous, and being vain, hiding your face with something

133

prettier than your exterior will ever be. And never, and I mean never, being allowed to remove it for fear the reveal will shatter the illusion of perfection you have worked so hard to build.

"But then the day of reckoning comes. After Mardi Gras ends, you are to repent and sacrifice for your misdeeds. We did the former, but not the latter, and I've been obsessing over the imbalance. We are skipping that step, continuing the party and ignoring the cleanup that always comes after.

"I told myself when I first stole that sad little corpse that I was afraid they'd find something, and it'd all be over for us. But deep down, I knew that's what I really wanted. The time had come to atone. I wanted this ruled a homicide. I wanted — *want* — them to investigate. And now I'm going to go back and turn myself in, and tell them everything, because I can't take all the lying and secrets anymore. I'll tell Marcia everything, beg her forgiveness, and then go to the police. I'm tired of hiding behind the mask of being a good person when I have proved, beyond the shadow of a doubt, that I am not. I will not indulge this masquerade of character any longer. I'd rather be imprisoned by bars than my conscience. Who's coming with me?"

"If we don't come, will you shoot us?"

"Still thinking about yourself, Theodore." Wes shook his head. "That's not in the spirit of Mardi Gras at all. You're no purple or green, and all gold."

"Huh?"

He scoffed. "Been living here your whole life, and don't even know what the colors represent. Purple — justice. Green — faith. Gold — power. And you think you have more than you've actually got." He cocked the gun. "Just get in the lifeboat, all of you. I'm taking the dinghy back. Goodbye."

Wordlessly the four filed into the lifeboat and watched as Wes set off toward shore.

"It'll take us all night to paddle back by hand," Candace grumbled.

"Will he turn us in?" Judith asked.

"I don't know. Where's his proof? It's still his word against ours." Theodore tried to feign confidence he didn't have.

Sebastian looked at his wet sock. "I don't think we're going back to shore," he said quietly as he pointed to the rips on the lifeboat bottom, where water was seeping in quickly.

The slices formed three letters: RIP.

MR DeLuca is a short story writer with over a half-dozen publishing credits to her name. She enjoys reading, crafting, and baking homemade desserts.

MARDI GRAS FOREVER AND THE BIGFOOT FIASCO

Rosalind Barden

"Hey, Bigfoot, dance!"

Mardi Gras reduced me to hitchhiking a desert highway in a tattered Bigfoot suit, suffering mockery from cars speeding past.

I, Josh, actor and noir detective, solved the murder but can tell no one.

My incredible, but always interesting, story began 48 hours ago.

Glumly, I wandered my Hollywood apartment building's hallways. My swishing raven locks, craggy chin, and Apollonian form landed me a shampoo commercial, but I got canned for a horse swishing its tail.

"The boy I wanted to see!" I turned toward a laughing voice oozing from my polka-dot-bowtie-wearing neighbor, accompanied by his poodle pair and his pretty boy, who was indistinguishable from his previous pretty boys, apart from being so blandly beige.

It was at bowtie idiot's Mardi Gras party last year that my life as a noir detective began. I nearly solved the murder, but got no credit. I tensed at the sight of him.

"Fired again?" he grinned. "I see you still have no shoes."

"And no pants," Beige-boy had to note.

"I can pull off this look." I flexed my thighs as they eyed my tee and undies. I can't afford shoes matching my persona, and I have one pair of likewise acceptable pants I must save for auditions. That's neither here nor there.

"Thought so. If you're looking for work, my aunt purchased a Palm Springs resort. She's filming ads for its new theme, 'Mardi Gras Forever,' a never-ending party." He cocked his head.

"What are you saying or meaning?" I inquired in my resonate, Shakespeare voice.

"I need a body for shooting today. You'll play Mardi Gras King."

I lifted my chin so the hallway lights caught my cragginess, my kingliness.

"I'll check my schedule. It pays? I won't take coffee cards." I've been burned like that.

"Pay equals your three months' past due rent."

I stiffened. How did he know?

"My aunt owns this building. Your pay will bypass you and go directly to your bill," Bowtie smiled. "I know you're doing nothing. Meet us out front in an hour."

With poverty gnawing my bare toes, I had no choice but to endure him for this important role. King.

"That all you're bringing?" Bowtie raised his eyebrows at my travel pouch as I slid into his backseat with the snuffling poodles. "Still no pants?"

"I travel Zen."

Beige-boy and poodles made a snorting laugh. I had no luggage appropriate to my artistic status. But the shoot should have supplies, and I'd borrow costumes for after-work relaxing at the Mardi Gras party. I decided this was my paid vacation.

As Bowtie merged onto the freeway, he took his hands off the wheel to sign papers where Beige-boy pointed. After furious truck honking, Beige-boy tossed the papers to me. "Contract for the shoot."

"I want the credits to reflect my new name."

"Changing names again? We go by what's on your rental agreement, though ads don't have actor credits," Bowtie smirked.

"I've told you, that is not my heart name. Call me McArd, Josh McArd."

Boyfriend and Poodles snorted.

"It reflects my hard-boiled detective career."

Bowtie muttered, "Not that again."

I pretended not to hear. "And rifts on my hard, artistic life."

"Thought it meant something else."

After Bowtie threatened to replace me with a lamp post, I signed and threw the contract at Beige-boy. "Not reading it? Or, can't read?" the boy sniggered.

I held my majestic head high, making the powerful decision to ignore them.

The city thinned until disappearing into desert. I swatted the poodles away with my travel pouch. Bowtie chattered about his aunt, how rich, how silly she was.

"So you've said," Beige-boy cooed.

Arriving in Palm Springs, Bowtie waved to a building in the walled, Spanish style. "It's there!" Workers decorated the resort with billowing green, gold, and purple fabric. Out front was a purple convertible, top down. A poster taped to its side read, "Mardi Gras Forever." Through the resort's gold-painted gates, I glimpsed a courtyard with sparkling pool and fountains.

The car kept gliding. "We aren't stopping?"

"We're shooting on location."

This was my first indication all might not be right. I ignored my gut instincts, an amateur mistake for noir detectives.

We reached a mountain outside the city. The car growled as it struggled up into cool air and pines, finally stopping at a picnic table and pair of cabins.

"Is this the set?"

"No! These are lodgings. That's yours." He pointed to the rougher cabin. It had no door. I peeked inside. There were two cots, one draped in spider webs. Another doorless doorway led out the back.

Bowtie ignored my despair. "We shoot till dark and wrap in the morning. Tomorrow night is the Mardi Gras blowout premier, invitation only. After that, ads must air to lure regular tourists because it's Mardi Gras every night."

I was startled when out from behind a bush stepped a thing: my height, my wavy raven hair, my build, my chiseled cheekbones, but not my perfection. My actor alarm flashed red alert.

"So, this is the tenant," it said. Before I could hiss a reply, another thing stepped from behind another bush.

This actor did not have my look: puffy face, puffy body in black coveralls. What was his part? My astute mind made connections. If he was dressed all in black, he was a crew member. Yes! I named him Mr. X.

Mr. X chatted up Beige-boy, until Bowtie inserted himself and handed Mr. X something. Cash? I couldn't tell. The man seemed dissatisfied, but Bowtie ignored him until Mr. X wandered back into the bushes.

Before I could demand I get cash too, yet another thing stepped from yet another bush: huge pink glasses, cropped candy pink hair, cropped candy pink top and short-shorts on her bird-like frame. "So, this is the tenant," it said in a heavy cigarette voice.

"My aunt," said a voice in my ear. I thought I'd met my spirit guide, then realized Bowtie was standing a little too close. "We call her Miss Pussy," he whispered. His friend, also too close, snorted. The poodles wiggled from the boy's arms and tried slathering my bare legs.

As I avoided poodle tongues, I noted the first thing was not avoiding Miss Pussy's slathering. "We call him Boy-Toy," Bowtie sniggered.

"Why is that thing here? You promised I'd be Mardi Gras King!"

"Relax. You'll be king, after a fashion."

Crowned and draped in a king costume, Boy-Toy was to lounge at the picnic table and sip a purple concoction from a plastic mug, then a green concoction, then a gold one that looked like a urine sample. Selling these drinks was how Miss Pussy figured to make Mardi Gras cash.

Me? I was to shuffle up to Boy-Toy, make begging motions toward his drinks, and say, "Want, want."

All while wearing a filthy Bigfoot costume, plastic beads around my neck.

"There's the backup costume, if you don't like what you're wearing." Bowtie yanked an even rattier Bigfoot from the poodles' teeth. "You are king, as promised: Mardi Gras King of the Bigfoot." He stapled a paper crown onto the costume I wore, stapling my head in the process. "If you want to quit, Miss Pussy can always evict you."

Thus threatened, I grunted "Want, want" to Boy-Toy while Miss Pussy beamed.

Bowtie filmed using a tripod and his phone, which had a polka dot cover matching his tie. He complained about "someone's stealing equipment" and darkly eyed Boy-Toy, who smirked. No sign of useless crew member, Mr. X.

All was going to script until Boy-Toy sipped the drink, spat it—on me—and shouted, "There's no liquor!"

He stormed to the other, superior cabin. Miss Pussy trailed behind, pleading, "It's to save money."

"It's colored water so he doesn't get drunk," Bowtie explained. "Plan B: you'll play both roles. We have a spare king outfit."

"This is why you should only hire professionals, like me."

"Not so fast, tenant!" To Bowtie, Miss Pussy hissed, "That thing," meaning me—how *dare* she— "will not be the star. This is Toby's role!" Toby must be creature's name. How boring.

"Either we use the tenant," Bowtie drawled, "or shut everything down, have no ads, no tourists, no liquor sales, and see if insurance covers this boo-boo. You did insure everything and everybody like I told you?"

"Yes! Don't sass back or no more allowance, freeloader!"

Interesting. Didn't know he was a kept nephew.

Miss Pussy dashed to the other cabin to comfort Boy-Toy, who sobbed, "You think I'm a baby!"

Bowtie used the fading afternoon to film me doing "Want, want," hoping he could edit in Boy-Toy's footage. "I knew this would be a disaster," Bowtie moaned to Beige-boy, who echoed, "Me too! Aren't you glad she got insurance?"

I embraced the role, adding operatic flourishes to my— dare I say—masterful grunting. Bowtie didn't stop me. "Perhaps we can screen that during the party."

In the middle of a particularly emotional grunt, Bowtie pulled his polka dot phone off the tripod.

"You didn't say cut!"

"It's too dark to record," he dismissed, pocketing his phone.

He and Beige-boy got snippy over hiding filming gear from Boy-Toy's sticky fingers. "It's not like it's super valuable and if we take it to the resort, we'll have to drag it back in the morning," Beige-boy complained, finally dumping the gear on the picnic table to Bowtie's eye-rolling sigh.

I interrupted with the obvious: "Weren't we staying here?"

"You, not us. There's no electricity," Bowtie said.

They were in the car and driving away; I did notice no lights winking on in the sun-setting gloom. It was getting cold, too.

"This is wrong!" I stumbled over pine needles, tripped through my cabin's dark doorway, to fall upon, to my horror, Boy-Toy sprawled on *my* cot wearing *my* spare Bigfoot costume. The last straw.

"Get out of my cot and my spare suit!"

He blearily rolled over. "It's cold. This suit is cozy. Me and Miss Pussy have a disagreement. I'll crash here. You crash there." He waved toward the spider cot.

I set upon him. But his Bigfoot face laughed in mine, blasting me with rum breath.

Fine. I'd use the other, superior cabin. Miss Pussy doubtless went to her resort, so it must be empty.

But I heard Bowtie in the other cabin. Wasn't he enjoying hot towels at the resort?

"I'll be the star instead of Toby." It was Miss Pussy.

"I warned you to forget that resort. You've mortgaged the apartments — where I live — and bet your ad campaign on Toby, a drunk ne'er-do-well."

"You're the ne'er-do-well! I'll evict you and that parasitic tenant!"

How dare she.

"Okay. I'll fix this."

A sniffing sob. "Maybe."

"I've discovered a use for that tenant. But he'll never be the star."

Beige-boy's voice piped in, "Not even a bitty star."

A happier sniff. "I'd like that."

Betrayal! I stumbled into the dark trees.

A flashlight beam blinded me. "If you want me back, it'll be another month's rent, or I walk!"

The beam lowered. It wasn't Bowtie. It was Mr. X wearing night vision goggles. The beam came from a light attached to a camera. He snapped my photo.

"Stop! If he told you to take stills, he pays me cash!" I swatted his camera to the pine needled ground. Its light shown up at his smiling face.

"Bigfoot. You really can talk."

"Of course, I can. I studied Shakespeare in Pasadena."

"Palm Springs Bigfoot is the rarest of them all. My heart despaired meeting you. You are magnificent."

That goes without saying.

"Please make sounds for me?"

I burst forth with my King Lear improvisation. I expected applause.

"No! Bigfoot hoots. Jump up and down. I need provenance." He snatched up his camera and clicked. He tried grabbing me, but I pulled back.

"You insult my art!"

I fled into the darkness. I heard him following. His camera beam blinded me again.

"I destroyed Pasadena with my soliloquies!" Sobbing, I pulled the paper crown, but forgot it was stapled in place. "I am not your performing monkey!" I wiggled my butt to make the point. "I studied classical dance in Burbank!" I launched into a leap that that was technically perfect, except for the bushes I fell into.

I heard Miss Pussy singing drunkenly. I steered by her voice until I saw my cabin's shape. But the thought of Boy-Toy happily asleep on my cot made me veer too sharply away. I fell upon the picnic table and filming gear. I hurled the gear into the darkness. That will teach them to demean actors! The cabin deserved my special anger. Gripping the tripod with my furry mitt, I flung. It sailed through my cabin's back doorway. Bullseye.

Satisfied, I curled up on the picnic table and slept, until screams woke me in the morning.

"Shut up!" The screams continued, joined by sirens roaring up the mountain. Did Bowtie change the script?

I approached an actor dressed, badly, as a plainclothes detective with a fake gun in a shoulder holster. "I was at this shoot first. I should play the detective."

He gave my Bigfoot costume an expressionless stare. "You are?"

I retorted with my classic noir detective stare, though the Bigfoot face may have ruined the effect. "Who are you, unknown actor?"

He changed tactics with a smile. "Tell me about your acting."

I did, at great length, because my artistry demands time. He wondered how I felt about this shoot. So much emotion poured from me, how betrayed I felt.

"So, this Boy-Toy upset you and ..."

Miss Pussy's cigarette voice, with a layer of hangover for extra thickening, shouted, "Toby! You're alive!"

I heard Beige-boy add, 'I see him too!"

Miss Pussy, utterly naked, flung herself on me, arms and legs wrapping my fur suit. It's not often I am rendered speechless.

"I am so glad that horrible tenant is dead. We'll be together forever."

I found my voice. "I beg your pardon?"

Instantly, she released me and tumbled to the ground. "You should be dead! Not my Toby!"

The detective actor watched with interest, but not closely enough because she sprang up, grabbing his prop gun holstered around his shoulder. She pointed it at me while it was still attached to him, and they both fell over.

"It's a prop gun. It doesn't work," I told her. She got it loose and it did fire, taking off a chunk of cabin next to my furry head. I scrambled around the corner. "I'll report you for bringing a real gun to this set!" I chastised the actor.

Ten actors dressed as police jumped on Miss Pussy. She threw them off. Ten more jumped on before finally subduing her. As they dragged her to a prop police car, she screamed, "I'll kill all of you!"

Bowtie materialized, poodles in arms. "She had both boys insured to the eyeballs. She'll come out a millionaire."

Before the actor got a word out, I seized the scene: "You did not tell me you changed the script and didn't let me audition for the detective, when you know I have real crime experience!"

Bowtie grinned insultingly, then turned to the actor detective: "The tenant I told you about."

"Ah," the excuse for an actor nodded.

Bowtie dismissed me with, "Filming's canceled. I have enough footage. Bye."

He turned his back to me as an actress in a white costume ran out from my cabin, which was crawling with similar extras, and held up something in a clear plastic bag that looked like a dish rag drowning in hot sauce: "Detective, look! The murder weapon must have made this impression when it struck the costume." Costume? Yes, it did look like the head of the spare Bigfoot costume Boy-Toy slept in.

"Something's imprinted in the blood! Acme Tripod," the actor detective muttered.

"That's the brand of my aunt's tripod. We left it on the mountain last night, and this is the sad result." A fake tear rolled down Bowtie's cheek.

My detective instincts buzzed: Miss Pussy swarmed by actor cops, but if those were actors, that meant a huge budget and this was a shoe-string shoot; something about Boy-Toy being dead instead of me; hot-sauce-soaked costume; then the final alert, Bowtie's fake tear.

"Boy-Toy was murdered!" I declared.

"Ignore him," Bowtie said to the detective. I realized the detective was only pretending to be an actor because he was undercover.

I stomped to my cabin to change. What I now knew was an actual cop blocked me from breaking through the "Crime Scene Do Not Enter" tape.

"Let me in!"

"Everything in the cabin is evidence. You can't touch it," she deadpanned.

"But my clothes!" I'd taken off my tee-shirt and undies to keep them fresh before I put on the costume. They were in the cabin, along with my travel pouch. "How can I walk around in this ape suit?"

"You already are, so you'll be fine."

My attention was drawn to the sound of Bowtie's car moving. I ran, fur feet slapping the ground. I stumbled and half fell into the open car window. Beige-boy pushed me out.

"You have to give me a ride down!"

"There's a trail," Bowtie said, waving toward trees. "Walk. The party is starting. Mardi Gras waits for no one." They tore off down the mountain.

I never hiked before, but maybe I could use it to create a bitter, one-man show about my life.

A police car rolled up alongside me. "Where are you going?" asked the officer at the wheel.

"I am going to win a Tony with my one-man show, after I go down this trail."

"People travel from around the world to hunt Palm Springs Bigfoot on this mountain. You won't make it down alive," said the second officer in the passenger seat

"But I've been abandoned."

"We'll drive you," suggested Officer #1.

I felt prisoner-like on the ride down, but it reminded me that I am a noir detective. I pondered why Miss Pussy wanted to kill me. Insurance? Or because my talent eclipsed hers and Boy-Toy's?

"If you pay me, I'll solve crimes for you."

"Oh?"

"My steel-trap mind is solving this murder: the motive was jealousy of me. That's a freebie."

"That's nice."

It wasn't close to evening when the officers dropped me off by the purple convertible, but the resort was boiling with nearly-naked people in glitter, masks, and beads. More streamed through the golden gates toward the booze-flowing fountains. Bodies splashed in the pool.

Inside the courtyard, my eyes were drawn to a huge screen. It was me! My heart soared, until I realized it was me stumbling through the woods.

My wiggling butt, sobbing about Shakespeare, falling, operatically grunting at the picnic table. It played in a loop like a horror show over and over.

Laughter exploded in the courtyard.

"Stop it!" I screamed and rushed forward, but two muscular men in black body paint, except for red "Sex-curity" painted on their chests, blocked me.

Bowtie, Beige-boy, and poodles materialized. "Go away. You're not on the list."

"I did not agree to that footage!"

"You did." Beige-boy pulled out the contract and fluttered it.

"Because filming's canceled," Bowtie added, "I technically owe you nothing."

"My back rent!"

"Fine. I'll waive that. But no ride to LA. Hitchhike."

Something wasn't adding up. Sex-curity had nearly pushed me out the golden gates when the pieces assembled in my steel-trap brain. "Only your aunt can waive rent. She's the owner, not you!"

Bowtie laughed. "When we stopped at the jail on the way here, she gave me power of attorney to handle her affairs while she's locked up. That's forever, so I'm the resort owner and your landlord."

It all made sense. "You all came back last night to trick Boy-Toy into sleeping in my cot so Miss Pussy would kill him instead of me, and you'd control everything!"

Beige-boy and poodles snorted. Bowtie rolled his eyes. "They stay on the mountain to do her nudist thing. Then she kept drunk calling, demanding we return to film her."

I was about to verbally fling the tripod at him, when I remembered it was me who'd flung it into the cabin.

My disturbing thought was interrupted by a familiar shape wandering by the booze fountains. Mr. X waved away a bartender-looking boy handing him a booze mug.

The final puzzle piece.

I pointed. "You paid him, Mr. X, cash to sneak-film me last night."

"Cash to that Bigfoot fan, when I can film you myself?" Bowtie waved his polka dot phone. "I gave him tickets to this party to get rid of him, but he's supposed to buy drinks."

"I'll shoo him out," Beige-boy volunteered. "I'll snap his photo for the cops, in case he slips back." He plucked Bowtie's phone away and disappeared toward the fountains.

Sex-curity tossed me onto the sidewalk.

All was not lost. I spotted two officers coming.

"Stop! My landlord is evilly plotting!"

As they came closer, I saw their badges were taffy, glitter caked their faces, and they wore no pants. They smiled enigmatically and glided into Mardi Gras.

All was lost. I shuffled down the hot sidewalk, despairing how I'd return to LA.

A car honked behind me. "Bigfoot!"

"Go away!" More honking. I turned and saw Mr. X driving the purple convertible. Its front grill sagged from a huge pair of hood ornaments shaped like candy-coated party boys.

"Get in!"

"If you take me to Hollywood."

"Yes! Hurry!" He patted the seat next to him, but his hands were so sweaty and grabby, I slid into the back.

The Mardi Gras poster rattled and flew off the convertible as Mr. X roared away.

A thought occurred to me. "Isn't this the resort's car?"

"No! It's mine. That man in the bowtie stole it."

"Figures."

It had been a long, crime-filled day. In the hot, open car, I dozed.

The road bumped. My eyes popped open. "We're off the highway." I saw an empty two-lane road, sand and rocks for miles.

"The scenic route."

I shrugged. An actor can't question free rides.

Pondering my clothing and footwear challenge, my eyes glanced to my fur feet. I spotted something on the floor. A tripod? If Mr. X wasn't a crew member, why was he filming? Or was he a secret talent scout filming the hot discovery, me?

My excitement dimmed when I realized it looked like the tripod from yesterday, and a dark something stained one end. The end that said, "Acme."

The car made a bigger bump as Mr. X pulled onto a dirt track. "Where are you taking me?" I demanded.

"You'll see." Mr. X steered the convertible into a maze-like boulder field.

He stopped the car and got out. "Don't be nervous. This will only take a moment."

A moment to kill me. "You cannot fool a crack detective!"

I leapt out, tripod in hand. "You are Bowtie's hired assassin. You two got Boy-Toy's insurance, but you won't have mine. I've foiled your plot because you carelessly left the tripod in back." I raised it overhead to illustrate his mistake.

Mr. X dropped to his knees. "Oh, please, Bigfoot, I'm no assassin. I brought you here because I love you." I flinched when he pulled something from his pocket. "Will you marry me?"

It was a ring with huge stone and huge band size. As huge and powerful as I am proud to say my hands are, I'd have to put three fingers together to keep that ring from sliding off.

Can I say, no one's proposed to me before? The size of the rock melted my heart. My eyes misted. I tossed back my head, though my raven locks weren't given their due inside the Bigfoot head.

I heard a clunk and turned to see Beige-boy spring from the convertible's trunk. With a polka dot phone, he snapped photos of me, tripod raised above kneeling Mr. X's head.

"Fools! You played into my trap!" He threw back his head, making the poodle snorting laugh. "These photos will prove the quadruple murder-suicide!"

My detective mind worked overtime. "That's not your phone!" I recognized Bowtie's polka dots. "Quadruple means four. Me plus Mr. X plus Boy-Toy equals three. And only one of us is dead."

"Look at you. Mr. Crime Solver."

Beneath the Bigfoot mask, I blushed. "Thank you."

More poodle laughter. "You and that bowtie fool made the fatal mistake of not reading the contract. He signed a will giving control of everything to me. You both signed a murder-suicide confession. As did Boy-Toy and Miss Pussy." He snapped another photo. "By dawn, you'll be dead and he'll be found drunkenly drowned in a Mardi Gras fountain with this polka dot phone in his hand."

I heard Mr. X shuffling away in the sand. Fine. I'd handle this crime alone. "I have the weapon you foolishly forgot in the convertible."

"Forgot? I planted it when I followed your Mr. X! I knew he'd search for you. He'll be dead too." Beige-boy pulled a second tripod from his beige pant leg. "I am not unarmed!"

"You stole equipment yesterday, not Boy-Toy!"

Grinning, he twirled the tripod.

"Ha! I am a Thespian trained in swordcraft!" I leapt about in classic stances, tripod poised. But the costume thwarted my athletic prowess. My furry feet got tangled. I tottered.

Beige-boy took advantage, bringing his tripod down hard, ripping a flap loose from my costume's backside. Desert air refreshed my naked, toned glutes.

Mr. X howled. He pounced, knocking me down. The tripod flew from my hand. The ring flew from his. Was he shielding me with his body?

Beige-boy seized his moment. "I'll take this valuable rock!" He snatched the ring with his teeth, grabbed my tripod. He twirled both weapons at us.

Mr. X ran one way into the boulder maze. I ran the other.

The setting sun threw crazy orange light through gaps in the boulder maze. I spotted Beige-boy's twirling tripods, heard his poodle laugh. Over there, Mr. X's black boots ran.

I ducked behind cacti when I saw Beige-boy in a boulder clearing.

He wasn't alone. There was another actor in a Bigfoot costume. Boy-Toy was alive? Then a slanting ray lit the actor. No, an actress, a particularly tall and husky gal.

Beige-boy's back was flat against boulders, arms spread, polka dot phone and both tripods at his feet.

Sun sparkled off the ring's stone clutched in his teeth. She saw it too and her eyes became soft and misty, rather like mine had when Mr. X proposed. Happy moaning escaped her lips as she pressed them to his, taking the ring.

She scooped Beige-boy up and slung him over her massive shoulder. I saw the ring glinting from her finger. Fit her perfectly.

Beige-boy and his secret femme fatale disappeared into the boulder maze. Beige-boy's voice echoed: "Oh, God!"

Ah, ha! It was the two of them all along.

By nightfall, I escaped the maze but could not find Mr. X or the convertible. Lost, I decided to power nap beneath the desert's thousand stars.

Screeching tires shocked me awake. I blinked in the sun. I'd fallen asleep on a road. The convertible's grill loomed near my face.

Mysteriously, the hood ornaments now sat in the front seat. Recognition hit me. "You're the police at the party, the police who drove me down the mountain. You're undercover!"

Officer #2 raised one eyebrow.

I spotted Mr. X in the backseat. "They rescued you too!" I hurried to him, but Officer #1 held up a warning hand. "He's dangerous."

Mr. X lunged, teeth snapping. I saw he was wrapped in a straitjacket.

"You're lucky you're alive," Officer #2 said. "This man operates a scam tricking Palm Springs Bigfoot with marriage proposals, only to lure them to his taxidermy shop."

"I'm the victim!" Mr. X yelled. "Fake Bigfoot swindled me!"

"The man you call Beige-boy convinced him that the genuine Bigfoot was acting in the commercial. That's how he got him to murder one of you," Officer #1 explained.

"I didn't kill him!" Mr. X sobbed. "I was about to, but someone threw a tripod on his head."

My heart froze.

I stayed cool, my actor skills kicking in. "Beige-boy is on the loose with his femme fatale."

The officers exchanged looks. "He won't be going anywhere anytime soon."

That didn't sound like adequate police work. "But Miss Pussy will be free." Then Bowtie wouldn't be my landlord.

"No. She put a dozen officers in the hospital. Then there's the matter of the wealthy widower gone missing during Mardi Gras twenty years ago."

Because I couldn't ride in the back, I clung to the grill as the hood ornament. They dropped me at the resort.

Bowtie ambled out with poodles and a new pretty boy, indistinguishable from his previous pretty boys, apart from bright red shoes.

"Can't get rid of you, can I?"

I rushed forward. "Help! I need clothes–vogueish only!"

Snickering, they slipped inside, locking the gates. The poodles slathered through the golden bars.

So there I was, actor, noir detective, murderer, hitchhiking to Hollywood in a bedraggled Bigfoot suit. Sun pounded, cruel traffic roared. Was this the end of my bitter, one-man show?

I collapsed to all fours.

Suddenly, a stylish sedan skidded to a stop. Fashionably inebriated people leaned out, their Mardi Gras beads clacking. "Poor puppy!" They waved mugs of purple booze to lure me inside, not that I needed luring. "Its butt is skinned raw. Let's take it to the Malibu house for pampering."

Sometimes an actor, a hardened detective, gets lucky.

Josh the actor and would-be detective makes his second appearance in Rosalind Barden's "Mardi Gras Forever and the Bigfoot Fiasco." Josh first appeared in her story, "International Vogue and the Pajama Fiasco Weekend," in Mystery and Horror, LLC's anthology *Mardi Gras Murder*. Ms. Barden's stories also appear in Mystery and Horror, LLC's *History And Mystery, Oh My!* (FAPA President's Book Award Silver Medalist), and six of the *Strangely Funny* anthologies. Her humorous Young Adult mystery novel set in Depression-era

Los Angeles, *Sparky of Bunker Hill and the Cold Kid Case*, is an Author Academy Award Top Ten Mystery Finalist and a Critters Annual Readers Poll Top Finisher in both Best Mystery and Best Young Adult categories. Dozens more of her stories have appeared in print anthologies and webzines, including the U.K.'s acclaimed *Whispers of Wickedness*. Ellen Datlow selected her short story "Lion Friend" as a Best Horror of the Year Honorable Mention after appearing in *CERN Zoo*, a British Fantasy Society nominee for Best Anthology, part of DF Lewis' award winning *Nemonymous* anthology series. *TV Monster* is her print children's book she wrote and illustrated. Her satirical novel *American Witch* is available as an e-book. In addition, her scripts, novel manuscripts and short fiction have placed in numerous competitions, including the Writers Digest Screenplay Competition and the Shriekfast Film Festival. She writes in Los Angeles, California. Discover more at www.RosalindBarden.com

GUSSY SAINT AND THE CASE OF THE THREE-BOOBED WOMAN

CD Gallant-King

I woke up in a brothel and stumbled out of the back room in nothing but my socks and boxer shorts. I expected some hard looks from the ladies and the madam, who did not take kindly to me passing out and taking up one of their beds for the night, and I was ready with a witty retort to put them at ease and call off their goon, a huge Polynesian man named Leakee.

I was not expecting to be surrounded by cops, and thus found myself for perhaps the first time in my life at a loss for words. My quip about polishing the morning wood would probably fall flat on these uncultured, humorless swine.

The brothel's parlor looked like a crime scene, probably because it was.

A body was splayed naked and face-down across the ugly red loveseat that had undoubtedly been the scene of countless lap dances and other illicit hanky-panky. It was my professional opinion as a detective and private eye that the fat, hairy man in the Loveseat of Cheap Love was most likely dead. Bloody footprints surrounded the corpse like someone had danced a cha-cha in his plasma.

"What the hell are you doing?" asked a woman's voice, asking a question I have often heard, though usually only in the ladies' restroom.

"Well, I'm no longer concerned about hiding my morning erection, thanks to that guy. Nothing like a bloated corpse to kill the mood."

"This is Gussy Saint," said Cleoniki, a dark-skinned, middle-aged woman in way too much makeup, and madam of the finest whorehouse in Louisiana. I'm not certain, but she may have been a transvestite. I've even had sex with her twice, and I still can't be sure.

"I notice you didn't add, 'my best customer.'"

"That's because you pay my girls shit."

This was true. "Yes, but I have also never beat up any of them, so that has to put me near the top of the list."

My name is Gussy Saint, Augustine to my dear departed mother and my parole officer. I usually ply my wares as a private dick in the seedy underbelly of Mount Vernon, Washington, but I make a special point of visiting The Big Easy every year for Mardi Gras. The reason for this is three-fold:

One, to visit Cleoniki's place. I'm telling you, it's worth the trip.

Two, because it's a sweet-ass party, and I have numerous program sponsors who will confirm that I love a sweet-ass party.

Three, it always falls conveniently just after Super Bowl Sunday. Since I inevitably make a truckload of bad wagers on the big game, it's nice to get out of town to let the heat die down a little after I get all my bookies arrested for illegal gambling.

"So, you're the famous private investigator Gussy Saint," the female voice said. It belonged to the chief detective in charge, a buxom blond woman whose buttons deserved a gold medal for the Olympic effort they were pulling off keeping her white blouse closed. Her tits strained at the clingy material like Mexican children in cages on the border. I spoke to the woman for several minutes, and I swear to god I couldn't tell you the color of her eyes. "They warned me about you."

Though I usually lived on the other side of the country, I may have had a run-in with the New Orleans police once or seven times. My reputation obviously preceded me. That's okay, because I knew who she was, too. I'd heard the fuzz at the station talk about the smokin' hot homicide detective. Rumor had it she had lost a leg in the line of duty, but I couldn't tell for sure in her sensible black slacks. If she had a prosthetic, she covered it well. This was the first time I'd seen her in person, if you didn't count me creeping on her Facebook page on the computer at the library. "Detective Stacy Williams, I presume?"

The detective wrinkled her nose, which was kinda cute, even if she was acting like I was a crusty sweat sock she picked up off the floor. "They told me you narrate everything happening to you under your breath."

Shit. I'd been working on keeping all that internal. I hope she didn't hear the part about her Facebook profile.

She sighed. "Would it be a waste of time to ask if you know anything about this?"

I glanced about the scene, quickly taking in all the pertinent details. "I think you have a dead fat guy on your hands, detective."

"I mean do you know anything about why he's dead?"

"I suspect he stopped breathing."

"Jesus Christ, did you see anything? Hear anything?"

I honestly had not. Last night, like most of my nights, was a total blur. "Unfortunately, I would not be a reliable witness. I'm in a twelve-step program."

She did that cute thing with her nose again. "You reek of alcohol."

"I didn't say I was good at the program. I'm afraid I'm going to have to start over at step one again today."

"Detective," said one of the CSI-types, a young man with frizzy hair and a crooked nose that did not look anywhere sexy enough to be in one of those TV shows. CSI: New Orleans would have the homeliest cast. "We found this. All of the girls claim it doesn't belong to them, and none of them recognize it."

The chesty detective held up the plastic bag with something frilly inside. "A bra? It looks weird."

"It's from a three-breasted woman," I explained helpfully. She gave me a horrified look, so I continued. "It's rare, but occasionally women are born with an extra breast. It's called polymastia."

"It's true," said the CSI-geek, who had already Googled it on his phone.

The detective looked back at me. "I don't suppose you know any three-breasted women in town, do you? I would very much like to ask her how her bra ended up in a brothel next to a dead man."

"The last two I know of were circus freaks passing through. But there is one more that might still be around. Who's the stiff, anyway?"

The detective sighed and shrugged. I had either worn down her defenses or she was giving into my animal magnetism. I've been known to score both ways. "It's city councilor Mark Ward."

"Wasn't he supposed to run for mayor next year?" New Orleans might not be my usual stomping grounds, but I liked to keep abreast of local politics. It was a good idea for someone like myself, who constantly found himself at odds with local law enforcement and bylaws. How was I supposed to know it was illegal to tie an alligator to a fire hydrant in Louisiana?

"He was. And he was one of the few city politicians who wasn't in the mob's pocket. Seems like a pretty clear case of someone removing a complication before it becomes a problem."

"Nothing is ever what it seems, sweetheart."

"Don't call me sweetheart."

160

"Sorry. Sugartits."

She glared at me, but I caught the hint of a smile. "My name is Detective Williams," she said.

"Of course, my apologies, Detective Williams. Allow me to make it up for you by buying you a coffee."

She raised a shapely eyebrow. "Are you asking me out?"

"No, strictly professional. Just for our ride over to see the three-breasted woman."

"You can just give me her address."

"I could, except if she gets a sniff that there's a cop showing up at her door to ask questions, she's going to disappear faster than a lubed-up hamster in a paper towel roll. She'll open the door for me."

"You often show up at the three-breasted woman's door?"

"Not often, but when I do she's appreciative afterward. Some people are freaked out by women with unusual assets, but I'm a bit more open-minded and sensitive."

She hesitated for a moment and shifted her weight from leg to leg.

"Sensitive? You?"

"As a hard-on, sweetheart. Sorry, Detective Williams."

"Fine. We'll go together. But I'm asking the questions. And you still owe me a coffee."

"Of course. But can you spot me a fiver? I spent the last of my cash on a tip for Madam Cleoniki's girl."

Detective Williams and I drove across the French Quarter to a cheap hotel behind a tram station off Canal Street. We took her car on account of my license being suspended due to a little incident involving a flask of bourbon and my piss in the gas tank of a highway patroller's car.

It was early, but Mardi Gras celebrations were already underway. Our route was detoured for the Zulu parade, and at one point we had to stop to wait for a crowd of colorfully garbed, barely dressed ladies to dance across the street. Despite the plethora of jiggly eye-candy, I found my gaze constantly drawn back to the dame seated beside me.

I liked letting the detective drive; it gave me more time to look at her and admire her curves. I enjoyed the way she gripped the wheel, her strong fingers confident and firm, and I could imagine her gripping a few other things I'd enjoy even more.

I wondered what it felt like to work the gas and brake pedal with a fake foot you couldn't feel, but she was certainly having no trouble. There wasn't a glimmer of hesitation in this woman; she knew what she wanted and wasn't afraid to go after it. I found that an incredible turn-on, and now I just had to figure out if we wanted the same thing.

We pulled up at the motel and I told the old receptionist Gertie that I had an appointment with the lady in room seven. The octogenarian, tattooed stoner said the occupant wasn't supposed to be back for hours but her door was always open for me, so she gave me the spare key.

"She just gave you the key to Maureen's room?" Williams asked me as we headed down the hall. "I thought you didn't come here often."

"I don't. But I may have gone down on the old bag a couple of times, so she's soft on me."

Williams rolled her eyes, but I saw her smile. Nothing like performing cunnilingus on an ancient crone to earn you brownie points. It's the "helping the old lady across the street" of the new generation.

I opened the door to room seven and let Williams in first, which was part gentlemanly and part in case Maureen was actually there and took a shot at whoever let themselves in. The small room reeked of pot and mildew, and the brown carpet and yellow walls had seen better days. The jaunty sound of the parade drifted in from outside.

"Charming place," the detective said, doing that cute nose wrinkle once again.

I couldn't stop myself this time. "You have a gorgeous face, you know that?"

"Smooth. At least you didn't start with my tits."

"Oh, they are tremendous, don't get me wrong, you must have a bra made from Kevlar to keep those bad boys in check. I just like to start from the top and work my way down."

She smiled despite herself, but it faded quickly. She sat down on the bed and looked away. "Well that's probably for the best. The top half is the nicest part anyway."

"I think all of it is nice. A pretty package, like a Christmas present waiting to be unwrapped."

"Aren't you going to be disappointed when you open it up and find your toys broken?"

She was showing me a surprising amount of vulnerability. I had seen this encounter going several ways, but none of them quite like this. I suspected the Detective was soft on me, but I never imagined she would let her guard down so quickly. My next move would decide which direction our little rendezvous went.

"See, I was never one of those kids who took their toys for granted. Every one was special, a few dings and scratches didn't hurt." Emboldened by the parade music from outside, which sounded like a sensual blend of accordions and soup ladles being pounded on cheese graters. I put my hand on her leg. I felt where her flesh met the plastic and metal of the prosthetic, and she flinched away. "You don't have to shy away."

Slowly, cautiously, she slid her leg back to where I could reach it. I put my hand back, could once again feel the place where the skin met plastic through her pant leg. I moved my hand higher up her thigh, to focus on her and show her it wasn't just a fetish for a fake leg. True, I had once made love to a woman with a glass eye entirely because she had another hole I could try out, but this was not like that. I liked all of

163

Williams, and wanted to see all of her, both what God and the doctor gave her.

I kissed her and she didn't pull away. She returned the kiss, hot and hungry, her tongue reached into my mouth to meet mine. Her breath tasted like coffee, the one she had to pay for because I really was broke, but I didn't mind. I always imagined cops tasted like coffee, so that fulfilled a particular little fantasy.

My hands traced her hips and slid down her legs until once again I brushed against the prosthetic. She flinched and her hands instinctively went to stop me, but I pushed them aside and pushed her down gently on the bed. I unbuttoned her sensible black business casual pants and pulled them off.

There lay the detective, in her rumpled top and white satin panties, legs spread for all the world to see. Her left leg stopped at the knee where it met the plastic cup thing that encased what was left of her limb. Her lower leg was replaced by a metal rod with a plastic foot on the end. Williams looked up at me, expectantly, waiting for judgement.

"What do you think?" she asked softly.

"You know, I thought your tits were your best feature, but I think you have the sexiest legs I've ever seen."

"Do it!" she hissed through gritted teeth. Being a gentlemen, I could only oblige. Let me tell you, you've never lived until you've fucked a one-legged cop at Mardi Gras to the dulcet tones of Zydeco music.

I woke up with a gun in my face. Some people would be freaked out by this, slipping from the gentle embrace of repose into the balls-squeezing shock of a .40-caliber Smith & Wesson muzzle pointed at your dome, but since I find myself in such situations on the regular, I barely broke a sweat. I mean, I was shitting my pants, but I wasn't going to let Williams know that.

"Gonna shoot me, Sugartits?" I asked, reaching over to the nightstand for a cigarette. I don't usually smoke, but I had to do something so the detective didn't see my hands shaking.

Detective Williams was dressed only in her bra and panties, a plain white bra that was performing a Herculean effort to keep her melons in check, and was only partly succeeding. She had put back on her prosthetic leg, but apparently I'd awoken before she could get the rest of her clothes on. "I will if you don't keep your hands where I can see them."

I held up my hands with a smoke in one and a lighter in the other. I impressed even myself with the rock-steadiness of my fingers; I could have performed a circumcision with those hands, which I did once when I went undercover as a rabbi on a case, but that's a story for another time. "Just a smoke, sweetheart. You want one?"

"That's your last request? A cigarette?"

"Well, I'd prefer another quickie, but I didn't think you were in the mood." I lit the cigarette and took a drag. It was awful. Who enjoyed this shit?

Williams smiled an evil, nasty grin. I didn't like it. "And I would have to put the gun down, wouldn't I?"

"Not necessarily. Wouldn't be the first time I had sex at gunpoint. Still, if you were going to kill me, why didn't you do it while I was passed out?"

"Because I had to know how you figured out it was me."

"Figured out it was you what?"

Her vile, sorceress grin turned even darker, though she was still showing her pearly white teeth. "Don't play stupid. You know it was me who killed Mark Ward."

I took another drag. "I didn't. Not for sure. Not until you just told me."

Her vindictive certainty wavered for just a moment, but she regained her composure pretty quick, which was a trait I admire in a woman dressed only in her underwear. "You seemed pretty certain while you were talking about it in your sleep."

Fuck. I had gotten pretty good at keeping my narration silent while I was conscious, but my drunken stupor was known to be chatty. "Well, I just found it awfully convenient that the three-breasted woman left her brassiere at the scene of the crime."

"It was a whorehouse. There was underwear lost behind and under furniture everywhere. And even if someone planted Maureen's bra there, how do you jump from that to me being the killer?"

"Because that's the second time you've mentioned Maureen's first name, but I never told it to you."

Now her certainty was gone altogether, and her hand started shaking. I would have felt a lot better if the gun wasn't still pointed at me, but I was working on it. "Of course, it was all still circumcisional until you just admitted it.

"Circumstantial."

"Sorry, I was just thinking about a bris. Anyway, obviously you knew who Maureen was, and you must have figured pinning the murder of a local politician on a three-breasted prostitute would draw a whole bunch of crazy attention to the case and away from you. Though I gotta say, it's kinda harsh for you to throw a fellow sister with a disability under the bus. I bet you figured everyone would be so quick to hang the freaky-chested hooker that your CSI-nerds might not even analyze those bloody footprints next to the body. And while I'm sure you were smart enough to buy some new, untraceable, disposable shoes for your little caper, you think they'll notice that the two feet have an odd gait?"

"Fuck you."

"You did. It was pretty good, too. In my experience murderers are always the best lays. Not that I would convict you on that alone; accountants are also surprisingly talented in the sack."

I remembered I was holding the cigarette, and I took a drag. "So why'd you do it, doll?"

"None of your fucking business."

"No, I suppose it's not. And I suppose it has nothing to do with when Ward's brother was mayor a few years ago, he cut a bunch of public services. Free clinics, safe injection sites, that kind of thing. A lot of people who relied on those services were left in the lurch. Some were really hard off. Some even died. Who died, detective? Your parent? Your lover? Your kid?"

I saw the glimmer of sadness and anger in her eyes. It passed quickly, but I must have hit close to the mark.

"You're a good cop. You just made a bad choice. Is it true you lost your leg pulling a kid out from under a tram car?"

Williams growled and shook the gun at me. "Despite his sterling reputation, Mark is even worse than his brother. He's just better at covering it up. He's dirty and corrupt and only in politics to line his pockets and the pockets of all his sleazy criminal friends. And his sights are even higher than this shitty town. Municipal politics in New Orleans was just a steppingstone for him on the way to the governor's office."

"Hey, don't get me wrong, Mark Ward was a shithead, and trust me, coming from a low-life like me, you have to be pretty friggin' awful for me to call you a shithead. And he probably even deserved to be stabbed in the back like a rotisserie chicken. But when a cop does it, it's kind of a bad look, you know?"

"He hangs out at brothels all the time; it wouldn't have surprised anyone if he turned up dead in one. Until you came along and fucked it all up."

"I am very good at fucking, it's true."

She shook her head and laughed, bitterly. "Shut up, Saint. Go to hell."

The hotel door burst open and a woman barged in with a gun drawn. She started to say "What in the fuck?" but only made it half-way through—to about "What in-"—when Williams turned and shot her. Maureen was quick though, and she got off a shot herself in the heartbeat between seeing the detective's pistol and William's pulling the trigger.

I was right about the three-breasted woman being trigger happy.

Both women hit the floor. The twin gunshots echoed in the small hotel room and I winced at the pain in my ears. I would like to say that I had planned it all; that I had purposefully kept Detective Williams talking because I knew Maureen was going to show up at any moment. But I did not. I probably should have been dead right now. Instead, I was getting a bit of a hard-on.

Two broads just tried to kill each other over me. Sorta. That was fucking hot.

Someone moaned and I realized that one or both women might still be alive. I should probably do something about that, but I was ashamed both of my unfortunate erection as well as the piss stains I had probably left on the sheets in my terror. I wondered whether I should call the cops first or change the bedclothes.

Being a private dick in New Orleans was always full of tough choices.

CD Gallant-King wrote his first story when he was five years old, and he made his babysitter look up how to spell "extraterrestrial" in the dictionary. He now writes stories about un-heroic people doing generally hilarious things in horrifying worlds. A loving husband and proud father of two wonderful little kids, CD was born and raised in Newfoundland and currently resides in Ottawa, Ontario. There was also a ten-year period in between where he tried to make a go of a career in theatre in Toronto, but we don't talk about that.

CD has published three novels, most recently *Psycho Hose Beast from Outer Space* in 2020.

Website: http://cdgallantking.ca

Amazon Page: https://www.amazon.com/C.D.-Gallant-King/e/B00XAZHYGA

Twitter: https://twitter.com/cdgallantking

Facebook: https://www.facebook.com/cdgallantking

In a Faubourg Far, Far Away...

Michael Rigg

On a crisp Friday night in late January, Janelle and Tamara—her Alpha Delta Gamma Big Sister at Ole Miss—ambled arm-in-arm along a dimly lit stretch of Frenchmen Street. Tam had told her all about it. Frenchmen was where New Orleans locals went to avoid the tackiness and high prices of Bourbon Street.

Butterflies tickled Janelle's stomach, partly from tequila shots at The Bunker. But mostly from thinking about the 'NOLA 101' lecture Professor Faulkner, their sorority's faculty advisor, gave the Alpha Deltas last week. In the Crescent City, one universal law—as undeniable as gravity or inertia—*must* be obeyed. Out-of-towners—especially college students—are to limit their revelry to approved festivities, like Mardi Gras parades. Or the French Quarter, where they'll be protected by bright lights and the watchful eyes of the NOPD Equestrian Squad.

Forsaking the Quarter, despite Faulkner's warning, was Tam's idea. She had talked about their adventure for weeks. When a saxophone in the Spotted Cat Music Club engaged in an unscripted duet with a cornet from d.b.a., an upscale café across the street, Janelle understood why. Great music. Cheap drinks. No cops hassling friends out for a good time. Even the scraggly guy sitting next to a blue bicycle and holding a sign asking for money added to the uniqueness, the freedom. You could do what you wanted, be who you were. No parents. No police. No professors. This was *real* New Orleans.

"I didn't like that last joint." Janelle's words seemed to linger in the frosty air. "The Bunker."

"Me neither. I hate sticky floors." Tam grimaced. "Some air freshener would have been nice. Smelled musty. Jesus, what kind of bar has a laundromat in the back?" She frowned. "And what-the-hell's with talking to that redneck playing video games?"

"Oh, the guy in the flannel shirt and baseball cap? Nothing. Asked me if I was here for Mardi Gras. Called it Carnival. Like in Rio, only better. Said he's in a marching parade tomorrow. Has a *Star Wars* theme."

"Screw Mardi Gras. Screw parades. And screw your Luke Skywalker. What a dipshit."

Janelle's face warmed, despite the cool breeze. "Seemed nice enough. Told me he was pre-med. Even warned me about using the john. Said it was filthy."

"Pre-med?" Tam rolled her eyes. "As if."

"Told him I would think about the parade. And he's right. The john *was* filthy."

"The john?"

"You know, the bathroom."

"Is *that* your name for it?" Tam sighed and rolled her eyes again. "Whatever. He looked pissed. I'm glad we left. Hope he doesn't follow us."

"Don't worry, Tam. Let's get out of the night air. Everything'll be fine."

"Some heat would be good right now. Besides, I'm so hungry I could eat shoe leather. Let's check out the saxophone place."

They huddled together at the open front door of the Spotted Cat, looking for a menu. Plaintive notes from the duet they heard earlier invited them to enter.

"Shit." Tam's voice was barely audible, like she really didn't mean to say aloud what she was thinking. "Music club is right." Her voice was louder, more animated. "They don't serve food. To hell with this place. Let's go over there." She pointed toward the Snug Harbor Jazz Bistro. "Looks like *they* have a restaurant."

As the two friends stepped onto the *banquette*—the sidewalk—on the other side of the street, Tam froze. "I saw him."

"Who?"

"Over there; in that alley between the buildings. The guy in the flannel shirt."

"I don't see him."

Tam shuddered. "Well he's there, goddammit." Her jaw quivered. "He's there, watching us. I know what I saw. Let's get inside."

Snug Harbor. Its name fit. Janelle shook off the chill as the front door closed behind her with a loud thump. The building blended exposed brick and wood from the nineteenth century storefronts it occupied with modern lighting and amenities. Its atmosphere exuded a warm, welcome-home vibe. An aroma of cayenne and filé gumbo filled the air. Just what they needed, a barrier between them and the outside world—and their stalker in the flannel shirt.

"Good evening, ladies." The *maître d'*, a thin, muscular man in his mid-twenties with flowing dreadlocks, greeted them with a smile. An oval badge above his shirt pocket revealed his name: Ian. "Welcome to Snug Harbor. Most versatile eatery in Faubourg Marigny or the whole city for that matter."

"Faubourg Marigny?" Janelle asked.

"It's the name of this area. Faubourg's the French word for neighborhood, that's all."

"Oh, I see," Janelle said.

Ian seemed to ignore her response, his gaze fixed on Tam. "So, ladies, what'll it be? Bar, restaurant, or jazz club? The ten-thirty show just started."

"Can we get something to eat in the bar?" Tam asked.

Janelle had seen that look in Tam's eyes before. She might be asking for food *now*. But later? She'd be demanding another kind of sustenance. Something more prurient than proteins and carbohydrates. Tam always moved too fast. She needed to slow down.

"Absolutely," Ian said. "Best small-plates in town."

"Then the bar it is," Tam said.

Ian escorted them to a table well away from the front window. Excellent. They wouldn't be as noticeable to any prying eyes outside. But Janelle could still see the front door and street. Maybe *now* she could relax and have some fun. Time for some appetizers and a Pimm's Cup. She had never had one, but it was what all her sisters at the Alpha Delta house told her she just had to have.

"Cleo will be your server tonight," Ian said. "I'll send her right over. But first, can I see some ID? Wouldn't want to lose our liquor license."

Ian's eyes never left Tam. Janelle had seen *that* kind of look before, as well. What was it about Tam and men? Such a double standard. Janelle couldn't even talk to a guy. But when Tam zeroed in? Nothing, and no one, had better stand in her way.

"Oh sure." Tam handed Ian a Mississippi driver's license.

Janelle followed suit. She glared at Tam. *No one* asks for IDs in New Orleans. They'll *never* catch on. Tam had *promised* her. Why could she never say 'No' to Tam?

"Thank you Ms. Davis," Ian said. "Or may I call you Bette?"

She retrieved her license. "Please don't. Call me Tamara."

"Tamara?" Ian seemed puzzled. "But your license says—"

"Yeah," Tam said. "Sounds odd." She looked at Janelle and then back at Ian. "Well, you see, our faculty advisor said we should make up identities when we're in New Orleans.

That way, if someone overhears us, they won't know our actual names."

"Hmmm." Ian studied Janelle's license. "So, Ms. Crawford, I assume I shouldn't call you Joan, right?"

She grabbed the plastic card from Ian. "It's Janelle." She bit her lip to avoid saying something she might regret later. Her face warmed in embarrassment. "Call me Janelle."

"Okay," Ian said. "Two twenty-one year-olds from Tupelo—with the same birthday—here to have a good time and catch some beads." He winked at Tam. "Welcome to the Big Easy. I'll let Cleo know you're ready."

Minutes passed rapidly, as the odd combination of Pimm's Number One, Ginger Ale, mint, and cucumber loosened Janelle's nerves. But she couldn't stop worrying. Had they done the right thing—ditching classes and heading south down Interstate Fifty-Five? Shouldn't they have gone to Bourbon Street like Faulkner told them? And fake IDs? So much could go wrong. Thank God the guy in the flannel shirt hadn't reappeared. Still, she needed to keep an eye out—just in case.

Cleo brought more appetizers and two more cocktails—another Pimm's Cup for her and a White Russian for Tam.

"Feeling better?" Janelle asked, after their server left.

"Yeah, I guess. The booze is great." Tam scooped a couple of barbecue shrimp onto her plate. "Food helps."

"I feel better, too," Janelle said. "There's something about being around other people. And tunes from the music room? Wow." She took another sip of her cocktail. "And it doesn't hurt to have your new boyfriend checking up on us—or at least on you."

"Ian's hot," Tam said. "I want him something fierce."

"I see how you two look at each other. But listen. Think it's wise? You just met him. What would your daddy say? The newspapers—"

"No. *You* listen to *me*."

175

"What did I say wrong? You need to be careful, that's all. We're supposed to watch out for each other."

"Don't worry about my *father*." Tam's eyes appeared ready to pop out, her nostrils flared. "What would *your mother* say about Luke Flannel-shirt? The publicity would be just as bad for her. Maybe worse." She took a drink of her White Russian. "I was starting to have fun again."

"Okay, okay. I got it. Let's just enjoy ourselves. No one knows who we are. We're invisible. We'll be fine as long as we stick together."

Maybe more alcohol was the answer. Janelle took a sip of her cocktail and signaled for Cleo to bring another round. "And you're right. Ian *is* cute. I think he wants to ... oh look, here he comes again."

"I hope everything's to your liking, ladies." Ian placed his hand on the back of Tam's chair, lightly, a hint, perhaps, of wanting closer, more intimate, contact.

Almost in unison, they assured Ian they were having a great time. But it was obvious that he was more interested in Tam's feelings. Jesus, it was as if their pheromones were dancing an invisible tango, readying the pair for the next step. They were going to have sex and nothing she could say would talk her Big Sis out of it.

Janelle closed her eyes. Why hadn't they had just gone to the French Quarter?

"Say, my shift ends at eleven-thirty, when the late-night crew takes over. Thaddeus—one of the cooks—and I are headed to The John. Don't suppose y'all would care to join us?"

Janelle opened her eyes, surprised by Ian's invitation. She and Tam exchanged glances. The bathroom? Really? Maybe Tam would finally tell him what a dick he was.

"Oh, join you in the bathroom?" Tam asked.

But she didn't seem angry. Rather, she smiled, flirting with Ian. "That's the first time I've heard that line. Must be a local thing. You get a lot of yesses?"

Ian held both hands in front of his chest, palms forward, as if in surrender. "Not the bathroom, The John. It's a hangout a couple of blocks up toward Rampart. On the corner of Frenchmen and Burgundy. Take a left out the front door and head past Washington Square."

"Well, I don't know," Tam said. "We just ordered drinks."

"Tell you what. After you finish, drop by. They're open all night before Chewbacchus. You might even see a Wookiee or a droid getting an early start on the festivities."

"Wow," Tam said. "A Wookiee. Or a droid. We'll think about it."

As Ian left the bar, Janelle leaned close to her companion and whispered. "Watching C-3PO get hammered? Are you nuts? How much have you had to drink?"

"No more than you have. But obviously not enough. That's for damn sure."

The pair drank, mostly in silence. Tam spoke first.

"Look, I came here to have fun. I'm going to meet Ian. You coming or not?"

"Don't do it. I have a bad feeling. You hardly know this guy."

The pair continued to argue as they paid the bill and walked to the restaurant's foyer. Janelle listened, but her mind kept drifting back to Faulkner's lecture about staying in the French Quarter — and the rest of the warning. *Especially after midnight, when the creepy nocturnals — those undeniably weird people who exist in the shadows — make their appearance in the world of the normal.*

"It's nearly midnight," Janelle said. "Professor Faulkner told us — "

"Who cares what that old biddy said? She tells us the same thing every semester." Tam shook her head. "And nothing ever happens." Tam sighed. "What is she, forty-five? Fifty? Hell, might as well be a hundred." She paused. "It's probably been so long, that she's forgotten what it's like to get laid."

I'm taking a Ride-Share back to the room." Janelle tapped on her phone. "At least let me drop you off."

"It's only a couple of blocks. By the time the car arrives, I'll already be there."

"Four minutes. It says the car will be here in four minutes. At least wait that long."

"Screw it; I'm leaving." Tam strode out of Snug Harbor and proceeded past the restaurant's large front windows up Frenchmen toward Burgundy.

What just happened? Why had Tam said that? Why couldn't she wait for a ride? Janelle hurried after her friend, who had already made it across the street and past the intersection with Royal Street. Tam walked rapidly— continuing up Frenchmen, along the tree-lined park at Washington Square. She stopped and leaned on a telephone pole. Was Tam about to be sick? Must not be. She started walking again.

Janelle's Ride-Share was less than three minutes away—at least according to the vehicle icon rolling along Esplanade Avenue on her phone's display screen. Movement in her peripheral vision shifted her attention away from the phone. In the sporadic street lighting, a figure turned the corner off Royal, moving parallel to Tam—but on the opposite side of Frenchmen and about twenty yards behind. Something wasn't right.

Another glimpse. Seconds this time, instead of a quick flash. Oh, God. It couldn't be. But she had seen it long enough to be certain. Sleeves of a red flannel shirt visible in the armholes of a down vest, a baseball cap blocking a clear view of the person's facial features.

"Tam, no!"

Janelle rushed past Café Marigny and cursed silently at its noisy brass band. Tam couldn't have heard her warning over the loud music.

"Stop! It's me."

Janelle ran, but not very fast. Too much Pimm's and tequila—very different liquors. And the spicy food. It wasn't blending together well in her stomach. She hiccupped, nearly vomiting at the acidic taste.

"Tam!" Janelle clinched her teeth and swallowed the bile crawling up her throat. "Please come back!"

No Tam. No figure in a flannel shirt. Janelle hesitated at the entrance to Washington Square—on the corner of Frenchmen and Dauphine—to catch her breath. She didn't want to hurl, but was afraid that she would. Cold sweat covered her forehead. Her teeth and tongue throbbed rhythmically, as if her heartbeat had moved from her chest to her mouth.

"Tam, where are you?"

Janelle turned toward a muffled sound behind her, from inside the gate—out of the darkness of Washington Square. No one should be there. The hours posted in silver reflective paint on a dark metal placard made it unmistakable: Park Closes at Dusk. But it didn't matter. Tam might be in trouble. She *had* to go. That's what friends do. No matter what.

It was as if she was being drawn by a magnet toward the narrow opening in one corner of the iron fence surrounding the Square. What a creepy place, more like a prison than a park. Janelle shuddered. A broken lock and portions of chain lay on the ground. But she couldn't stop moving forward. Mesmerized, she inched her way through the gate. Its rusty hinges squeaked in the breeze. The throbbing sensation had migrated to behind her cheeks and in her forehead. Cool air stung her nostrils. At least the acidic taste was gone and she didn't feel like throwing up.

"Tam, is that you? This isn't funny."

Janelle squinted, hoping it would help her eyes adjust to the shadows. She flinched. Rustling leaves maybe. Or a twig breaking. She swiveled to her right, eyes wide open.

"Who—"

The blow landed on the left side of her face, between her temple and lower jaw. With hardly enough time for the pain to register, Janelle crumpled to the ground. Stars flashed behind her eyelids — just before her world turned black.

Janelle awoke to the sharpness of gravely soil and uncut grass underneath her torso and head as she was dragged feet first away from the gate. Her shoes were gone.

Her face scraped against a rock and she tried to yell, but couldn't open her mouth. She struggled even more, feeling a rough stickiness on her cheeks. Her arms, immobile, were bound tightly on either side of her body.

Janelle attempted to move her legs apart, but they seemed glued together. Duct tape. She kicked at the shadowy figure tugging on her ankles and strained to see what was wrong.

"Hold on, Missy." The voice was ragged and smoky, but sounded more youthful than she expected. "Won't do any good to fight. It'll just make it worse for both of us." A slight pause. "But mostly for you."

The outline of the figure — angular and thin — seemed to be male, but long hair gave her assailant a more feminine appearance. Regardless, he — or she — was strong enough to overpower Janelle and then drag her into the void, without much effort or exertion. The figure turned around. A man.

"Look, I'm going to ..." He seemed to be thinking about how to respond. "Don't matter what you do, I'm still going to do my business. And the more you resist, the more I have to ..." He flashed a yellowed-toothed grin. "... The more I have to discipline you."

Scattered beams of light, filtered by the trees surrounding the park, reflected through some sort of glass wall. The resulting rainbow images, distorted yet also beautiful, seemed out of place. Otherwise, the landscape was dark and barren. A combination of body odor, alcohol, and

180

tobacco — or maybe it was weed — wafted in the breeze and made her gag.

"Don't worry, this won't take long."

It already seemed like forever. Through the tape she mouthed, "Please don't hurt me." It came out a garbled mess — sounds, not words. Tears cascaded across her face, the resulting sinus drainage making it more difficult to breathe. Suddenly, the dragging stopped. He lifted her onto a blanket. Janelle relaxed into the softness, but knew that it was to make it more comfortable for *him*, not her. *Soon*, she thought. *Soon this will be over.*

She had stopped crying, but any false security from the softness evaporated at the sight of her assailant's right arm dangling at his side. Oh, God, no. A knife. With a click, what appeared to be about a four-inch serrated blade shot out from the handle.

Janelle strained to breathe through her mucous-clogged nostrils, the tape still blocking her mouth. She squirmed, backing away in serpentine fashion by alternating her shoulder blades.

"Worried about this little thing, are you?" Her assailant placed the weapon in front of his chest.

Janelle continued her slow backward movement.

"Well, don't be — unless you move off that blanket."

Janelle stopped squirming.

"That's better." He kneeled beside her right leg, near her feet. He placed the tip of the blade lightly on her left knee. Then he traced the outline of her leg, slowly and with agonizing detail. The soft touch of the blade tickled, but Janelle lay frozen like a statue, fearful that any movement would make her attacker angry. He stopped at the gray adhesive wrapped around her ankles.

"I'm going to cut you loose. Don't move and everything will be fine."

Janelle nodded and mouthed a silent "Okay." She watched in helpless horror as he sliced through the restraint, restoring full circulation to her feet. Next, he unzipped her jeans.

"Don't worry. I won't hurt you if you cooperate. You still okay?"

Janelle nodded. Tears filled her eyes. What the hell did he think she would say? That he's the love of her life and she'd been waiting for this moment?

"And now your arms."

Janelle's face and body tingled. Despite finally having use of her limbs, she was paralyzed. Her arms seemed to weigh a ton, her legs twice as much.

"That's right. Just lie back. I'll do everything. Let me show you."

Janelle disconnected from her physical self as much as she could. She was strong. She would live through it. It would be over soon. She clamped her eyelids together and clenched her teeth.

"No," he said. "Look at me. I want you to look at me."

Janelle opened her eyes and glanced to her left. The knife. He had put the knife down. But her arms still weighed a ton. She couldn't move as he tossed her jeans aside.

Then, suddenly, the adrenaline kicked in, her arms no longer heavy and useless. Everything seemed to happen at once—and in slow motion at the same time. Janelle pushed him away and grabbed for the blade. A warm wetness, visceral and salty, spread across her sweatshirt and bare legs. And what was that metallic odor? Whatever it was, it masked the stench that caused her to gag earlier.

As if he were a marionette pulled by an invisible wire, her attacker jerked upward, flailing wildly. For a brief second—in a blur—he looked like a Hindu god, one with multiple arms and two heads. Making a gasping sound, like air was escaping from his lungs without control, her dual-headed, multi-armed assailant staggered backward until he bumped into the glass wall.

Janelle curled up like a newborn, her body still energized, too warm for the cold air to register. Then, for the second time since coming to New Orleans to celebrate with her sorority Big Sister, she fainted.

Janelle's body seemed lighter than before, as if she were floating. And she no longer ached from the hard-scrabble surface. She was warm, enveloped by a heavy, but very soft, cloth sheet. The duct tape was gone, replaced by a clear plastic mask covering her nose and mouth. Oxygen flowed gently through a long tube. She blinked at bright lights greeting her when she opened her eyes. Overlapping voices and fuzzy images of other people multiplied her confusion.

What was this place? Was she still in the park? Was she still alive?

After a few seconds, surrounding images came more into focus. Two figures, both wearing dark blue jackets, towered over her. She smiled when she read the patches sewn to their sleeves: New Orleans Emergency Medical Services. She *was* alive. They must be here to help her. She tried to sit up, but straps across her chest and legs kept her from moving. Why was she restrained? How long had she been knocked out?

Janelle rolled her head to her left. A group of people—maybe three or four—stood a few feet away, looking toward something on the ground. A body? She squinted to make sure. Yeah, a dead man. Her attacker, his face frozen in a mix of pain and surprise, sat motionless against the circular cut-glass and steel panels she had seen earlier. A rectangular piece of wood with brass edges—most likely a knife handle—protruded from under the right side of his rib cage, partially concealed by the folds of a heavy hunting shirt. Thick pools of crimson liquid surrounded him. Despite oxygen flowing into the mask, Janelle's nostrils stung at the same salty, hot-metal odor from before.

She wondered whether this was what it was like to kill someone. Tears dribbled down her cheeks. It must be. How could she have done it? But she didn't have any other choice. She had to. Janelle shivered. Maybe they were here to arrest her.

One of the EMTs, a female, called out. "Hey, Lieutenant, she's conscious."

A tall, muscular woman who had been part of the group looking at the body, hastened toward Janelle.

"Hello, I'm Detective Sprance from NOPD. Glad to see you're awake. You had us worried. Some people don't regain consciousness for a long time after something so traumatic."

"It was ..." The words seemed garbled by the mask. She wanted to remove it, but her arms were still under the straps.

Sprance motioned toward the male EMT. "Smitty, can we loosen the restraints?"

"Sure thing," he responded. "You want that we should sit her up, too?"

Sprance nodded. "Yeah, that'd be great." She inched closer to Janelle. "You recognize the decedent?" She cocked her head toward the corpse. "The body leaning against the City's AIDS Memorial?"

Janelle nodded. "But I don't know his name."

"Can you tell me what happened.?"

"I was looking for Tam. My friend, Tam. She left alone from Snug Harbor. I heard a noise in the park. The gate was open. When I went in, someone hit me."

"Did you see who?"

"No, I passed out. But when I woke up, that dead guy was dragging me. I was tied up with duct tape."

"And then?"

Janelle described the rest of the attack, but stopped before describing the final seconds of her ordeal. Her jaw quivered and her eyes remained locked on Detective Sprance. Janelle breathed deeply before continuing.

"... I reached for the knife ... everything happened so fast ... I fainted."

Janelle gritted her teeth, hoping it would hold back the tears. "The knife." She hesitated, her eyes moistened. "He's dead. But I don't know how I—"

"That's okay. Let's not think about that right now." Detective Sprance put her notebook down. "We think we can link this guy to three sexual assaults in the last month. We located a bike in a corner of the park. Probably his. There was duct tape and a pair of bolt cutters in one of the side-baskets."

Janelle pointed to a man sitting on another hospital gurney taking deep breaths from an oxygen mask. He had an aluminum emergency blanket draped around his shoulders. She hadn't noticed him before. "Who's that?"

"Oh, him?"

"Yeah," Janelle said. "That's the guy who was stalking Tam and me. The guy in the flannel shirt and baseball cap. The guy from The Bunker. It's him. I know it's him."

"He's the reason you're here talking to us."

"I don't understand."

"Name's Jimmy Copeland. Former Navy Corpsman. Pre-med at Tulane. Works part-time for the Coroner's Office."

"But why's he here?"
"His weekend off. He's in the parade tomorrow. Lightsaber Sub-Krewe. Says he saw you and your friend at The Bunker. Talked with you briefly."

"I remember. Told me about Mardi Gras."

"Well, he had a bad feeling about you."

"A bad feeling?"

"An intuition. Said it's something he developed in combat. Like a sixth sense. An inner voice that told him when something bad was about to happen. That one of his colleagues would need medical attention."

"So he followed us? Me and Tam?"

"Well, let's say that he kept an eye on you two."

Janelle's face felt like the blood had drained away, replaced by ice water. "Tam. What about Tam?"

"He followed her to The John. When it appeared she was safe inside, he sprinted back down Frenchman to find you."

"Is Tam okay?"

"Yes. Both her and her boyfriend. My partner's interviewing them at the bar. Initially, there was a question about who she was. Something about a driver's license for an old movie actress."

Janelle's face was no longer frozen, warmth returning as embarrassment again spread across her cheeks.

"That guy, Jimmy. What did he —"

"He fought with your attacker. And let's just say that Jimmy's medical — and military — background taught him how to inflict the most damage."

"But why would he …? It sounds so strange."

"Strange?" Sprance said. "This city runs on strange. Tomorrow night, we'll be invaded by alien creatures of all shapes and sizes parading through The Marigny." She looked at the corpse and then back at Janelle. "And in my line of work, we run across all sorts of strangeness, even when it's not Mardi Gras. Some good. Some bad. Maybe some in between, like getting fake IDs and heading for Frenchmen Street."

Sprance paused, as if to let the point hit home how stupidly she and Tam had acted.

"But, the scumbag who attacked you is definitely strange in a bad way. Maybe as bad as it gets. What makes a person hide in the shadows, hoping for someone like you to come along? He's not crazy. He knew exactly what he was doing. But he damn sure isn't normal. Strange might be the best word for it.

And Jimmy — your Jedi Guardian — isn't exactly normal, either. I don't know about his sixth sense. This inner voice. Or what made him risk his life for someone he barely knew.

What I do know is that *something* led him to be in the right place at the right time. His good kind of strange saved you from a world of hurt." She sighed. "Hell, maybe one day I'll figure it all out and write a book. Make a million bucks. Right now, I'm just a detective doing her job."

Janelle nodded. "Thank you. I'm so sorry …" Her voice trailed off.

"That's all right. No need. You've been through a lot." Sprance motioned to the EMTs. "I think I have enough for now. These guys will take you to University Hospital for an examination. I'll drop by later and we can talk some more."

Choices. As the EMTs wheeled Janelle away from the crime scene, she contemplated her choices and her decisions — good and not so good — since leaving the more bucolic surroundings in Oxford for New Orleans. One decision nagged at her the most. Maybe watching Wookiees and droids get drunk wouldn't have been so bad after all.

Michael Rigg, a retired Navy Judge Advocate, plies his trade as a mild-mannered civil servant and attorney by day, then morphs into a nascent mystery and thriller writer by night. When writing "In a Faubourg Far, Far Away," he drew upon a long legal career of dealing with the darker side of the human character for valuable insights. And Mike leveraged his direct experience in navigating the craziness and confusion that characterizes New Orleans during Carnival, as well. He belongs to three Mardi Gras Krewes, has marched or ridden in numerous parades, and can throw beads and trinkets with the best of them. Mike is a member of Hampton Roads Writers, along with the Sisters in Crime national organization and its Southeastern Virginia Chapter — Mystery by the Sea. He and his wife live in Virginia Beach. Visit him online at www.facebook.com/michael.rigg.author.

UNHOLY BEADS

Nancy Brewka-Clark

"Michael Savant served at St. Botolph's for only eighteen months before leaving the priesthood." Josephus Marchand, New Orleans police detective with twenty-eight years under his belt, studied the papers before him. In that small pile were photographs of the murder scene. Never before had there been such a bizarre garroting committed in broad daylight while thousands reveled in the streets and bars and hotels and alleyways of his beloved city. "The reason given for his departure was that after working with the underprivileged youth of the parish, he wanted to pursue a more active career in social justice."

Felicio Jijio sat back in the creaking wooden chair. He kept wanting to put his big feet up on the interrogation table because it beckoned him to. Still, he knew better than to take advantage of his long friendship with the man across from him. "This Michael Savant, this ex-priest, what reason would my son have to murder him? I'm telling you, none. You know in your gut I'm right, Joey. So, you will let the boy go, right? And nobody's sad, or mad, and the world will keep turning."

"Your youngest isn't a boy anymore, Felicio." Marchand shook his head, grizzled and gray from the constant onslaught of the ones who came to him, trying to convince him of a loved one's innocence. "If Bali has committed a crime, a man's portion has to be served to him. Only fair."

Marchand sensed that Felicio held back the desire to squirm. Truth did that.

"Yes, I understand." Felicio held his chin up. "But he didn't do it."

Marchand went on in the same calm and reasonable voice he used on all agitated relatives. "Now, you know I see you taking the side of your son because that is what any father would do. But an eyewitness described Bali right down to the tattoo on his right arm, my friend, and that is why he is in a holding cell. And that is why he will remain there until under law I have to release him to your custody. I know you see the logic of this, the good sense of it."

"I see no such thing." Felicio rubbed his brow. "I'm the one who raised him to honor and obey the law, not to even go across the street when the little red hand is flashing. Yes, once or twice he got in trouble. But he straightened out as soon as he started playing horn."

"A juvenile record is not a forecast of the future," Marchand agreed. "It's sealed for that reason."

"Thank God." Felicio spread his callused hands. "Besides, he was playing his trumpet at the time. Terpsi-Chorus may be the newest of the parade krewes but already their float, their music, so colorful, so lively, draws thousands to dance in the streets. Who is this eyewitness?"

It was just like Felicio to try to sneak up on him to pop such an important question. But Marchand held no grudge. Who wouldn't try to extract as much information as possible? Marchand knew that by revealing any information at all, trouble might ensue. There were those always waiting to muddy the waters, should they hear of anything beyond strict police protocol. Even so, he was interested in what Felicio's reaction might be, regardless of his words. When defending a child, no matter the age, it was a parent's right to explore all avenues while the trail was fresh.

"The eyewitness is a young woman by the name of Arlene Nous." Marchand jerked his head. "She's down the hall, going over her statement. She swears she saw a man with a tattoo of musical notes on a scale running up the entire length of his right arm push his way through the crowd at the corner of Napoleon and St. Charles. About five-ten, one-forty-five, straight black hair in a ponytail."

"She's a liar," Felicio said. "Bali was on the float playing his trumpet."

Marchand could remember Felicio as a young man in dreadlocks and dashikis. Now the beam from the overhanging lamp was shining off his bald head like summer sunlight, and his jeans and chambray shirt were the uniform of the working poor. "Yes, the world saw the band members and heard their sweet music. But they were masked and made up, my friend. Men as girls, beautiful girls, and the singer, such a pure falsetto. Who knows who was really beneath those feathers and beads, eh?"

"Well, hell, yes, who knows? And that is just exactly why you can't keep holding him. The street was packed. And so were the balconies, the windows, the rooftops. A hundred murders could have been going on, and nobody would notice." Felicio made a point of pulling up his wrist to study his watch. "Time's running out. If you can't charge him, you have to let him go."

The detective looked down at the scarred tabletop. Its heavy oak had been pounded, slapped, slammed, scratched, cut, carved into and sometimes even scalded in its long precinct history. In fact, it was just like the victims he tried to give some dignity to, some sense that justice, no matter how late, had been served. When he was a kid, he always dressed up for Mardi Gras like Superman with a big S on his chest. He had no sense of shame that his costume consisted of underwear dyed blue that his grandma drew upon with magic markers. He'd smelled of chemicals from their popsicle colors, sucking in the fumes like a drunk. The stink had always been a favorite odor of his, promising power. And all these years later, the S was still on his chest, at least in his mind. And no amount of blood or guts or torn skin or broken bones or bullet holes or any other horrid thing could turn his stomach like a killer getting off. Never.

"Felicio, how do you know Michael Savant was a stranger to your son?" Marchand asked. "I know he said so. But …"

"You mean a hook-up," Felicio said flatly. "Bali has a steady boyfriend. Three years now, and counting. They're talking about getting married."

Marchand studied him with lidded eyes. So many times the Church had covertly sanctioned what others justly condemned as a mortal sin. All of his own boyhood he had loved and venerated his parish priest, Father Justin Dupuis, and had never countenanced a single act of unkindness. And yet, the good father had been accused of untoward advances toward a bevy of boys who'd thought it amusing to bandy about false gossip. Sadly, this had come at a time when all clergy had to defend themselves from charges that would have been considered perverse themselves.

The urges of the youthful mind, what his dear friend Felicio was trying to defend in a grown man, often led to unforeseen consequences, and had since the beginning of civilization. How many parents, his own included, had joined in holy matrimony because there was an infant on the way, unsanctioned until a ritual of men provided a shield of honor from the judging world? And how many others, sworn to celibacy, had borne a secret longing for one of their own sex? Only in recent times had that sort of union for the layman met with society's approval, and even then, there were dissenters, some willing to try to turn back the hands of the clock by getting blood on their own hands. As for marriage with a woman, ironically, that too was still forbidden within the

Church. Altogether, it made for excruciating choices for someone hungry in both body and soul.

Marchand deliberated for a long moment before sliding the stack of photographs toward his companion.

"Oh, my." Felicio's face registered shock. "Are those truly Mardi Gras beads?"

"Yes." Marchand sighed. "Strange use for them, no question."

"But I don't understand." Felicio studied the dead man's distorted face and bulging eyes, that painfully thrusting tongue lapping at its own death. "Those beads are cheap. How could they not break?"

"Re-strung on something strong, like fishing line."

"Clever." Felicio laid the photo back on the top of the stack. "But I know for certain that Bali would never bother to concoct such a crazy way to kill a man."

Marchand gave a noncommittal grunt.

"Oh, come on, bro." For the first time Felicio appeared to be scared. "This is a crazy scene. Yes, Mardi Gras is known for crazy, it's supposed to be crazy, but it's for fun, for joy, for life. Nobody thinks about killing a man when he's blowing a horn, man. Jazz, it's a purifier, like sunlight. That's what my boy said when he was first learning from his elders, and when I heard it, I knew he was saved, Joey."

Bali Jijio hadn't been a wild kid, not by anybody's standards. Just a very unhappy child after his mama died of a heart attack on her twenty-ninth birthday, baking a cake for herself with his help. Marchand had done as much as he could to step in and help guide the boy, but maybe that had been too much guidance. Sometimes he wondered if he should just have stayed out of it. He was the father of three girls with a wife who showered love on them all. What did he know about sorrow? Or lost boys? Well, yes, except that he did. His own folks had died before he was twenty. He'd made his way through the law enforcement system with the help of an uncle in the force, dead himself now these past nine years.

Marchand said slowly, "Thing is, this young lady identified him like there was no doubt in her mind."

"How? Who is she to smear my boy?"

"She's a fan," Marchand said.

That was like singling out a grain of sand on Coconut Beach over in Kenner, he knew. So many bars and bistros and out-of-the-way corners and holes-in-the-wall, and the police knew only so many of them because they came and went like the tide. The big established places in the French Quarter and the tourist spots on Bourbon Street all had their share of names. But the younger musicians, those just trying to find their way in the Big Easy music world, they had their auditions wherever and whenever they could. There was Snug Harbor on Frenchmen Street in the Marigny, and then there was the grassy venue of Crescent Park. There was something in the air here, and people had known it for centuries. Even Hurricane Katrina couldn't drown the spirit of that music, Marchand reflected, and his old friend's son was blessed to be a part of it. What a shame that he was now entangled in something that Marchand hoped with all his heart was a big mistake.

As if he'd just read the detective's mind, Felicio slapped the long-suffering tabletop. "Fan? She's accusing a man of murder and she calls herself a fan?"

Marchand was on the verge of delivering a philosophical comment on the vagaries of success when there was a tap on the door. "Come."

"Sir," the young woman said, "Detective Devaneau is asking for you." She held the door wider. "Interrogation Room Three."

Not for the first time, Marchand thought that the department should find another way to reference what was often merely a private space for taking statements and not an oubliette. Well, two spaces, actually, the interrogation room being brightly lit and the observation room cast in darkness. They were separated by a wall containing a long window.

People who attained their knowledge of police procedures through old movies referred to it as a one-way mirror. The less dramatic truth was that it was only the lack of light that made it difficult for the suspect to see the observers.

As he stood, Felicio kept his eyes on his old friend's face. "If you want to wait here," Marchand said, "that's fine with me."

"Thank you."

Seeing the shadow of anxiety cross Felicio's face, Marchand sadly revised his opinion of just exactly how these rooms in the basement affected people. As he took the short walk down the airless corridor he thought that although no blood was spilled, they were indeed torture chambers of a kind that could inflict more pain than any devised by the most zealous minds of the Spanish Inquisition.

"Just a sec, Joe. Let's talk in here," Devaneau said, appearing in the doorway of the observation room.

"What do you have for me?" Marchand squinted as his eyes adjusted to the dark. As the younger detective shared his information, Marchand nodded soberly. A petite female with all the colorful beauty of a souvenir doll was sitting on the other side of the glass. "Very good," he said, keeping any emotion out of his voice. "Now we will see what we will see."

"I told the other officer all I know." Arlene Nous looked up guilelessly through huge hazel eyes fringed with thick black lashes. Her skin glowed with what appeared to be simple good health, although Marchand knew enough about women to know that some very expensive beauty products were involved. Rich, thick masses of shining black hair were lifted in a deliberately artless tumble, some strands curling about her bejeweled ears. Skin-tight jeans, a V-neck silk tunic in various hues of greens and blues, and five-inch heels of turquoise leather accentuated her lithe figure. Voice honeyed and low, she asked, "So, please, sir, may I now go?"

Inwardly praising Devaneau for his keen powers of sensing disparity, Marchand made no attempt to disguise his interest in Arlene Nous's hands. Those slender fingers wore no rings. The tips bore pale circlets of hardened flesh. The nails were their natural color and clipped short. "The hands of a devoted musician, eh?"

Her eyes widened, this time involuntarily rather than as a seductive message. "I play a little guitar, yes."

Marchand pointed. "And a lot of fiddle."

Her hand flew to her neck. The gesture was one Marchand had seen in many a theatrical production when his middle daughter got starry-eyed about playing ingénue roles in high school. This wasn't merely a melodramatic movement, though, but a fruitless attempt to cover a small oblong of raised flesh. Despite all the makeup, a similar blotch was visible on the left portion of her jaw. "Is that a crime, officer?"

Marchand asked, "Ms. Nous, you say you recognized the alleged assailant because you are a fan. Have you ever played in a band with Mr. Jijio?"

"Me? No."

The detective saw defiance in her eyes tempered with relief. "But you do play professionally?"

"Play?" She rolled her eyes. "Cajun fiddling is a calling."

"Ah?" Marchand cocked his head. "Like the priesthood?"

"I wouldn't know about that." She looked at him directly, a small smile playing around her lusciously painted lips. "I, sir, am not a naughty girl, so I have no need for confession."

Marchand studied her without returning her smile.

"Oh, dear, what have I said?" She splayed her hands in another theatrical gesture meant to convey helpless confusion.

"The victim was a man of the cloth."

"What? You mean a priest?"

"Ex-priest. Apparently he'd left the priesthood to work with underprivileged youth."

She laughed. "I don't qualify."

Marchand had come in empty-handed, but Devaneau's briefing was as detailed in his mind as if he had it laid out before him on a sheet of yellow lined legal paper. "So, the name Michael Savant means nothing to you?"

She shook her head.

"How about Alphonse Reveille?"

Silence gathered around her like a cloak. She might have been a mannequin, gorgeously appointed for a display window less forbidding than that of a police interrogation room.

Marchand smiled gently. "He's one of the finest up-and-coming Cajun fiddlers around, wouldn't you say? At least Michael Savant thought so." Marchand nodded as if to reassure her of the truth. "His cell phone had some dates where all he put was the name Reveille. He had quite the schedule. And, do you know what? Bali Jijio, the man you accused, played with that fellow, too."

"So what?" Her voice rose. "Why are you talking to me about all this?"

Marchand went on. "I hope to jog your memory a bit, Ms. Nous. I know you musicians pick up jobs on the spur of the moment. You might even have played with this Reveille at one time."

"Your guess is as good as mine." She stood so fast Marchand was taken off guard. "Nobody wears an ID."

Drawing a breath to still a middle-aged heart that was suddenly racing, he knew that behind him the window was filling with cops. Raising a hand to indicate that they should stay where they were, he said, "We are not done. Please sit down."

"Listen." She shocked him further by lunging forward. "I don't know this priest." Resting the heels of her hands on the table, she brought her face close to his. "And neither does Alphonse."

Marchand's steadying heart sped up again. "So this Alphonse, you do know him then?"

Her eyes glittered with unshed tears. "We're birds of a feather."

"Because of the fiddling?"

"Pardon me, officer, but your detective skills suck." Once again she brought her face closer to his. "Look deep. Solve the riddle." She dropped her voice to a whisper. "We're hermaphrodites."

Cross-dressing could almost be called the native costume of his beloved city. But never before had he encountered, well, what, exactly? Thanks to long-ago high school biology classes, images popped into his head of snakes, dissecting the formaldehyde-soaked flesh of a native cottonmouth while the teacher—Mrs. Benoit with her dyed red hair and enormous bosom—talked about how the creature contained both eggs and the genetic material to fertilize them and produce offspring by —what?—a word that reminded him of ancient Greece—partheno-something—and Mrs. Benoit saying never to call it 'virgin birth' because that was blasphemy.

Marchand said carefully, "I would very much appreciate learning more."

"There are newer words, like intersex. But I'm not sensitive. Poor Alphonse, though, he struggles with it. He's very handsome, you know, and men, they come on to him. He's very picky. But he chose wrong with that pervert. He called Alphonse a freak. Who knew he was a priest? Though now that you say so, it makes sense." She heaved a sigh. "Imagine running out of a place with your pants half-down around your ankles just because you got some of each."

It might have been a moment of high comedy, a farce that Marchand would laugh at for years to come, but for the fact that a murder had been committed. Quietly he asked, "And Bali Jijio? How does he fit in?"

"He told Alphonse to tune his fiddle, not once, not twice, but three times."

Marchand shifted slightly in his chair. "And he took offense?"

"Yes, officer." Tearing off the wig, she tossed her shaven head as if she still wore a crown of luxuriant hair. "I did."

"Thank you, my old friend." Felicio released his grip on Marchand's shoulders. "You showed me great courtesy." He turned to the handsome young man standing next to him. "We're lucky, eh?"

Bali Jijio nodded. "I guess." He laughed when his father punched him on his arm, right on a G clef. "Yes. Thank you, Uncle Joey, for taking such good care of my old man."

"I'm sorry you had to go through all this, both of you." Marchand smiled. "I wish with all my heart that all my cases would solve themselves so easily."

"Beads on a fiddle string." Bali shook his head. "Some murder weapon."

"And some murderer. Arlene Nous, my butt." Felicio brandished a fist. "Alphonse Reveille, Donald Duck, Minnie Mouse, the madman doesn't know who or what he is, or should be. Or should I say madwoman?"

Bali shrugged. "These days, nobody cares. Or at least that's what you think, until something crazy like this happens."

Marchand thought of all the people he'd met over the years, some the accused, others the accusers, all of them struggling to hide bad relationships, bad decisions. New Orleans seemed to produce more creative ways to murder a fellow human than most places. Could it be because death was always so close to the surface? No burial place was safe from water, no crypt too strong to withstand the encroaching gulf waters. Living on the edge of extinction made people do strange things, often violent acts but even more often acts of love, or call it passion, that sometimes had endings that no one could ever have predicted.

Mardi Gras brought out the drama in people, no disputing that, which was why eager participants threw off their staid lives to dance with the devil. Michael Savant, an unworldly soul going from one extreme to another, and not finding peace in either, was just one of the many whose hoped-for celebration of life ended in unexpected death. The ex-priest and the fiddler who'd been born between two genders were two more characters in the endless parade of lives that wound through the ancient streets of New Orleans, dancing, dancing, dancing as if the music would never stop.

Nancy Brewka-Clark's recent short fiction has appeared in *Yellow Mama, Close to the Bone, Eastern Iowa Review, Litbreak, Every Day Fiction, Twist in Time, The First Line, Enchanted Conversations*, the Gothic murder anthology *Exquisite Aberrations*, the ultimate pizza horror anthology *Tales from the Crust* and *Best New Writing 2018* among others. Kelsay Books published her debut poetry collection *Beautiful Corpus* in March 2020.

THE BRASS MENAGERIE

DG Critchley

It was Twelfth Night, the start of carnival season, better known to the tourists as Mardi Gras. 1959 had not been a good year for me so far. Between Castro in Cuba, Khrushchev in Hollywood, and Sputnik in orbit, every strange noise, misplaced shadow, and stranger was suddenly a communist plot. It was funny at first, but I'm a detective with the New Orleans Police department, not a spy buster with the FBI.

I had spent the start of my shift dealing with the aftermath of a knife fight on Bourbon Street. Then I got to spend an hour explaining to Widow Archambault that someone stealing her garden gate was a prank, not proof that the Reds were infiltrating the city. The knife fight had been less annoying. I was heading back to the station when the radio crackled with a reported dead body in the French Quarter. I was nearby. It was going to be one of those Mardi Gras.

Knowing what the French Quarter looked like this time of night, I parked as close as I could get and fought my way through the crowds. Every Mardi Gras, I requisition a billy club, and every year they turn me down. The crowds thinned out as I turned onto Toulouse, which I'm sure had nothing to do with the fact it was notably empty of bars and too narrow for the krewes to consider for parades. I found the house—722 Toulouse Street—hoping it was just a passed out drunk sleeping it off. Instead, I got Mickey Le Saundre, a local who freelanced as a night watchman. Mickey was an excellent choice in security when he was sober. So, most of the time, you hoped for the best.

I followed him into the building. As we entered, I finally figured out where I was. This was the old flophouse where Tennessee Williams had an apartment before he hit it big. It had been purchased a couple years back, and the owners were turning it into some sort of art gallery.

Mickey led me through the lobby, filled with construction supplies. In the back was a storage room with the door ajar. The room was filled with shelves of metal bric-a-brac. In the middle of the room was a body. I didn't recognize the corpse, because there was a massive brass door knocker where his face used to be. So at least I knew the cause of death. His suit told me he was a little too well dressed to be a cat burglar. That was a complication, and I was not a fan of complications. Dead Guy was wearing a white and light gray plaid suit with pegged pants — expensive and the new fashion rage. I'll stick with good old houndstooth. It's a little warm for New Orleans, but it hides stains beautifully.

I radioed for the meat wagon and a crime scene photographer. I looked around. The dead guy, snappy dresser or not, did not appear to have any tools to jimmy the door, suggesting he had a partner. I assumed the room was storing material for the museum being set up. It was mostly a collection of animal sculptures with a few vases added for good measure. A second door knocker sat on a low shelf with a gap next to it. That meant the knocker was used as a weapon, and my dead Beau Brummel didn't accidentally pull it off a high shelf onto his face. This was a homicide.

I talked to Mickey. He looked pretty steady, meaning he had already uncorked something. "Well, Detective, I arrived at midnight to check the doors and windows. The front door was unlocked again, so I came in to check things were okay."

"What do you mean—the door has been unlocked before?"

Mickey glanced back at his jacket outside on a fence post. Now I knew where his bottle was. "I don't want to get anyone in trouble."

"Mickey, we already got trouble. There's a stiff in there with a chunk of brass where his face used to be, remember?"

Mickey just nodded.

"Could the door be unlocked because the last one out forgot to lock it? Who's the contractor doing the work in here?"

Mickey licked his suddenly dry lips. "Emile Richeau."

Emile was Marty Richeau's kid, the one Daddy wasn't talking to. Emile had decided to go into carpentry rather than the family business of selling booze that had mysteriously lost its federal excise tax stamp. So, it was probably a smart decision on the kid's part, even if Marty refused to talk to him. Still, mentioning Marty Richeau was enough to make most people nervous.

"Okay, Mickey. Tell me how to reach the owners, and you can go home."

"The Williamses. They live around the corner in the old Merieult House on Royal. But they ain't here. They're off on a European cruise collecting antiques."

I sent him home and waited for the medical examiner to show up and take my new best friend to the morgue. Then maybe we all could get out of the French Quarter by sunrise. The DA could figure out how to contact the owners in Europe.

Johnny Kay, the photographer, arrived first. While he took the first batch of shots, I looked around the storage room at the brass menagerie. I didn't see a damn thing worth killing someone over, and there were no other obvious gaps on the shelves to suggest a burglary gone bad.

Johnny was wrapping up, so it was time to play detective. I delicately reached inside the bloody coat and pulled out the victim's wallet. Johnny took a photograph, and we opened it up. His driver's license said the deceased was Louis Dieudonné Lévesque IV. His business card said he was a literature professor at Lafayette College in Slidell. It still didn't explain why he was dead in New Orleans, but at least I had a name.

The ME showed up with a stretcher and his latest intern. Johnny already looked a little green around the gills. As long as he'd been doing this job, he never got used to taking certain photos, such as when they pulled the body out of a wreck or lifted a chunk of metal out of a face.

Doc turned to the body and nodded to his assistant. They put on rubber gloves, grabbed the knocker, and hoisted it off the remains. Johnny flinched. He took the shots silently and looked at me. I looked at the Doc. He glanced at the decidedly queasy looking photographer and nodded. Johnny's exit was neither graceful nor leisurely.

Doc watched him go. "I'll give him credit. He's lasted longer at this job than I thought he would." He gestured to the intern, who opened the stretcher.

He examined the remains. "Victim is tall, maybe six feet, and weighs about 150 pounds, normal for his height. Cause of death appears to be blunt force trauma, but I think you knew that. The weapon appears to be a brass object of some sort, possible an antique doorknocker like you'd see on one of the mansions in the Garden District, weighing approximately 30 pounds. I'll check for any other damage at the morgue, but at first glance, there are no signs of defensive wounds. I'll look closer when he gets his turn on the slab."

I looked at the knocker. "I'll have the crime lab dust for fingerprints, but I'm not optimistic." I watched the stretcher head to the wagon, then closed the door and sealed it with crime tape. I sealed the outside door as well and glanced at my watch. It was just about 3 AM as I walked back to my car. The crowds were starting to thin, but only because it was the first night, and most of the tourists were out of practice from last year's boozing and whoring. Give them a few days to get back in shape, and the NOPD would be looking for overflow holding cells again.

I radioed the station and had them look up Emile Richeau's address. He was not happy to see a cop at his doorstep at 3:30 AM, but when I told him there'd been an incident at his job site and he and his crew were not allowed in until I cleared the crime scene, I think he relaxed. A cop rousting him over something unrelated to his old man's bootlegging was probably a novelty for him. He thanked me, and on that note, I called it a shift. A Richeau thanking a cop is weird even by Mardi Gras levels of weirdness.

The next morning, I drove to Slidell and paid a visit to the dean of Lafayette College. Dr. Roget ushered me into his office. I sat in a leather chair that cost more than my car, overlooking a desk roomier than my apartment. He smiled like I was a potential donor. "How can I help you?"

I slid Louis Lévesque's business card across the desk. Roget looked at it, and the smile vanished. He sighed. "What did he do this time?"

"Well, he was breaking and entering a structure in the French Quarter and —"

Roget sighed again. "Let me guess. The old Tennessee Williams residence again."

I nodded. "Yes. Only this time somebody killed him."

Roget stared. It took a moment, but he recovered quickly. "Shot as a trespasser? What a terrible waste."

I let him think that it was that simple. "It's an ongoing investigation. We don't know all the details yet."

The dean sat back. "Damn you, Louis. I warned you your obsession was going to be your ruin."

I leaned forward. "Tell me why Professor Lévesque was so obsessed with that building."

The dean took off his glasses and polished them as he collected his thoughts. "Tennessee Williams began feuding with his landlady from the day he moved into that attic room. Then, *Glass Menagerie* opened in Chicago, and everyone knew that play was bound for Broadway. Williams was still living on Toulouse and hating it, waiting for the first check big enough to move."

He sat back. "That's all the background you need to understand Louis Lévesque. Years later, Louis heard a rumor that Williams suspected the landlady was rummaging through his trash, looking for notes, scribbled out revisions, basically anything handwritten. Williams believed that she thought his discarded paper might have resale value once he was a Broadway playwright. Unwilling to accuse the woman without proof and get evicted before he was ready to leave, he took to burning his rough drafts in the stove. When it was too hot to light a fire, he hid the papers to wait for cooler weather.

"Louis was convinced Williams may have forgotten the hidden documents because of how quickly he left for New York."

I didn't get it. "So there were work notes from Tennessee Williams. So what?"

"These make-believe papers, if they existed, would have offered insight into Mr. Williams's creation process. But it's an urban legend. You might as well claim the *rougarou* ate the notes."

"So why didn't he ask Williams directly?" I still didn't see the appeal, but my idea of literature came with a centerfold.

"Oh, he did. Louis was at every public appearance that Mr. Williams attended. Finally, Mr. Williams filed a restraining order against him."

Now I understood. "Your professor wouldn't take no for an answer."

The dean nodded, "Louis was obsessed. He was convinced that denials were proof that whatever was left behind would ensure his academic legacy."

Half my arrests were obsessed people, so I understood the type. "It sounds like your professor, to use a highly technical police term, was a few crawdads short of a gumbo."

"Louis was actually an outstanding literature professor. And this Tennessee Williams thing has been going on for years. In retrospect, I can see now that it had probably gotten out of hand."

"There's an understatement for the ages, Doc. Did he have any enemies other than Tennessee Williams' lawyers?"

"Not really. Although Kemper called me about Louis several times."

"Kemper?"

"The owners of the property, Kemper and Leila Williams. No relation to Tennessee, by the way. They're converting the building into a museum for their art collection. Apparently, Louis has been bothering them for permission to search the attic where the apartment was. When they called to complain, they repeated what they told Louis. It's been 15 years since Williams moved out. The room has been remodeled repeatedly, mostly after former tenants trashed it. There's never been any evidence that the story of the scrap paper was true."

"I take it Professor Lévesque was still not taking a hint?"

"The Williamses are also generous benefactors of Lafayette College. Kemper finally told me if they had to complain again, they would end their generous annual donation. So, I point blank told Louis that if we lost their donation, he would be unemployed. That seemed to quiet him down."

"Until he found out the Williamses were taking a cruise. So he decided to take a look anyway."

"Do you have any suspects, Detective?"

I stood up. "I have no suspects, no motive, and an impressive headache forming."

As I drove back, something in the back of my head said I was missing something. That was not unusual, but this time, it felt like I was missing something so obvious I would hate myself when I figured it out.

I got back to the station to find two notes waiting. The first one was from Doc Charles, asking me to pop by the morgue. The second one was more surprising. Emile Richeau wanted me to swing by the house again. Suddenly, Mrs. Archambault's missing garden gate was looking like the highlight of Mardi Gras for me.

I walked down to the morgue, bracing myself for the usual assault of smells that the disinfectants couldn't quite mask. Doc met me at the door.

"Let's make this fast; I'm buried in bodies this morning."

I decided he was in no mood to make the obvious pun and followed him into the closet they called the Medical Examiner's Office. I sat down as he opened a file.

"I'm listing the cause of death as blunt force trauma to the head and face. There is so much damage I can't tell which part of the injury specifically killed him. And I already have two alcohol poisoning victims, a suicide, and a botched robbery waiting in the morgue this morning. It's Mardi Gras. I don't have time to narrow it down. All you need to know is it's officially homicide."

I started to stand. He gestured me back into the chair.

"There's one odd thing, which is why I wanted to see you. Your victim had perimortem bruising on the anterior deltoid."

I looked at him. "In English, Doc?"

He rolled his eyes. "He has a bruise on his shoulder that happened right before death. The attacker grabbed the victim by the shoulder from behind with one hand. He spun the victim around and smashed in his face. Whoever you're looking for is very strong. That's a lot of damage for swinging a heavy object one-handed."

I thanked him and went upstairs. A weapon of convenience was used, but the killer could have easily bashed the professor's head in from behind. He was sending a message.

I pulled up in front of Emile Richeau's house. He was sitting on the porch, watching several children play on the lawn. I noticed a .45 tucked in his waistband. I assume he had heard the "incident" was a homicide and was being cautious. I didn't blame him. He stood up as I approached.

"You woke me from a sound sleep, and I didn't think of it at the time. Last night, I got a prank call about 11:00 telling me the house on Toulouse Street was on fire, and I should get over there."

"You didn't go."

He grinned. "When your father is Marty Richeau, you don't rush anywhere on an anonymous phone call. I called a buddy at the Fire Department. They had no reports of fires in the Quarter. So I assumed it was a prank and went to bed."

He shifted in the chair, stretching his long legs. Something finally clicked in my head. "Mr. Richeau, how tall are you?"

"Excuse me?"

"Humor me. I'd say about 6 feet and 150 pounds."

He looked at me. "6'1" and 160. May I ask why?"

"I'm just thinking out loud. Do you happen to own one of those new white plaid suits?"

He looked surprised. "My wife made me buy it. How did you know that?"

I looked at him. "Mr. Richeau, there's something odd going on." I handed him my card. "Call me if you think of anything, or get any more call. And avoid Toulouse Street."

He sat there. "Let me guess. My father's in another turf war?"

I shrugged. "I don't know. But I think it may time for me to have a chat with your old man."

Emile looked at me. "I assume you know where to find him?"

I nodded.

As I left, he looked at me. "You will explain this all to me?"

I nodded again and drove home. I considered visiting the French Quarter, but I had been civil to about as many people today as I could stand.

At ten o'clock the next morning, with a lot of apprehension, I walked past the street cleaners attempting to make Basin Street not look like a confetti factory explosion. I turned onto St. Louis Street. Overriding my survival instincts, I walked into Blanche's Café Au Lait. Everyone knew Blanche. She made the finest beignets in the French Quarter, and probably the entire state of Louisiana. That's all she made. She was now semi-retired, so she opened at 6 AM and closed when the beignets ran out. If they lasted until 8 AM, it was a slow day. A half-dozen beignets and her fresh chicory coffee blend were proof there was a loving God. Back when I was a patrolman, I spent a lot of time in a corner booth "writing reports." I'm pretty sure the sergeant never got a report from me that wasn't covered in powdered sugar.

She looked up from the cash register as I walked in.

"Hi, Blanche!" I tried to sound a lot more cheerful than I felt.

She looked up and smiled. Her fake smile was better than mine. "*Mon chere*. It's been too long. But you know I'm out of the good stuff."

"I know. I need to talk to Marty."

A very large man stepped out of the side door. "And what if Mr. Richeau doesn't want to talk to you?" His accent was French, not Cajun. A Canadian gunsel in New Orleans? What was the world coming to?

I walked over to him, wishing I was about a foot taller to look him in the eye. I was about to say something I'd undoubtedly regret when a voice rang out behind the wall of muscle in front of me.

"Behave, Little Pierre. Like all law-abiding citizens, we welcome visits from law enforcement."

The mountain moved aside, and I stepped into the office of Martin Richeau. The room was Spartan—a few chairs and a desk. Blanche's Café Au Lait was probably the only legitimate business Marty Richeau owned, famously so because he bought the building just to keep Blanche in business. Such was the power of Blanche's beignets. A grateful city tended to overlook a lot of Marty's sins for a good beignet. With Blanche showing her age a little, he suggested she eliminate the sit-down dining area. Marty ripped out the booths, put up a wall, and used it as his office. Whatever illicit operations Marty was currently involved in didn't take place in the cafe. He ran that operation strictly by the books, again proving the power of Blanche's beignets.

I sat down. "Marty, I have an odd question to ask, and then I'll be out of here." He nodded. "There was a murder over on Toulouse Street."

He started to say something. I cut him off. "There's no connection to you or your businesses. It was a college professor trespassing in the building."

Marty looked at me. "If I'm not a suspect, why would this unfortunate matter concern me?"

I paused. "Because the building is under construction, and Emile is the contractor." Marty sat there without expression.

I continued. "The victim was the same height and build as Emile, and wearing a suit similar to one Emile owns. And he was attacked from behind in a dark building, so the attacker never saw his face. You can see where I'm going with this."

Marty remained expressionless. "You think someone knocked off the egghead, thinking it was my boy."

I nodded. "So, my question to you is simple. Besides Feds, is there anyone else currently pissed off at you? I mean, angry enough where they'd go after you through Emile?"

Marty looked at Pierre and then gestured at the door. He lumbered out of the room and closed the door. Marty watched him go. "I don't talk shop in front of him. A couple of beers, and he'd tell you anything. Good help is hard to find."

He sat back. "As you may have heard, I have several local business interests."

I nodded. Everyone knew Marty, besides his signature excise tax dodge, had his fingers in any number of additional vices.

"I do have competitors, but certain agreements are in place. One of the most important ones is 'no one goes after the family.' However, we have a new competitor, Richie Diodati. This young punk thinks he can stroll into New Orleans and start carving out a piece of the business like he's still in Chicago. That's not a problem by itself. After all, this is New Orleans, and we take care of our own. But this piece of garbage has no respect for how things are done."

"Has he threatened your kids?"

Marty shook his head. "No, he's not stupid enough to go after me first. But Sammy Duvall had discussed potential conflicts of interest with the kid, and Sammy accidentally broke his knuckles on Mr. Diodati's face. Several nights ago, someone torched Sammy's car. He thought it was a warning. I thought it was just someone tossing away a cigarette. Now, I'm not so sure."

I stood up and headed toward the door. "Thank you, Mr. Richeau."

He smiled with teeth that must have made his dentist very wealthy. "Keep me in the loop. And please, call me Marty."

I nodded and stepped back into the café, Blanche walked over with a grease-soaked bag. She handed it to me with a wink. "For old times' sake."

Three things occurred to me as I headed back to the police station. The first was that, even five hours old, Blanche's beignets were still the greatest thing in New Orleans. Second, I shouldn't eat beignets in the car. Powdered sugar and houndstooth do not play well together. The third thing would require a return trip to the morgue. I hoped the beignets tasted as good coming back up.

I walked into the autopsy room to find Doc elbow-deep in someone on the slab. "Doc, can I ask you a quick question about my victim?"

Doc looked up. "Yes, but make it quick. This accidental alcohol poisoning case has a stomach full of rat poison, so Lieutenant Marceau is about to find his nice neat case has unraveled."

I didn't volunteer to get any closer than the doorway. "Doc, you said the assailant was strong because of the bruise. Can you calculate the guy's height from the handprint?"

Doc pulled a glass jar out of his current guest. It was filled with a rather unpleasant looking collection of fluids, and the stink was drifting my way. He put it down and cocked his head.

"Interesting question." He put the jar down, went over to the drawer, and pulled out the professor. He peeled the sheet back and examined the shoulder. That meant he uncovered what was left of the face. I could feel the beignets filing a protest. Fortunately, he put the body away quickly and turned back to me.

"Well, not precisely, but most of the finger outlines are in the front, below the clavicle. That means he was taller than the victim."

I forced the bile back down my throat. "And you're sure?"

Doc nodded. "If he were shorter, most of the bruise would be on the trapezius. I mean, I can't say how tall, but tall enough to reach down to grab the victim by the shoulder."

I thanked Doc and went home. Between powdered sugar and the Eau de Autopsy cologne, I needed a shower and a change of wardrobe. I felt sorry for Mr. Lee when I dropped the jacket off at the cleaner. As we were chatting, I had a clever idea. A quick talk with Mr. Lee, a quick agreement, and I went home. I was almost in a good mood. I even fought the crowds on Bienville Street and got an order of gumbo to go at Arnaud's. I ran a couple more errands and headed home. I settled in for the night with good gumbo, bad bourbon, *Gunsmoke* on the Philco, and an underlying sense of doom.

I hadn't shared my plan with the lieutenant. There was no way he would green-light anything as poorly thought through as my plan, based on a hunch. My concern didn't stop me from dozing off on my chair, because Jack Paar was trying to be funny when the telephone woke me up.

"Detective? This is Emile Richeau. I just got another phone call. This one claimed to be from a neighbor who said he thought he saw lights moving around inside my job site."

"Okay, I was expecting you'd get another call, just not so soon. I'm going over there now. Do me a favor. If you haven't heard back from me in two hours, call the police."

There was a pause on the other end. "Aren't you the police?"

"Yes, but I have a plan that is such a terrible idea that I couldn't risk telling anyone at the office."

"Okay. Be careful?" Richeau sounded doubtful as he hung up. I agreed with the sentiment. I grabbed my revolver and made sure it was loaded. You only make that mistake once.

I stepped out into the street. The only difference between midnight in the French Quarter during Mardi Gras and a riot was most rioters were sober. I assumed Emile's "helpful neighbor" was not on Toulouse Street when he made the call and still had to get to the house. Having patrolled the French Quarter before making detective, I knew the area. I drove down to St. Louis Cemetery and parked the car. The last half-mile would be faster on foot. I crossed Rampart and worked my way through the merrymakers. The crowds in the back streets were a lot thinner than Bourbon Street, the intuitive way to reach Toulouse, and I was hoping that bought me some time.

I reached 722 Toulouse faster than I had hoped. I picked the lock and stepped into the building. Now we'd see how clever I really was. I turned on a work light between the door and the brass storage room. I stepped into the storage room, partially closed the door, and laid my trap. About ten minutes later, I heard the floor creak. In my best Emile imitation, I called out, "Anyone there?"

No answer, which did not surprise me. I ducked down and waited. The door opened slowly, and Little Pierre stepped in, which again, was no surprise. He looked to the back of the room, where I had a surprise for him. Mr. Lee had let me borrow one of his mannequins, which I had dressed in a white jacket from the thrift shop (I wasn't about to buy one of those ugly white plaid suits). It stood in the shadows, a hat on its head, looking away from the door, I hoped the lighting was poor enough to fool Pierre into thinking it was Emile. Sure enough, he charged forward, surprisingly fast for such a giant. He grabbed a large brass vase off the shelf as he passed by and swung it at "Emile's" head without breaking stride. The dummy exploded under the impact. Pierre looked confused.

I stood up with my gun pointed at his gorilla chest. "Pierre, you're under arrest."

Pierre swung the vase, and I barely ducked. I emptied my gun into his chest. He looked down at the shots and looked at me. He stepped toward me, and I began backing toward the door. If I survived, I was going to send a terse note to Colt about the stopping power of a police .38 Special.

He grabbed a brass elephant and hurled it at me. I blocked with my forearm, in which I could feel the bone shatter. The impact knocked me flat on my back, and my head hit the floor hard. By the time my eyes cleared from the dancing lights, he was standing over me to deliver the finishing blow.

Suddenly, a shot rang out. A red hole blossomed on Pierre's forehead. He looked surprised, dropped the elephant, and fell backward. I was helped to my feet. I turned around to see Marty Richeau.

He looked at Little Pierre. "Last time I hire a Quebecois for muscle. The bastard was working for Diodati."

He helped me to a chair and handed me a gun. "Lucky for you, you carry two guns." I took it in my good hand. My head was not clearing.

"But how?"

Richeau smiled. "Emile called me. It's the first time we've talked in two years, and I owe you for that. He thought you were about to do something stupid, and he was right."

I looked at the gun. He said, "Webley .45 automatic. Has more recoil, but definitely does more damage."

He took the gun and placed it in my useless hand. I barely felt it. That was shock setting in. "I need your fingerprints on the gun. And don't let them look at too closely at it. The serial number appears to be missing."

My head was starting to swim.

Richeau looked at me. "Okay, a concerned citizen is about to call in a report of gunshots, so your pals should be here soon. And I mean it, I owe you one."

I sat there and decided to close my eyes for a moment.

When I woke up, I was in Charity Hospital with my neck in a brace and my arm immobilized with enough stitches to qualify as a patchwork quilt. The doctor said something about concussions and comminuted fractures and metal rods. I wasn't listening very carefully — the painkillers were quite efficient.

By the time they let me out, I could almost lift my arm without wanting to weep in pain. I missed most of Mardi Gras, which almost made it worth the near-death part. I left the hospital a legend. I think some nurses even got a little teary when I was discharged. I assume it was that daily delivery of still-hot beignets I shared with them, not my shrieking like a teenybopper at an Elvis concert during my rehab exercises.

I heard they fished Richie Diodati out of Bayou St. John. Doc called it a tragic fishing accident. I have no reason to doubt him. After all, this is New Orleans, and we take care of our own.

DG Critchley's most recent stories have appeared in anthologies such as *Mid-Century Murder* (Darkhouse Books), *The Killer Wore Cranberry* (Untreed Reads), and *Pulp Adventures* magazine.

Unfiltered

Teresa Trent

I sipped my drink—a hurricane, of course. I mean, what else do you serve at a Fat Tuesday party? Frankly, I took a moment to congratulate myself on showing up here, even if I had to work hard to tamp down the smoldering anger inside me. My boyfriend, Josh, said I have anger issues, but really, why would I subscribe to pop psychology he probably learned off the internet? I know how I feel. Not that I have anger issues as much as I know when I'm right, I'm right. Why shouldn't I speak out? If you don't want to hear my opinion, don't listen. The reason I was "smoldering" on Fat Tuesday? Of all the gin joints in town, I was celebrating Mardi Gras at the restaurant of a man I despised.

Revelers who had gathered in small groups looked like they were having the time of their lives. Why wouldn't they be? They had survived the direct hit of real hurricanes and were now holding their own with the watered-down version of New Orleans' "signature drink." Local politician Everett Wilson stood in one corner surrounded by a crowd, hand on his chin as he listened to potential voters' concerns. No doubt he hoped someone was capturing this moment with a cell phone. So natural, so endearing. Our former mayor had left office for health reasons and the election for his replacement was underway.

In another corner, Arlo Guidry was in full throttle with some story, his face animated and his drink sloshing all over the bar. It was his party, so he could make himself the center of attention. He wore a white jacket with purple feathers on the lapel and a mask covered in purple feathers hanging from a strap on his chest.

"How you doin', darlin'?" Josh, who was already in the slight sway of early drunk, stood before me. Shiny beads in rainbow colors hung around his neck, and he wore a sloppy grin on his face. He'd begged me to come to this party because he was one step away from snagging Chez Arlo accounting work.

Arlo Guidry and I weren't friends and never would be. I had tickets to the Rex Ball this year, the ultimate Mardi Gras party ticket in New Orleans, but no, I was here, drinking an essentially virgin hurricane, listening to canned Zydeco music. Ooh wee. What fun.

"Oh, you're pouting," Josh said. "Don't be that way."

"You know what I think of Arlo Guidry. Just because I wouldn't put his cookbook in my window at the bookstore, he sets out to ruin me. Yelp reviews can take down an independent bookstore, you know. Do you know how many chefs in New Orleans have a cookbook? If I put his in the window, then I'd have to make space for all the others."

"Sure," he said. "But, tonight, you're besties, right? He's about to give me his account and I don't want to screw this up."

As if his ears were burning, the great Arlo Guidry himself stepped over, his latest boyfriend on his arm.

"How nice of you to come, Joshua. And you brought the esteemed Caitlynn Robson, owner of Robson Reads. Too bad no one buys print books anymore, dear."

"Especially cookbooks," I shot back. Did he seriously think he could hit me with his passive-aggressive crap?

Arlo stiffened. He was used to getting away with sliding in an insult here and there. Not with me. Today or any day — and now he knew it.

"Yes, well, the sales of my cookbook have been glorious, with or without your little store."

"Really?" I tried to feign surprise. "How many copies has your mother bought?"

Arlo's cheeks flushed a delightful shade of red. I was really getting under his skin and enjoying every minute of it. Did he seriously think I would let this issue between us slide? I was born for this.

"Honey, you're a mean and vindictive woman," he said. His boyfriend nodded, a bit of parade glitter still on one eyebrow.

"I just tell it like it is. You want to talk vindictive? How about the reviews of my bookstore you posted online?"

"I don't know what you're talking about. What reviews?"

"Oh, I'm thinking of the one that said I had pushed aside *Cooking with Arlo*, the best cookbook in New Orleans, for a politician's book in the window. You're the only person in town who would refer to his own cookbook as the best."

Okay, I probably went too far, as evidenced by Josh's hand on my elbow. This was more important to him than it was to me.

"I take great offense to that." Arlo's eyes slipped to Josh. "Joshua, darling, I'm afraid I can't think about business tonight. It's been a long day," he glanced at his boyfriend, "and I've decided to keep anything that stresses me at bay."

The boyfriend smiled and lifted his chin.

"My therapist insists I maintain good boundaries with people who upset me, and Caitlynn is upsetting me. Now that I think about it, turning my accounting over to you might be a bit risky to my mental health. I simply can't weaken my boundaries. It's really too bad — I thought we'd make a great team."

"Arlo. Please," Josh begged. "We've all had our fair share to drink and things got heated. I know you don't want to make a decision that important at a time like this. You're not yourself."

"*Au contraire*, my friend. I'm very much myself and lately I'm finding strength in places I never knew I had."

Arlo looked over to the corner where Wilson's crowd was breaking up, smiled, and waved to another diner. Without another word, he made his way across the room with his boyfriend tagging behind him.

Josh put his fingertips to his temples. "I can't believe what just happened. Just like that, a chance to double my revenue up in smoke."

"I'm sorry," I said, although I didn't feel the slightest bit guilty for calling him out on the Yelp reviews. There was no way I was going to let him get away with trying to tear down my business because of a lousy cookbook. "I can get him back. I'll apologize."

Josh let out a sigh. "You could try, but I doubt it will make any difference."

"You said it." Another man walked up. "Arlo is the king of grudges. Believe me, I know. Luke Bridges." He extended his hand and Josh shook it. "I've been Arlo's attorney for years." Once he introduced himself, I knew who he was immediately. He worked for other French Quarter merchants. He was a strapping big guy with a shock of blonde hair who looked like he would be comfortable at a Louisiana State University game or a charity ball.

"I should also confess Arlo and I used to be an item," Luke added. "That's how I know about his ability to hold a grudge. I'm only still his attorney because I know more about him than most people."

"Nice to meet you," Josh said. "Unfortunately, he'd just hired me, but hadn't yet turned over his books."

"He goes through accountants as frequently as boyfriends and the latest fashions. You aren't the first he's fired. Not even close. Something about counting money makes him angry. Hyper-focused. He puts on this happy-go-lucky face, but his god is money. How else do you think he's made this restaurant a success?"

"And my attack on his cookbook didn't help Josh's chances at the account," I admitted.

"Lord, no. He'll get you back, but in little ways. Like Yelp reviews or making sure you aren't invited anywhere he's going to be. That's Arlo. Rather than directly confront you he sticks the knife in little by little, but I guess you know that by now."

"I need another drink," Josh said, eying the bottom of his empty glass. "I may as well eat, drink, and be merry because tomorrow I'm back to being a struggling accountant."

I put my arms around his shoulders. "Let's just leave. I never wanted to be here to begin with."

"No, just a little longer." He kissed me. "I promise."

"Okay." Josh made his way through the crowd, dense with revelers, to the bar.

"Don't worry," Luke said to me. "You're not the first to suffer the wrath of Arlo, and you won't be the last." He raised the index finger on the hand holding his glass. "Looks like your man is going in for a second try."

I returned my gaze to Josh, who had positioned himself next to Arlo. At first it was impossible to hear them over the din of the crowd, but then they began to yell.

"I said we're done," Arlo yelled.

"That's ridiculous. You're ridiculous."

A waiter stepped in front of us. "A secret admirer has sent you a drink, madam."

"Perfect timing." I reached for the drink and downed it as I watched my boyfriend not only seal the loss of a deal, but with that many witnesses, likely stifled other prospects as well. Oh, what a night. A Fat Tuesday to end all Fat Tuesdays.

My head hurt like a bad brain surgery. Not only that, my back hurt. It felt like I was lying on bricks. I tried to turn over, causing an ache to shoot through me. I could smell urine and stale booze and as I attempted to open my eyes, I realized dawn was breaking. Dawn? How could it be dawn? We'd only been at the party an hour.

The party.

I clenched my fist and realized I was holding something. Something sticky. I slowly raised myself up and looked around. I wasn't in Arlo's restaurant. I wasn't even inside.

Had aliens abducted me? Was this what 'missing time' meant? Where was everyone? The music? The laughter? Looking at the muddy grey walls, I realized, for some reason, I was in an alley. As I looked around me, my gaze hit upon another person lying near me. I suddenly recognized the white jacket with purple feathers on the lapel. It was Arlo — and based on the amount of blood splashed across the fabric, he was dead. I looked at my hand. I was holding a knife. A bloody knife.

My head was fuzzy. Had I killed Arlo Guidry? It was like reading a true crime novel I'd sell in the store. I had the motive, and as I stared down at the red-stained knife, I had the means. He'd been such an ass. Had I killed him for it? I looked more closely at the knife. It was a standard steak knife from the restaurant. I would have had easy access to it. But so would anyone else at the party. Oh my God, I had killed Arlo. The police would come and arrest me. I was covered with blood at a murder scene. What had I done? Why couldn't I remember anything?

I pulled myself up from the cold concrete and examined my clothes. Considering the amount of blood around Arlo, it was odd that I'd only picked up blood on one side. If I'd stabbed Arlo, wouldn't I have blood spatter on the front of my blouse? I've watched plenty of CSI. Was there splatter on my face? Did I look like some kind of Mardi Gras ghoul walking down the street?

I should call the police. I would expect anyone else to call the police at this point. I would tell someone they were wrong if they didn't call the police. Innocent people don't get arrested. But was I innocent?

I had to get my fingerprints off the knife. Arlo didn't just look dead, he looked gray. Wait—even if I cleaned off the knife, there was still a chance some over-eager forensics tech would find my DNA. No, I had to take the knife with me and try to dispose of it. But where? Maybe the sewer, or I could drive off the causeway over Lake Pontchartrain and dump it. Whatever I did, I had to get rid of it. It was the one thing that connected me to the crime.

"Where've you been?" Josh said, sitting up in bed rubbing his bloodshot eyes. "You went wild last night and then just disappeared. It worried me sick."

I was wearing one of his old LSU t-shirts after pulling off my clothes and stuffing them in a trash bag.

How could I tell him I wasn't sure where I'd been? Just off murdering an annoying chef. "Oh, well, not that it's any of your business, but I went out for a walk and guess I fell asleep in somebody's courtyard."

Josh looked at me like I was lying. I *was* lying, or at least making something up to fit the situation. If I wasn't sure what happened, then technically it wasn't lying. It was helping to clarify and make the other person settle down. Besides, I was here now, so there was no reason for him to make an issue out of it.

"You fell asleep? Seriously? Like with the bums out there?"

Okay, now he was getting on my nerves. "Don't you have an Ash Wednesday mass to go to or something?"

He ran a hand through his hair. "I don't know what's going on, but I feel like there's something you're not telling me."

"Give it up, Columbo. I got drunk. I went for a walk. I fell asleep. I'm here now. Get over it."

I crawled into bed next to Josh and turned away from him. I didn't want him to see my face because if he did, he'd know I was lying.

When I signed into the cash register that morning, I looked at Everett Wilson's book in the front window. With Arlo Guidry dead, his cookbook would become very popular here in town. Especially with the Mardi Gras tourists. I picked up a stack of Arlo's cookbooks and walked them to the front window. I guess that snippy chef got his way after all. His book was front and center in my window. As I put the last book in place, Josh entered, wearing a dark suit.

"After what you said to that man last night, I can't believe you just put his book in the window." Josh had an ashen mark of the cross on his forehead.

"How was church? Big crowd?"

"Not this early. There will be more at the noon mass, I expect. I like to get my confessions in early, beat the crowd. So, are you feeling guilty for tearing him a new one last night?"

"Uh ..." It was then I realized I'd made a mistake. Why would I put his book in the window if I didn't already know he was lying dead in the alley behind his restaurant? "Yeah. I was too hard on the guy."

Josh's eyes widened. "Am I hearing right? Are you telling me you were out of line telling someone—how do you put it?—'If you don't like it, you don't have to listen'. Glad I went to church because you backing down is a sure sign of the Rapture."

I threw my hands up in the air. "Whatever. I've never been that way. I'm a kind person."

"The hell you are. You love to take people down insult by insult. It's an art form for you."

Josh made me sound like a monster. Was that how people saw me? Was I that much of a bitch that a normal person wouldn't want to be around me?

The bell on the front door rang and the paper deliverer for the *Times Picayune* stepped in and plopped a stack of papers on the counter. Yes, we're in a digital age, but my regulars like to have something they can touch, fold, and line the bird cage with from time to time.

"Got us a Mardi Gras murder," the man said, chomping on the cigar in his mouth. "Right' cher in da French Quarter it was."

There on the front page was a picture of Arlo Guidry. The same picture featured on the cover of his cookbook. They had found him.

As Josh and I sat in the police department waiting area, it was a bit like the party all over again. Except it wasn't a party. No food, no music, and no laughter. I guess not everyone from the party was there, but anyone who had interacted with Arlo was lined up against the wall like a suspect line-up. Luke Bridges was there, with his arm around Arlo's boyfriend, whose name I never picked up. Phillip? Geoffrey? They reminded me of two ex-wives at a funeral. Everett Wilson sat next to us with another man in a finely tailored suit who had 'lawyer' written all over him.

As my gaze wandered his way, he raised his chin. "I never got a chance to thank you for putting my book in your window. I appreciate your support for my campaign."

I gave a weak grin. "I was happy to do it. You're a lot better than the other guy who's running for mayor. Good luck with the election."

He puffed out his chest a bit. "Glad to hear it. Together, we can change things."

His response sounded a little canned, as if he had said this to anyone who said yes to him. I had to wonder if he gave his speech to the pizza delivery guy. *Together we can change things, and here's your tip.*

"I'm just sorry we have to meet like this." I raised a hand to indicate the waiting room.

"Yes, well, I never thought much of the man. A feeling I know we share. He was rough on you with those reviews. If I'd had a little more to drink at the party, I would have told him off the way you did. I admire a person who isn't afraid to speak their mind, and from what I hear, you're just that."

"Yeah, well too bad he had to go and get murdered right after that," the boyfriend said from behind a white handkerchief. "It's all your fault he's dead. You turned the crowd against my Arlo, and someone murdered him. That is, if you didn't do it yourself."

"There were other people there who had motives besides me," I blurted out. There was no way I was going to be the scapegoat for this. I was probably sitting next to the murderer, and this was the perfect opportunity to get the attention off me.

"Yeah?" The boyfriend looked around the room. "Who else hated Arlo enough to kill him?"

I felt a panic rising in me. "Well, Josh here lost his chance to do Arlo's books. Arlo fired him right there on the spot."

"Caitlynn," Josh said, a shushing in his tone. Why had I brought that up? It was the first thing that came to my mind and instead of filtering, I just slammed it on out. *Think first, then speak.* Why wasn't I doing that?

Luke Bridges chimed in. "Yes, well, accountants are a dime a dozen with Arlo. He obsessed over money to the very penny." Luke looked to Everett. "Didn't you have some trouble with him after that Thanksgiving supper for the homeless?"

Everett stiffened. "Not that I know of."

228

"Oh, come on" Luke said. "Arlo went on for days about it. He likes his tax deductions and went into a range when he was told his donation wasn't tax-deductible. I mean, why else would he help the poor? He sure didn't care for poor people. He called them the crawfish scum of New Orleans parish."

"Regardless, I don't know what you're talking about," Everett said, "and I for one want to help the poor and homeless. I want to build a foundation in our city of people of all economic levels — "

"Oh, can it. I've heard your stump speech before and I'm voting for the other guy," Luke said, stopping him short.

"So, we hear you had a lot to drink that night."

"Not really, just two drinks."

"Then they must have been pretty big drinks, because from what we hear, you were the life of the party." Detective Leonard Thibodeaux removed his glasses and polished them on the edge of a cheap polyester tie. I had been the second person called from the waiting room, the first being Arlo's boyfriend. Was I that high on the suspect list?

"Can you tell me where you went after the party?"

There it was — the million-dollar question. If I'd been taking a polygraph, this would be where the squiggly lines would start to zig zag. I had to come up with something plausible.

"I went home."

"And what time would that be?"

I stumbled slightly with my words. "Who keeps track of what time they leave a Mardi Gras party? Two? Three? Four?"

"According to Mr. Guidry's boyfriend, Geoffrey," *so that was his name*, "you fell asleep in a chair in the restaurant and then you were gone. No one knew where you went."

"There you have it." I couldn't tell him how much relief I was feeling in that moment. I was in a chair. Not in the alley with a knife killing Arlo.

229

"About that same time, Arlo left and no one knew where he went. How do you explain that?"

"How do you want me to explain it? I have no idea where he went. I wasn't exactly following him around all night. If you really want to know, I didn't even want to be at that party. I only went because my boyfriend was trying to seal the deal on getting Arlo's accounting work. Then, because he was such an obnoxious man, Arlo fired him right there in front of everyone. I felt so bad for my boyfriend. Who does that kind of thing?"

"So, you were furious with Arlo?"

"You bet I was. He had no right to humiliate Josh like that."

"You had a history with Arlo? Negative reviews of your bookstore?"

It was then I realized I'd said too much. Way too much. Me and my big mouth. Sometimes knowing when to shut up is more important than making a point.

The police found the bloody clothes in the trash bag when they searched my house. They also tracked my cellphone and found I went over the causeway and then right back. It isn't often someone makes a twenty-four-mile trip across a bridge and then turns around and returns unless, of course, they're ditching a murder weapon. As they sentenced me to life, I noticed Everett Wilson out of the corner of my eye. He was trying to get my attention.

As we rose to leave the courtroom, Everett stepped closer and slipped a piece of folded paper into my hand. When I opened it later in my cell, all it said was:

Thanks for serving our fair city and keeping my record clean. No wants a murdering mayor. Hope you enjoyed the drink. Arlo never agreed to the campaign contribution I skimmed off that Thanksgiving supper and was about to do to me what he did to you. But because you like to tell it like it is, you just became the driving force to put me in office. The world needs more people like you. At least I do. Together, we can make a change for a better New Orleans.

Teresa Trent is the author of the *Pecan Bayou Mystery* series that features Betsy Livingston, a single mom who writes a helpful hints column and solves murders in a tiny town in Central Texas. Teresa also authored the *Piney Woods Mystery* series for Camel Press that follows Nora Alexander and her life as an innkeeper in an East Texas oil-bust town. She gets cozy with Tuck Watson, local lawman, and together they solve murders centering around the hotel's guests. Teresa is currently working on a historical mystery series set in the 1960s.

KEEP YOUR HEAD UP
Tom Andes

All the other times her boyfriend, Larry Smalls, had hit her, Mandy Gannon figured it was because he was an abusive creep, and she hadn't done anything to deserve it. This time, if he ever caught up to her and laid into her like he'd done in the past, at least she'd have it coming. She'd taken half a kilo of cocaine in a Wilson duffel bag from their apartment in Laplace, Louisiana, left a note saying she hoped the gangsters who'd fronted it cut his nuts off, and hopped a Greyhound for New Orleans.

It was the Tuesday before Mardi Gras, and all the hotels were booked. She ended up in St. Vincent's Guest House, a hostel on Magazine Street, where she paid cash in advance for four nights in their last bed. She was sharing the room with three sorority sisters from the University of New Hampshire who'd come down for Carnival. Kristy was the party girl, and the slut: anybody's when she drank. Naomi was the smartest of the three, which meant Mandy liked Naomi the most, and also that she was the most dangerous. Jacqui was the Barbie doll blond and seemed to be in charge of the group— "the Alpha," Larry would've said.

The second night, Mandy broke out a little bit of Larry's product, and they partied in the room. A butterfly knife in her pocket, and if one of those girls went for the duffel under the bed, Mandy would've stabbed the bitch through the hand. Jacqui sucked the stuff up like a Hoover, talking into the small hours about Trump and Me Too, long after her friends had gone to sleep, or more accurately, assed out. Mandy didn't give two shits about Donald Trump or Hillary Clinton, and she could've told Jacqui about Me Too, but Mandy kept her mouth shut. *No personal information.* She was going to find a buyer, unload the half kilo in New Orleans, and use the ten grand that ought to net her to start fresh on the West Coast, where Larry Smalls need never darken her door.

But then her curiosity got the better of her.

"Where're you from, anyway?" Mandy asked. Near dawn, they were sitting on the patio. Fifty-five degrees, and it had rained earlier, the courtyard shiny under the moonlight. For the first time in months, Mandy felt good, and she wanted to know everything about this other woman. The more loaded Jacqui got, the thicker her twang.

"Tennessee," Jacqui said. And she explained she was from Brentwood, outside Nashville, probably a suburb with people like her with their perfect teeth and their polar fleece vests.

"How'd you end up in New Hampshire?" Mandy had never been north of her grandma's place in Natchez, Mississippi, and now she was leaving Louisiana forever. And though she'd achieved escape velocity, she didn't know if she could go through with it.

Jacqui waved, like there wasn't much of a story.

"After I went to rehab, my mom thought I should get away from all my so-called friends."

"Rehab?" Mandy laughed. Rehab was for people with meth teeth and pocked faces, but Jacqui looked perfect, not a hair out of place, not even after putting half an eight ball up her nose. Must be what money did for a person, but Mandy wasn't one to judge. Not much better than trailer trash, herself, least not the way most people saw things. But she'd never met a stranger, and she wasn't one to cast the first stone.

Jacqui was holding her hand.

"What about you?" she asked, her face close to Mandy's. "Where're you from?"

And so in spite of herself, Mandy told her all of it, or most of it, anyway: the old man, Warren, coming to her bed at night since she was thirteen, and she'd jumped out of the skillet and into the arms of Larry Smalls, who'd picked her up those six months she'd been waitressing at Fatty's Seafood Restaurant in Slidell. Mandy's mom was still alive, sure, living in a trailer in Mandeville on the North Shore of Lake Pontchartrain, but she was deep in her Evangelical bullshit and didn't want to mess with Mandy. Old Warren, the fat fuck, had cashed out a few years ago, and good riddance.

"I'm really sorry that happened to you," Jacqui said, and Mandy shrugged.

"You're not the one who needs to be sorry." She lit one of Jacqui's Marlboro Lights.

"Let's do one more bump," Jacqui said. "Yeah?"

Girlfriend was fiending, about to gnaw her lip off. But Mandy couldn't think why say no. Couldn't believe how much she wanted to open up to Jacqui, how good it felt to tell her things.

"Okay. But just one more." Mandy handed Jacqui the rolled-up dollar bill and went back in the room to get the duffel from the footlocker at the end of her bunk.

She'd also stolen all the money she could find in the apartment, and after she'd paid for that bed, she still had two hundred bucks, so the next afternoon, she walked to the Walmart on Tchoupitoulas and treated herself to a few pairs of clean underwear. Bought a change of clothes, a raincoat, and a new pair of shoes, righteous Chuck Taylors in the colors of her favorite football team, the New Orleans Saints, duh: black and gold, baby, yeah. Standing in the parking lot, looking at her new kicks, she felt happy for the first time since Larry had taken her to the Zea Rotisserie in Metairie for her twenty-fourth birthday last year, one of those rare, sweet gestures, which he'd managed to ruin by getting in a fight with their waiter and punching the guy in the face because

Larry thought his ribeye was overcooked, and he couldn't stand to be disrespected.

That night, because she couldn't help herself, because she felt like gloating, and because having made it this far, maybe she could do anything, she called Larry. He answered after the first ring.

"Bitch, where are you?" He was already mad enough to spit.

Now that she'd made this break, his bullshit seemed that much more predictable: when his anger didn't get him what he wanted, he would try bargaining, until all his pretty words and his promises of better things dissolved into the rage she knew so well, but what could he do to her over the phone? Still, maybe she shouldn't have called. Her knees felt weak, and she reached for the wrought iron fence outside the hostel, which had once been an orphanage, though it seemed like the kind of place that would terrify children, or maybe that had been the idea.

"I don't think you need to know that," she said.

She was safe, she said—to herself as much as to him. That was all he needed to know.

"Safe?" Larry let forth an ominous chuckle that she knew from experience was supposed to strike terror into her heart—and even thirty miles away in New Orleans, it did. Six years ago, when he'd walked into Fatty's, he'd promised her everything: to take care of her, to protect her, to give her a life that wouldn't involve blistered feet, a sore back, and managers three times her age trying to cop a feel when she was at the register, and maybe even time to do her art, the pen and ink anime drawings she'd abandoned years ago. Now, she felt like one of the Manson kids, like a cult member who was being deprogrammed. "Little girl, you won't ever be safe again. Did you stop to think about that? You're going to spend the rest of your life until I find you looking over your shoulder."

He was gearing up to yell again, so she cut him off. *Bitch. Little girl.* All those words calculated to undercut her self-esteem, just like she'd watched Dad with Mom. Pops had been a long-haul trucker, working 25 years for JB Hunt, and Warren had liked the little boys he'd picked up at the truck stops. And maybe Larry was like her old man in that respect, too.

"I hope you're enjoying your nuts," she said, "while you still have them. Hope you can get a few more little boys to diddle you while I'm gone."

She wasn't sure about the one, so she was spit-balling, but she'd always had a funny feeling about Todd, the high school track star who was Larry's distributor at St. Charles Catholic. The two of them spent a lot of time together with the door closed in Larry's room, and maybe not all of that involved counting money, weighing out product, and playing Grand Theft Auto. After all, she washed Larry's shorts, which gave her certain insights.

She'd said that to goad him, to push him those last few inches over the edge into a full-blown tantrum, but what scared her was the fact he got quiet.

The Magazine Street bus rolled past, the warning signal beeping, the brakes hissing, and the automated voice calling for a stop at Race. When the bus pulled away, its red lights disappearing into the fog, Jacqui was standing on the corner. She was crossing the street with a Rouses shopping bag when she saw Mandy, changed course, and walked her way. *Shit.*

"Keep your head up," Larry said, which was a reference to his favorite Tupac song, and if he hadn't quoted "Hit 'Em Up," the infamous diss track on which Pac had bragged about banging Biggie Smalls' wife, and if Larry was obviously no relation, since Larry was white—though he did like to claim to be a distant cousin, something about ancestry being all mixed up from slavery days, as if—well, it was still a threat. Dude loved that nineties hip-hop, which was one of many ways Mandy had come to realize he was, well, old, or anyway, thirty-six, which was practically forty, which might as well be dead. Mandy felt sick, which only got worse when Larry hung up.

That didn't stop her from calling him a faggot and a cocksucker, yelling into the empty phone that maybe she finally understood why he liked her hair short. Once, when he was giving it to her from behind and trying to get her to let him film it on his iPhone, so he could post it to his Pornhub channel, the dude had told her that she had hips like a fourteen-year-old boy.

By the time Jacqui reached her, Mandy had managed to pull herself together. But she was still shaking.

"Are you okay?" Jacqui asked, and though Mandy wanted to collapse in the other woman's arms, she shrugged. She would not cry. *I'm a tough bitch*, she thought.

"Yeah," Mandy said. "I'm fine."

Lying, but she didn't want to have to depend on anybody, and especially not a rich, cokehead sorority chick who looked like she might've been one of the baddies who made Lindsey Lohan's life hell in *Mean Girls*.

"You called him, didn't you?" Jacqui shook her head, Mandy already regretting telling her as much as she had about the situation.

"Don't worry about it," she said. It wasn't Jacqui's problem, and not her business, either.

"As long as he doesn't know where you are," Jacqui said, "and you're safe, it's okay."

Like they were in this together—partners in crime, Thelma and Louise or some shit.

Mandy had been eighteen when she met Larry—a kid. Still living at home, where she slept with her door bolted and a breadknife under her pillow, at least when Warren was around, with her mom calling her a lazy so-and-so, even when Mandy was pulling doubles every weekend, saving up so she could get out of that house. "I don't think I know what to do without him." The truth of it hit her when she said it.

The wine bottles in Jacqui's Rouses bags clinked as she put her arms around Mandy, and they stood in the middle of Race Street, locked up in an awkward hug, until she pushed Jacqui away. Mandy didn't want anyone's pity. Around them the early paradegoers were walking to St. Charles, the drums like an invading army in the distance. Brass. Cymbals crashing. The rat-a-tat-tat of the snare like machine gun fire.

"Enough," Mandy said. Still no tears.

"We're going to the parades," Jacqui said, holding her arm, "if you want to come."

By now, Mandy should've been on a Greyhound out of town—that was the plan—but as much as it pained her to admit, the truth was that she had no idea where to go, and hardly any scratch to get there, anyway. As much as Mandy loved her shoes, she'd been an idiot to spend what she'd spent today. And with that grandmother in Natchez being long dead, it seemed to her that Jacqui was the only friend she had, and maybe the only person she could trust in the world.

"Yeah." She touched Jacqui's hand. Squeezed. "Maybe I will."

Back in the room, Kristy was drying her hair. She was wrapped in a fuzzy blue bath towel she must've brought with her from New Hampshire, since the ones at the hostel were like cardboard laced with sandpaper. Naomi was sitting on the bottom bunk, reading a book, *Catch and Kill*.

"You coming with?" Kristy shut the hairdryer off and set it on the counter. That first night, she'd brought a boy home from the parades and gotten laid—noisy, sloppy drunk sex—in the top bunk on her side of the room. Last night, she'd ralphed, and after three days in New Orleans, her face was puffy, a spiderweb of broken blood vessels in her cheeks giving her a sickly red color. *Slow down, girlfriend, it's only Thursday.* But Mandy didn't say that. Didn't say it was a marathon, not a sprint, either.

"Yeah," she said, "I guess so."

Naomi's watchful brown eyes were studying her over the top of the book.

"Yay!" Kristy jumped up and down—no joke—and clapped, like a happy little puppy.

"Cool." Naomi marked her place, closed her book, and set it on her lap. She yawned. "We could use a tour guide who's a native."

Mandy sat on the bottom bunk and hugged herself, scratching her arms, feeling out of place in that room, with those girls, who probably had normal boyfriends, or at least dated guys their age, not wannabe players pushing forty whose idea of a good time was driving into the swamp with their cousins and getting shitfaced while they bagged nutria—guys who thought intimacy was farting under the covers and pulling them over a girl's head, what Larry called "the old Dutch oven." Hunched over, Mandy picked at a zit on the back of her arm, and in spite of herself, she laughed. Larry could be a jackass, sure—but he meant well, didn't he?

"I'm not sure how much of a tour guide I'm going to be." She had gooseflesh on her arms. It felt nice to be valued, to have something to offer those girls, and she liked that they saw her as a native, as being *of* this place, even if she came from thirty miles up the river, which was a different world. She chewed her thumbnail, which was bitten down to the quick. "But I can try."

No, in point of fact, Larry didn't mean well. He was an abusive creep, a genuine POS, and probably a closet case, too.

Jacqui had opened a bottle of wine, and she sat next to Mandy and put an arm around Mandy's shoulders. "I'm sure you'll do fine."

Mandy almost wept with gratitude—she didn't know what she'd done to earn such faith—but if she could put her finger on the other two, Jacqui mystified her. Kristy was going to marry money and have lots of affairs, while the other night, Naomi had said she had a boyfriend, a guy studying environmental science she really liked, and who she'd probably settle down with. Mandy figured both of them for houses in the burbs, subdivisions, maybe gated communities, life as it was promised to certain people, or at least those who didn't live in duplexes with cars up on blocks in the yard — those who didn't grow up under Warren Gannon's roof, and who didn't get involved with scum-sucking, sociopathic sacks of human feces like Larry Smalls.

"You okay?" Jacqui still had her arm around Mandy's shoulders, and she was brushing Mandy's bangs out of her eyes, Jacqui searching Mandy's face. Jacqui had a clean, baby powder smell, like the talcum, the Johnson & Johnson Larry used on his balls, and Mandy froze up, experiencing a second of spiraling panic. Across the room, Naomi blinked, and again Mandy had that feeling of danger, like Naomi could see right through her — but apart from the ten grand worth of blow in that locker at the foot of her bunk, what did Mandy have to hide, anyway?

"Yeah." Mandy forced a smile. Lying again, but she still wasn't sure about these people — wasn't sure she trusted three college girls from New Hampshire, a bunch of Alpha Phis, with her life. Her face was hot, and she felt herself turning red. "I'm great."

She broke out a little more of her stash, and they had a couple toots in the room. Then they were walking across Race Street in the early darkness, with a cold, drizzly rain spitting in their faces, joining the throng of people moving toward the parade route on St. Charles Avenue, where carnival was more of a family affair than it was in the Quarter: a few drunken college pukes, sure, but otherwise it was kids, their parents, and middle-aged couples holding hands. Mandy's phone buzzed in her pocket, and she knew before she looked — knew before a second text arrived, and it buzzed again — that it was Larry.

Hope you enjoying Mardi Gras. That was the first text.
Ill b seeing you. That was the second.

Standing in Coliseum Square, she swallowed the lump of terror in her throat. Jacqui's bus, the automated voice announcing a stop at Race and Magazine—could he have heard that, or was he a mind reader, and did he have supernatural powers, actual, serious voodoo? Or maybe it was just a lucky guess—after all, where else would she have gone but New Orleans?

Oh God, oh God, oh God.

Had she thought that or spoken aloud?

"What is it?" Jacqui asked.

They were on the corner of Prytania, across from a rambling Victorian behind a wrought iron fence, floats passing a block away on St. Charles. Across the street, Kristy was walking the curb with her arms out like a tightrope walker, like she was testing her balance. Naomi had brought a camera, and she was taking pictures of a kid with a Radio Flyer wagon full of trinkets: multicolored beads and LED lights, the little guy mugging for the photos like he'd just won the Super Bowl.

"Nothing," Mandy said. Thinking: *the son of a bitch*. She would not let him do this to her, would not let him terrorize her, not when she was so close to getting free. She felt faint, and if not for Jacqui holding Mandy's arm, Mandy might have fallen.

"You can trust me," Jacqui said. "I know you're scared of this guy Larry, but you can tell me what's going on. I know we only just met, but whatever it is, I'm here, and I can help, yeah?"

Mandy had that butterfly knife, which she could feel in the pocket of her cutoffs, next to the tiny key to the footlocker, and that was what she trusted—her own resources, that cold steel, which she'd stolen from Larry's dresser drawer, and which she was going to stick between the dude's ribs if she saw him. Her legs were bare, and she was freezing, shivering in the cold and the wet. A moment ago, Jacqui had been talking about a boyfriend, a guy in Philly who wanted to marry her, but there was a problem, or she wasn't interested — Mandy had only been half-listening — so how had they gotten to this?

"I don't know what to do." She wiped her nose with the back of her hand. Bitter as it was to admit, she didn't know how to unload half a kilo of cocaine, didn't have the connections or the street sense. Besides which, her potential buyers would've all been Larry's hoodlum friends, and he would've put them on notice as soon as he found her note back in Laplace.

"I can't help you," Jacqui said, "if you won't even tell me what's happening."

Maybe Jacqui was right, and Mandy had to trust somebody. She felt like she was about to bust apart, trying to keep all this bottled up inside, and wasn't that what Dr. Phil and all those people on the daytime talk shows said, that you had to ask for help before you would get any? Though she wasn't sure this was what they meant.

"He's coming for me." She showed Jacqui her phone, the text messages from Larry.

Jacqui's forehead creased, her face pale in the glow from the screen. "You have to go to the police."

Which was just about the most basic, white girl response to the situation, and exactly what Mandy had been afraid of. Dude hadn't even threatened her, not explicitly, so what was she supposed to tell the cops, anyway?

"No." Whatever world college girl Jacqui was living in, where the po-po were your friends, that wasn't the world Mandy came from. Might've been white, too — but she was still trash, not from any hifalutin Brentwood, Tennessee. Besides which, Larry's cousin worked for the sheriff's department, and one time when Larry had blackened her eye, and their neighbors had called in a serious domestic disturbance, the cousin had helped him to cover it up. "No cops."

Never mind the fact if she got the cops involved, she was probably going to prison, too. After everything else, it would've been the ultimate unfairness, the worst cruelty. She deserved better.

"I don't understand." Jacqui was shaking her head. "Why not?"

Hard not to credit Jacqui's exasperation, but Mandy wasn't about to tell girlfriend she had ten grand worth of blow in that footlocker back at the hostel, not when she could see how Jacqui was fiending for more—not when the contents of that duffel were her ticket out, the only thing she had if she was going to start over someplace, maybe out west: Seattle, say, where she imagined herself waiting tables in a café that overlooked the sea, with her hair grown out and dyed a different color, and she would be living under an assumed name, like a woman in a movie. She would wear a kerchief, live as a redhead, and serve eggs and hash in a diner, and maybe after five or ten years, she'd marry one of her customers, an older gentleman, divorced or widowed, a decent guy who would never put his hands on her in anger, who would be grateful for her attention, and who would never demean her in public, call her a whore, or shout in her face in the aisle of a Walmart that she was worthless trash. After putting up with Larry's shit for six years, she'd earned that much, hadn't she?

"I stole something that belongs to him," she said, "and he's going to come after me because he wants it back. But he's not getting it back. Do you understand?"

She didn't flinch when Jacqui touched her cheek, and Mandy was too startled to move when Jacqui leaned in and kissed her full on the mouth. Jacqui's tongue tasted of red wine, and it was thick in Mandy's mouth, probing Mandy's cheeks. Jacqui's throat tasted of cocaine, bitter, burnt post-nasal drip. *So, this is what she's after.* Furious, Mandy shoved Jacqui, and they broke apart. Up the street, Naomi was watching them, something dark in her face, like she'd been expecting this, the corner of her mouth curling into a wistful smile. Shaking her head, she turned away.

"I don't do that," Mandy said, her palm on Jacqui's chest. She was too pissed off to make sense of her thoughts, and she wanted to push Jacqui over and kick her in the ribs. She should've known Jacqui was after something—but this? "I'm not like that." She was stammering, couldn't get the words out. And then she did. "I'm not a fucking dyke, dude."

Her anger burned through the haze from the wine, her pulse pounding in her ears, and whether it was the adrenaline, the coke, or the noise of the parade, she felt like she was drowning. Behind Jacqui, the orange lights on the bridge, the Crescent City Connection glowed over the buildings along the river, traffic backed up all the way to the West Bank. From the parade route, the music swelled: brass, bass drums, a high school marching band.

"I'm sorry." Jacqui bit her lip, but if her feelings were hurt, she didn't show it. "I shouldn't have done that. I'm not like that, either." She pulled her bangs out of her face, a gesture Mandy had come to recognize as being characteristic, a kind of tic. Mandy laughed. *Then what are you like?*

"You and Naomi?" she asked, that dark look Naomi had given them making sense. But Jacqui shook her head. In her purse, she had one of the bottles of wine she'd bought at Rouses, and she pulled it out, yanked the cork, and splashed wine into a plastic cup she'd taken from the room, offering it to Mandy. Mandy sipped, but the wine didn't take the edge off her panic—or her anger.

"What did you steal?" Jacqui took the cup back from Mandy and gulped it before she splashed a little more in, corked the bottle, and dropped it in her purse. Wine stained Jacqui's lips. Mandy could feel it coating her teeth.

"Something that's worth a lot of money," Mandy said.

Like Jacqui didn't know—but maybe she just wanted to be sure.

"Never mind," Jacqui said. "I guess I can figure it out. How much of it did you take?"

Bitch, I'm not telling you that.

Enough.

"He's not going to find me." Mandy wasn't sure whether she was trying to convince Jacqui or herself. "He's just trying to scare me. He's trying to trip me up, so I'll do something stupid."

But that silence on the phone and the way Jacqui's bus had pulled up right before Larry hung up — an hour and a half had passed, maybe two, which was long enough for Larry to make the drive into New Orleans and maybe even navigate the parade traffic, park, and find her. Farfetched, yeah, but it was still a possibility.

"You're cute." Jacqui leaned in, Mandy turning her head at the last second, so Jacqui caught her a glancing blow, pecking her on the corner of the mouth. "Let's do another bump."

"Later," Mandy said.

They walked up to the parade route. Somehow, without Mandy being aware of how it happened, they were holding hands, and she took her hand back, pushing Jacqui away.

Rolling down St. Charles that night, the Thursday before Fat Tuesday was the Muses parade, the all-female krewe whose prized throw was a sparkly, hand-decorated shoe. Mandy was so keyed up, so anxious about seeing Larry that she stared for several seconds at the gangly kid on the other side of the parade route with the pencil-thin mustache before it clicked with her who he was. *Jesus Christ, no*: it couldn't be. But it was. Todd stared back at her for several seconds before he recognized her, too. When he did, his face broke into a goofy smile, so she wondered if he was there with his family — the kid was only seventeen, after all — instead of hunting her with Larry. He was a good-looking kid, light-skinned, with a Billy Dee Williams, Lando Calrissian-style mustache on his upper lip, and he was wearing a St. Charles Catholic T-shirt with a couple strands of beads around his neck. Todd waved, grinned, made a gesture like *wait right there*, and disappeared into the crowd on the other side of St. Charles.

"Jesus Christ." Mandy grabbed Jacqui's arm.

"What's up?" Jacqui said. Her face was lit up, pale with the lights and the cocaine, flushed from the exhilaration of the parade.

One of the floats rolled past, masked women pitching beads from the top deck, and Mandy rubbed her eyes. Had she imagined the whole thing? No, that was Todd, and if he was here, Larry wasn't far behind.

"Larry's friend." She'd come so close to making a clean break, and she couldn't let Larry catch her now. She could run to the hostel — and then what? As the plan came to her, Mandy felt calm, and she took the key from her pocket and pressed it into Jacqui's hand. "Go back to the room, get my bag, and meet me at the bus station."

That key was her whole life. Could she just let go of it? Well, she had to trust somebody, and might as well be Jacqui.

"Okay." Jacqui took the key. Pecked Mandy on the lips, stroked her cheek, gave her a long, fond look pregnant with longing or another meaning Mandy couldn't puzzle out, and turned her back and walked through the crowd. And just like that, she was gone, taking everything Mandy owned in the world apart from a stolen butterfly knife and those brand-new black and gold Converse with her.

Mandy's gut dropped. What had she done?

Down the street, Kristy was talking to the guy she'd brought back to the room the other night, Naomi snapping photos of the parade with that Canon Rebel.

Mandy took the knife out of her pocket, and she flipped it open, the cold steel pressed against her leg, the air sharp in her lungs, watching through the floats and the marching bands for Larry's face to appear in the crowd on the other side of the street.

But when Larry finally did walk through the crowd on the neutral ground, what surprised her was the fact she didn't think about all the bad shit: not Larry yelling at her and calling her a piece of worthless trash in the aisle of that Walmart, or trying to slam her head in the closet door that day she'd confronted him with a pair of his stained boxers and asked him what he and Todd really got up to with the lights off and the door locked while they were supposedly weighing out product in the bedroom, doing whatever they did on her bed, too, no less. Or, yeah, to be fair, she did think of all that. But it passed through her head like pictures floating across a movie screen, and it was gone. "Son of a bitch," she whispered. Years ago, after one of the worst of their fights, Larry had started crying and crawled into her arms, telling her how his mom had whupped up on him when he was a kid, making him stand in the corner until he'd peed his pants and sit in his piss-soaked skivvies until he started shivering from the cold. Old Lorraine had made him walk around in his wet tighty-whities until the insides of his legs chafed, he'd told Mandy, his mom making him wear those wet undies until his little boy's thighs were rubbed as raw and pink as a couple of ham hocks. All those years Mandy had been willing to make excuses for his bullshit, like he was still that damaged child, but when was he going to take responsibility for what he'd done, the harm he'd caused? And was she really going to blame his mom for the loser Larry had turned out to be? Screwed with all her life, buddy, and Mandy had never taken it out on anyone.

A marching band was going past, Warren Easton High cheerleaders in their blue and yellow uniforms, their sparkly shoes, with their silver pompoms. How many of those girls had been messed with the same way Mandy had: betrayed by the people who were supposed to love, protect, and care for them, instead of turning them out like street whores?

Every damn one of us. Mandy bit her lip. *Every damn one of us messed with. Every damn one of us traumatized.* Even Larry? Another voice asked her that. And Christ, she really did sound like Dr. Phil. *Yeah, even Larry.* She guessed so. *But screw him, too.*

"Come on," she said under her breath. That knife was pressed up against her bare thigh so tightly it was probably going to leave a mark, if she didn't cut her leg. All those nights Larry was out ripping and roaring, she'd sat up with it, teaching herself to open and close it without smashing her fingers or slicing a knuckle.

"Hey." He waved to her. After the band passed, during a break before the next float, he crossed from the neutral ground, and the dude definitely had a walk. Wasn't enough, even, to say he strutted or that he strode. Lips pursed, like he was whistling, he crossed St. Charles Avenue like he had all the time in the world, and Mandy felt that familiar thrum of terror all the way down to her toes, cold as they were in those brand-new Converse shoes.

Run, a voice told her. *Go. Get the hell out of here.*

But she stood her ground. Where was she going to run? Besides which, she couldn't have moved if she'd tried.

Dude walked like he was king of the world, just like the first time she'd seen him, and here was a man who could take care of her, who could fix anything, but he was faking it. He was as scared and pathetic as Warren or any of the rest of them. Every one of them scared he wasn't big enough or hard enough, and the only way they could prove it was to come at you like Larry was coming at her now, like they were going to shove you up against the wall and take what they wanted, whether you meant to give it to them or not.

"Where the fuck is my product?" Larry stood in front of her in his cargo shorts, in a T-shirt that had a decal of an AK-47 bedecked with Mardi Gras beads. Stood close enough she could smell the sweat, the body odor rising off his chest, and he leaned down, putting his face in hers. Dude's breath stank, but he'd always had total shit breath, hadn't he? Been putting up with it for years, since the first time she'd kissed him in the parking lot behind Fatty's, when she'd decided not to say anything because she didn't want to hurt his feelings. Because that was love when she was eighteen: swallowing everything, stuffing it down her throat, all for the sake of sparing this loser who'd probably get butthurt if she told him to floss.

"Your breath stinks, dude." After sitting on that for six years, it felt so good to say it. When his face fell, she laughed. Been sparing him all this time, but not anymore.

"Listen." Larry wiped his face, pantomiming exasperation, like he was all put out with the inconvenience of having to deal with her. Not that it was his mom's fault Larry was an asshole, Larry's pops being a royal piece of shit, too. Bobby and Lorraine owned dozens of properties in Laplace, including the dump where Mandy lived with Larry, who was supposed to be the property manager. That's how pathetic Larry was: wannabe gangster pushing forty who lived in a building his parents owned and worked for his mom and his pops, who were the biggest slumlords in town. "I'm going to ask you one more time, and I'm not responsible for what happens after that. Where is my stuff?"

Her knees were shaking. A career loser, of course he was, but what did that make Mandy, if she was the idiot who'd fallen in love with him?

"It's gone." For all she knew, she wasn't lying. By now, Jacqui would've made it back to the hostel, and who knew what she was going to do when she opened that footlocker and found a duffel with more cocaine than she'd probably seen in her life, like "Big Rock Candy Mountain"? Bitch had been to rehab, after all. Not like she was exactly trustworthy, and Mandy had seen that look in her eyes: like a fiend.

"No." Larry shook his head. Had to blink and look again before she believed it, but tears were in his eyes, and the sight made her dizzy with joy. Once when she'd made out with one of his friends on the couch because she was mad at Larry, he'd started crying, and that pain had quickly turned to anger, but since then she hadn't thought it was possible to hurt him. "These people I bought it from, do you know what they're going to do to me if I don't give them their money? These guys are gangsters, babe, some really bad motherfuckers, and they mean business. They're nobody we want to play with."

We. Like they were in this together. Like they'd ever been in anything together. Like it hadn't always, and forever been about Larry, Larry, and Larry.

"Don't act like we're on the same side of this." She was raising her voice over the sound of the music from the next float, the hundredth rendition of "Iko Iko" she'd heard that year. "Don't try to pretend you ever did any of this for me."

"Babe." He looked like he was about to drop to one knee there on the parade route, like he was going to beg, like he might pop the question and put a ring on her finger, and wasn't that what she'd always wanted? "Haven't I always done for you? Haven't I always done just what you asked and taken care of you, however you liked?"

As much as she'd thought about it, she did know what was going to happen to him. He'd bought the stuff from a couple hard cases he'd met in Houston, serious players who'd brought the blow across the border through Brownsville, and who were probably going to kick Larry's ass into next Sunday. Might even break a few bones, take a finger or couple teeth, or hell, maybe a couple toes. And didn't the dude deserve it, after all he'd done to Mandy? Didn't Larry have a beatdown coming?

"They're probably going to kill you." Truth of that didn't hit her until she said it, and it surprised her to discover she didn't care. She shrugged. Might not have wanted that for

251

him, but couldn't say he hadn't earned it. Did he really deserve any better? "I hope they do." She leaned closer, getting a whiff of his BO and that breath, like something had crawled in his mouth and died. "And Larry? I hope they make it hurt. I hope they cut you once for every time you put your hands on me, so you know what it's like."

Wanted him to know how it was to be that powerless, out of control of his own body. Like the way he'd made her feel all those times he'd raised his hands against her.

"Cunt." When he grabbed her neck, a space seemed to clear around them, like the two of them had become the spectacle as much as the parade was. One of those massive, double-decker floats had stopped on St. Charles, and masked women were hurling beads into the crowd. Bodies pressed against Larry and Mandy and pulled away, a gulf opening and closing again, like they were in a pool of churning water, like they were back in the mosh pit at that heavy metal show he'd taken her to for her birthday last year, her favorite band, Wolves in the Throne Room playing at Gasa Gasa on Freret Street, which was the last time they'd come to New Orleans.

"Let go of me." Mandy was choking, and she swiped at him once with the blade and missed. She was on the verge of bringing that blade up and into the dude's throat when Larry snarled. Mandy followed his eyes. Naomi was standing at the edge of the crowd, the lens of that Canon Rebel pointing at Larry. Around them in the early darkness, one flash and then another popped. People were pointing cellphones, two, three, four of them, the tiny fisheyes of camera lenses showing through the holes cut in the backs of their protective cases. Behind those phones were the faces, people staring at them like they didn't know what to do, whether to help Mandy or turn away.

"Whoa." A pair of hands was on Larry's shoulders, pulling him away from her: Todd, whispering in Larry's ear, maybe telling him to cool it, man, to live and fight another day, or telling Larry he'd gone too far. Larry was grinning, like it was all one big joke, ha, ha, ha, him trying to kill her on the sidewalk on St. Charles Avenue, laughing it off just like that time he'd tried to choke her when they were boning because he'd seen it in a video on Pornhub. Todd was holding his shoulders, and Larry shrugged, holding up his hands like it was cool, nothing to see, folks, all good. And when he looked at her, it was with such hatred, the air felt cold. Given half a chance, he would kill her.

But what about her; did she want Larry to die?

"Dude," she said, catching her breath, touching her throat to be sure he hadn't cracked her windpipe. "Why couldn't you just let me be? All I ever wanted out of my life was a little peace and quiet, a chance to do my art. All I ever wanted was someone to be nice to me, to not treat me like a piece of shit."

Hell, Mandy wanted what she'd always wanted: a little bit of kindness, and a little bit of freedom. The space to walk through the world like she was in charge of her life, without taking anything from anybody else, like Lucinda Williams in that song Mandy had loved since she was three, her mom blasting *Car Wheels on a Gravel Road* from a boombox next to a vase of purple asters in the kitchen window: "Never take nothing don't belong to me, everything's paid for, nothing's free."

But she'd taken that bag and everything in it, hadn't she?

Well, she'd paid for that bag with six years of her life.

And when she walked away from this, that debt would be settled.

"I'll find you, baby girl." He did that thing where he pointed at his eyes, at her, like DeNiro in *Meet the Parents*: *I'm watching you.* He seemed confident, playing it off, like he knew something she didn't. But he couldn't hide the desperation in his face, like a nine-year-old crying about getting his favorite toy taken away.

"You do that." Couldn't say she wasn't scared because she was shitting bricks. But maybe that would never go away. "I'll be ready." Folded the knife, shoved it in her pocket, and walked, the rat-a-tat-tat of the snare ringing in her ears, the cymbals crashing, smoke from the flambeaux rising into the streetlights.

At the hostel, the footlocker was empty, Jacqui gone. Naomi and Kristy had followed Mandy back, Kristy holding her guy's hand and a sparkly pink shoe, which she'd caught at the parade.

Naomi scrolled through her photos. "I've got pictures of the whole thing. Should we call the cops? Are you okay?"

Numb with cold, Mandy closed the footlocker. Would Jacqui be waiting at the station, or had girlfriend made off with Mandy's coke? Years later, when Mandy finished at Portland Community College, she would quit waitressing. That same year, she would enroll in the visual art MFA program at Portland State, take a gig doing advertising for a biotech, and when she put down a payment on a house in Beaverton, that would be the end of Larry's money and his influence in her life, even if she never would stop looking over her shoulder, not even when she had the husband and her twin boys, not even when she was long since shut of Jacqui, who would go back to Tennessee after six months and another trip to rehab out west. Now, emptyhanded, Mandy only knew she was leaving, Seattle in her future, and she was never coming back to Louisiana. "Gotta go."

Hands in her pockets, Mandy walked toward the station in the rain.

Tom Andes' writing has appeared in *Best American Mystery Stories 2012*, *Xavier Review*, *Shotgun Honey*, *Atticus Review*, *TOUGH: Crime Stories*, *Valparaiso Fiction Review*, and many other places. He won the 2019 Gold Medal for Best

Novel-in-Progress from the Pirate's Alley Faulkner Society. He has taught creative writing privately, as well as at San Francisco State University, the ADVANCE Camp for Young Scholars, and The Walker Percy Center for Writing and Publishing at Loyola University New Orleans. He lives in New Orleans, where he works as a freelance writer and editor; teaches for the New Orleans Writers Workshop, which he co-founded; and moonlights as a country singer. You can find more at the sporadically updated tomandes.com.